CHAPTER 1

Ethan lashed the last length of hemp around the maiden's supple wrist, turning her flesh pink against the crossbar.

Her tears spent and her voice hoarse, she murmured her protest. "Stop. I beg you."

Reaching under her auburn hair, he tightened a gag around the back of her neck to silence her. Then he climbed off the stool, careful to avoid disturbing the tinder he'd piled below her feet at the foot of her cross.

The twenty iron bars he'd mounted between the ground and ceiling provided an impassable barrier, except for the single moveable rod which he lifted out of his way through the floorboard above his head. As he slid under the bar and then let gravity bring it down behind him, he glared at his captive. "I'm sorry that I must do this to you. I truly am."

Her eyes grew black as she launched a muffled scream into her gag.

"If I survive my pending battle, I will dispose of you quite quickly. I promise." He stepped across the medieval home's basement floor and then darted up the stone staircase. At the top step, he hurried to a window. Although the sun was low, the men he expected before moonrise were absent.

But they would come. They always had, for the last two hundred years, and they would continue forever unless stopped.

For the first time in two centuries, he welcomed their arrival. For the first time, he would stand and fight. In preparation for the night's full moon, the spirit that dominated his life had given him a nonverbal command to hold his ground.

Instead of running, he would kill those who hunted him.

If not, he would welcome death as freedom from his fate.

For two centuries, he'd viewed himself as the bad one, the selfish one, while those who hunted him by some self-proclaimed holy right were the valorous ones in his mental narrative. But damn the concept of good versus evil. His world had evolved into survival–endurance of the strongest–and if he defeated his hunters, he would embrace his destiny of liberating souls from their bodies to assure his longevity.

Brimming with the possibility of self-acceptance, Ethan gazed through the glass. From the direction of Canterbury, he expected them to ride, but his farm's abandoned wheat field was empty. As darkness crept over the forest at the edge of his property, he lamented that he might have to switch to his habitual tactic of killing the maiden and then running away.

But his patience had eroded for running from the hunters. He needed to face them and accept the consequences of his death or of his distasteful enduring existence.

His hopes rose with the dust he saw rising from the road as two silhouettes on horseback appeared. A tremor of terror shook Ethan, but then he calmed himself.

He wanted this.

His Master spirit had ordered it.

It would happen.

He stepped across the oaken planks to the house's far side where he'd built a fake wall over the basement stairwell. Lacking a visible handle, the door opened when he shoved it, and he wrapped the fingers of his gauntlet around its edge. Jerking his arm, he flicked the door towards him while extracting his hand, exposing the small space.

Less than a foot wide, the secret standing area held slits through which he could see everything in the house above the basement. As he backed into it, he pulled the fake wall shut with an interior knob and checked his fields of view.

To his left, he saw the home's main entrance and the window through which he'd discovered the approaching riders. Straight ahead, through the false wall, he saw the kitchen, the dining area, and the bedroom loft.

PROPHECY OF CHAOS:
A SUPERNATURAL PSYCHIC THRILLER

WRAITH HUNTER CHRONICLES: BOOK 3

By John R. Monteith

His crossbow pressing against his leggings, he shifted his weight to unconstrict his blood flow. The air became stuffy, and sweat stuck to the tunic he wore under the chainmail that seemed to double in weight while he stood still.

To give himself a slight reprieve, he pushed open the door and felt the fresh air against his face. He pulled it closed again in time to hear the galloping hooves.

The galloping subsided as the horses slowed to a trot. The silence became eerie as Ethan assumed the hunters circled his house, scouting for the traps they'd expect him to have set. But he would disappoint them, since he'd foregone his habitual tricks to delay and deter them in favor of new lethal traps.

He hoped to get lucky with a single-person trap as splinters burst from the entrance door. Wearing barding armor, the horse lowered its head and stepped into the house, and its leg caught the rope Ethan had strung across the entry. Tethered to the high rafters, a blacksmith's anvil plummeted towards the animal, and the spikes tied to the iron mass pounded the flanchard protection under the furry neck.

Though the armor deflected the deadly sharp iron rods, the mace trap succeeded.

Frightened, the horse bucked and backed away from the source of its pain. Outside in the encroaching darkness, it raised its front legs and neighed, and then it fell backwards.

The nimble rider leapt from the angry beast and showed his strength and balance by staying on his feet. As the horse darted away, the hunter ran to the broken doorway and peered into the house.

Aiming his crossbow, the intruder scanned the empty room. Behind him, the second rider approached and nudged his horse into the house. His face exposed under his helmet and chainmail coif, the mounted man appeared young and determined. "What happened, Father?"

The dismounted rider's weathered face betrayed his age. Ethan frowned as he realized the elder hunter's abilities defied the number of winters he'd seen. A supernatural force seemed

5

to give his adversary energy and dexterity. "A mace trap. I thank God my steed took the blow."

"Any sign of the wraith?"

"None."

"I shall check the loft."

"No. If one of us is to die in a trap, let it be me."

"Go then, and I will cover you. I can see much of the loft from my mount."

From his hidden space, Ethan had heard his hunters call him 'the wraith', a title that both sickened him and flattered him. He'd given up his humanity to become a life stealer, but he'd also evolved into a semi-immortal being.

He rationalized himself as special. He assured himself that divine fate had selected him for long life as he watched the elder man seek to destroy him.

With impressive speed, the elder hunter climbed the ladder to the sleeping area. He jumped to the bed, inspected it, and then descended back to the ground floor. "Nothing, lad. Hurry to the basement."

Staying mounted, the younger hunter turned his steed towards the basement door. Urging the animal forward, he forced it to rise and then lower its hooves into the wood. The door splintered open behind the wraith, out of his sight.

As hooves clopped against the stone steps descending below Ethan, he admired the skill of the rider, who must have ducked low to the animal's nape. He watched the elder hunter trot across the floor and take a position behind the descending horse.

Knowing the scene in the basement would confuse his adversaries, he hoped they'd move deeper into the subterranean room to explore it. They'd expect the maiden lashed to the cross, but the bars blocking their approach was a trick of the wraith's newest trap.

The primary blow would come from a collection of three logs lashed together behind a basement crossbeam and connected by chains to the ceiling's center beam. Fearing the horse may absorb the brunt of the blow, Ethan waited for sounds revealing the hunters' reaching their prime compromised position.

Failing to find their prey, the hunters spoke to each other, betraying their locations in the basement's center. Their voices were muffled but discernable.

"I don't see him anywhere, Father."

"Neither do I. Beware of traps."

"The virgin could warn us, if she could speak."

"What is this new devilry?"

"You mean the bars?"

"Indeed, lad. Can you reach the maiden's gag with your sword?"

"Perhaps. I shall try."

As the hooves clopped, the wraith seized his moment. Bursting forth from the door, he sprinted over the floorboards to a wooden chair that faced a dusty dining table. One leg of the chair ran up its back and served as a lever through the floor that restrained the logs below him. Against the friction of wood holding back massy wood, he struggled, but the lever gave.

The chair tilted, the logs under his feet broke free, and the main crossbeam moaned under their weight. Below his floor, chains swept the heavy wood and spikes across the basement.

After a deep thud, the horse roared, and one man howled. Unsure if he'd disabled both adversaries, Ethan faced his fight or flight decision. Since he'd never see a better chance to break the line of those who oppressed him, he chose to fight.

Crossbow extended, he scampered down the stairs. To his relief, the elder hunter slumped over the logs hanging from the ceiling, and the gored and motionless horse pinned the younger hunter's lower body below it.

As he marched towards the pinned hunter, he lowered his crossbow to the ground and withdrew his sword from its sheath.

The stunned and crippled rider groped for his weapon, which had fallen on his mount's far side.

When he reached the animal, the wraith raised his boot over

the rider's hand and pressed it against the horse. "Don't bother for your crossbow. If you stop fighting, I'll hasten your passing."

The hunter moved his mouth but failed to speak.

Probing the fallen rider with his sword's tip, Ethan lifted his enemy's chainmail coif and revealed a leather necklace and pendant. Cutting sideways, he sliced the amulet free.

As the amulet fell, the hunter transformed from a human into something supernatural. The azure humanoid figure and its backlit sky-blue aura mocked Ethan with its angelic hues. Eyes of pure white stared at him with a peaceful acceptance of its death.

Like he'd promised, the wraith delivered a merciful death and drove his sword into the hunter's neck. The white light waned from his enemy's eyes, and the angelic aura died. Although the being dying before him had been his mortal enemy, his adversary's passing mesmerized him.

The searing pain in his hamstring brought his focus to the elder hunter. Spinning, he saw the man drop his dagger, utter an incantation in Latin, and collapse to the ground.

Ethan removed a gauntlet, probed his wound, and palpated the gash. It went deep, but his tendons appeared intact as he was able to move his leg and put modest weight on it. He remained standing while working the tip of his sword under the man's chain coif. "I commend your attempt to hobble me, failed as it was. But how dare you curse me."

The old man's voice was stronger than the wraith thought possible for a dying man. "You're already cursed. I did something much more extreme."

Ethan scoffed. "Come now. A man of your supposed chivalry shouldn't be issuing false threats on his deathbed."

The doomed hunter coughed blood. "No falsehood. I intermingled my blessed blood with yours when I cut you with a blessed blade, and I said a prayer for you, to free you from your bonds."

"What bonds, you fool? I'm the freest man alive."

"Bonds of evil." The man coughed blood and then continued.

"I deliver you from evil. I've failed tonight's virgin sacrifice, but you will invoke the fruits of my prayer with the next virgin."

The wraith felt a supernatural fear confirming his adversary's claim. The blessing had been real, and somehow, it mattered. "Damn you."

Smiling, the hunter mocked him. "You cannot. I may not have succeeded outright, but I've done my duty, as did my son. We are redeemed." After speaking, the punctured man died.

"Bastard." Ethan picked up the man's bronze dagger, examined it, and found it eerily similar to his own sheathed and charmed relic. He tucked his enemy's knife into a satchel, and then he limped upstairs.

In his kitchen, he found a jug of water and rinsed his wound. Wrapping a clean cloth around the gash, he slowed the bleeding. Returning to the basement, he lifted the moveable rod, pushed it all the way up into his dining area, and then started the sacrificial ritual.

First, he set up the candles in a circle in front of the hanging maiden. Then, he recited his memorized recitation to his Master spirit and unsheathed his bronze dagger. His own stench mingling with the scent of his prisoner's fear, he squeezed the handle and waited for the blade's sanguine luminescence.

A rush of satisfaction soothed him as the ancient artifact cast a red orb throughout the subterranean room, signifying the weapon's adherence to the rite. Fifty years separated him from his prior dose of immortality, and the knife whetted his appetite.

The virgin squirmed, and restricting ropes abraded her wrists. The cellar's stone walls swallowed her gagged and muffled screams, and her horrified, pleading eyes probed the wraith for solace, which he met with true compassion.

"I'm sorry, but only one of us can live another fifty years. It will be over quickly."

His Master, the dominating spirit of his bronze dagger, ordered him forward, through the circle of candles and towards the woman whose death would renew him.

Ethan climbed the stool and aimed the knife at her chest. Spurred forward by his selfish need to live, he raised the blade. Running his free fingers down her supple flesh, he counted bony contours from her collarbone, turned the knife sideways under her fourth rib, and pointed it at her left ventricle.

He slid the metal into her heart.

Like flame, pulsating crimson light shot from the blade, and the killer bathed in its oscillating glow. A dizzying rush of euphoria overcame him as he ingested her life.

Success. "Thank you, Master."

He stared at the knife and watched dark blood pour over it and down the woman's tattered gown. The dying body warmed the dagger as stolen life flowed from the victim, through the handle, and into him.

His strength grew, and a youthful torrent of vigor, bordering on invincibility, pervaded him. The dagger's light receded, yielding the cellar to tiny dancing flames, and Ethan withdrew the weapon from the corpse.

His wound seemed to heal with impossible energy, and his movements became less strained. He reached for a candle and set it to the tinder below the cross, begetting a slow burn.

After grabbing his satchel filled with money, food, and the commandeered blessed dagger, he trotted up the stairs. He gulped his fill of water from the jug in the kitchen, quenching his thirst. As crackling tinder revealed the growing of the flames below him, he hastened his departure.

Renewed for fifty years and freed from harassing hunters, he stepped out the broken door to seek a new land where he could spend the next half century until his subsequent sacrificial rite.

The last sensation he would remember about the three people he'd killed was shame. Though he succumbed to the temptation of immortality, vestiges of his humanity knew homicide was wrong, and the dishonor weighing on him worsened with each stolen life.

CHAPTER 2

Fifty years later, Ethan kicked rats from the edge of the corpse pit. The Black Plague sickened him with its ravaging of victims, and he appreciated his Master's gift of immunity.

In return for the gift, he assigned himself the duty to labor for those who suffered as he traveled between the villages of Yorkshire.

Having broken the line of hunters and taken possession of their blessed dagger, he knew he'd escape persecution from their harassing ilk for centuries. His Master's silent concurrence verified it. And with the plague taking countless lives, he expected unparalleled ease in finding, killing, and disposing of tributes.

Over the past two and a half centuries, he'd been murdering three tributes every fifty years, under summer's full moons.

Tonight's full moon started a new, brutal killing cycle.

As the sun set and firelight illuminated the grave, an elderly nun with a cloth covering her mouth lifted a torch over the deep trench of the plague's fatalities. "Put him here in the corner."

Two masked men carrying a stretcher with the town's latest victim sidestepped to the pit's edge and then dumped the corpse atop another body.

The elderly woman glanced at their work. "That's the last one for this layer. Start a new layer with the next unfortunate soul."

Beside her, Ethan lamented as the overload of wasted life weighed on his soul. "So much death. How can this not be the end of days?"

The woman turned towards the barn which had become a makeshift infirmary and called out over her shoulder. "It's only the end for the deceased. Let's get back to tending for the living."

Following the nurse, Ethan entered the structure and scanned the dozens of victims who awaited death. Knowing the locations of the young women who succumbed to the sickness, he passed several patients until reaching the lady suffering the worst. Sitting beside her, he saw beads of sweat glistening on her brow, and her acute fever signaled the end. "Poor, dear. It will be over soon."

She stirred. "It's so hot."

"No. Don't struggle." He reached for a cloth, moistened it in a bowl, and folded it above her eyes.

"Thank you."

"You must feel horrible."

"This is unbearable."

"Your family has abandoned you, have they not?"

"I freed them from the obligation of comforting me. I don't want to endanger them."

"That was wise and selfless of you."

"Why do you tend to us?"

The truth of his supernatural immunity was embarrassing, and he formulated a half-lie. "It's my divine calling."

"The nuns, the monks... I understand. But laymen like you who help? Why do you tempt the Black Death?"

"I must be here. I have my reasons."

"You're a martyr?"

The conversation with the tribute he planned to kill deepened his shame, and he sought a new subject–a preemptive dose of forgiveness. "Yes, I am a martyr, of sorts. Why do you think God forces you to suffer so horribly?"

She turned her head and coughed blood.

He removed the rag from her brow, rinsed it, and wiped her mouth. He then folded the cloth and cleaned the discharge from her pillow.

"I accept God's punishment."

Frowning, he countered. "But if God would ease your suffering, you'd welcome it, would you not?"

Straining for breath, she gazed at the ceiling. "If God's will would allow it, I would welcome death."

Relieved, Ethan left the cloth beside her bed, hoping her fever would render her unconscious to simplify his alleviation of her suffering.

He moved between other victims, feeling the epidemic's crushing weight as it snuffed England's life. During a glance back to the feverish woman, he noticed she'd passed out.

Returning to her side, he pulled her sheet over her head. He then brought a stretcher to her bedside and shoved it underneath her shoulders and buttocks. She stirred but then fell motionless.

The wraith spied the nearest monk and strode to his side. "She's gone. Please help me carry her away."

The young cloistered man appeared disappointed. "Another?"

"Yes. It's tragic."

The wraith brought the young monk to the stretcher and stood by her head. "Lift."

At her feet, the monk aimed his buttocks at the woman, grabbed the handles, and lifted. He then led Ethan through the barn doors and towards the nearest unfilled mass grave. He then lowered her to the earth beside the pit.

As the monk said a prayer for the maiden's soul, Ethan held his breath, hoping she'd remain still. She did, and he volunteered to handle the remainder of the burial. "I'll carry her into the center."

"By yourself?"

Ethan looked at the bodies he'd have to walk upon to reach the heart of the plague pit. "It's an unpleasant task, but I can manage. No need for both of us to endure it."

The monk shrugged. "Thank you, brother. There are others inside I shall tend to." He walked away.

The wraith squatted and reached under the woman's armpits. Though light, she was a clumsy mass, and he strained dragging her backwards into the grave. His footing became precarious over the corpses as he yanked her over them.

When he reached the middle of the pile, he looked up to verify his solitude, and then he reached under his tunic for his bronze dagger. Quickly, he withdrew it, knelt, and drove it into her beating heart.

The knife turned red, signaling his Master's acceptance of the tribute. He extracted the blade from her chest, wiped it on the cloth covering his victim, and then sheathed it.

Having broken the line of those who hunted him, he sensed himself safe to remain in the same town–giving him access to new tributes for his lording spirit and an environment in which he could hide his gruesome task in plain sight.

Under the next full moon, Ethan repeated his task with another sick maiden, giving his Master a second tribute.

Then, under the subsequent full moon, he offered his third tribute of the killing cycle.

Twenty-nine days after the third tribute, he reflected upon the three latest victims he'd offered in tribute to his Master. With a constant influx of sick patients, the effort had been trivial.

But he worried about the final sacrifice from whom he'd gain his next dose of life. The full moon was coming tonight, and his dagger's lording spirit withheld the identity of his virgin.

He buzzed around the infirmary second-checking the women who awaited death, finding none who appeared to his eyes as candidates for the kill. But as he passed by the barn's entrance, he saw a sickly young maiden dressed in peasant's rags. Hopeful, he greeted her. "Are you sick?"

Alone, she walked to him and looked up with a somber countenance. "I have the Black Death."

A rush of energy flooded his body, and he saw a red aura rise around her. The sanguine light blossomed in his vision, and the dying woman became an intoxicating view of enduring life. To his relief as the full moon's rise loomed hours away, his Master was painting her as the next sacrifice.

The red illumination receded, revealing a mundane scene of the visual spectrum. "I'm dreadfully sorry. We'll make your stay here as comfortable as possible."

"I have three tumors on my leg. The largest is the size of an egg. How long do I have? Some say I won't last two days."

Based upon the plague's progression, he understood she could survive the sickness a week. But based upon the stabbing of his blade, he expected she'd survive twelve hours. He lied. "You have time. With God's mercy, you may even recover."

"Don't offer me false hope."

"I never will again. I promise."

That night, as torches dimly lit the barn, he found the new maiden in her bed. He brought her an extra pillow, placed it on the small table beside her bed, and reached for her back to help her lean forward. "Come, let's try a second pillow for comfort."

Trusting him, she curled her torso.

He scanned the shadows for prying eyes and saw his fellow caregivers tending to other patients. Assured of his privacy, he lifted the dagger from its hidden sheathe, grabbed the blade in his hand, and used the knife's crossguard as a club against the woman's skull.

She collapsed to her bed.

With shallow cuts on his palm from gripping the blade, Ethan returned the weapon to its storage under his tunic, and then he summoned the young, gullible monk. "This one has passed. Can you help me carry her away?"

The young man joined the wraith. "Was she not a new arrival?"

Ethan lied. "I'm not sure. They all become a blur."

"True. So sad. I'll get a stretcher."

Beside the stinking pit, the monk finished his prayer and helped Ethan roll the woman into the trench of corpses.

The wraith helped the monk return the stretcher into the

infirmary, and then he grabbed twine from a storage cabinet. He walked to the plague pit where the unconscious woman squirmed as she awoke. He lifted her and dragged her to the hole's far side.

He strained as he hoisted her to his shoulder, and then he trotted towards the forest with her bouncing by his ear. Moving deep into the trees, he found a long, fallen branch and lowered the virgin beside it. With his twine, he lashed the branch to a trunk, creating a cross. Then he lifted the semi-conscious maiden to the crucifix and wrapped her limbs against it.

As she regained her awareness, she protested. "What are you doing?"

He convinced himself of his merciful compassion. "Easing your suffering."

She drew breath to verbalize her disbelief.

Before she could speak, he punctured her heart.

Like flame, pulsating crimson shot from the blade, bathing Ethan in its oscillating glow, and the familiar dizzying rush of euphoria overcame him as he ingested her life.

His strength grew, and then the dagger's light receded. But as he withdrew the weapon, he noticed something amiss.

A lingering feeling of incompleteness nagged him as he poured a small flask of oil over her soiled dress. Withdrawing a flint stone from his pocket, he smacked his dagger against it until sparks ignited the combustible fluid and begat a fire.

As he strode deeper into the dark forest, the familiar excitement of stealing fifty years of life drained from him. Falling to his knees, he clutched his dagger with both hands and begged for insight. "Master? What have I done wrong?"

In a flash of understanding, the silent answer came.

Fifty years ago, he'd let a blessed dagger cut him, he'd let the elder hunter's blood into his flesh, and he'd let his dying enemy pray for his deliverance from evil.

Deliverance meant interruptions in his ritual of immortality. It meant chaos.

The fifty-year duration of his doses of enduring life had ended.

His future killing schedule had been compressed–a lot–and he'd need to dole out death four times for every blood moon throughout the duration of his life.

If the silent update from his Master failed to convince him, the ghost appearing before him appeared poised to erase any doubt.

Floating above the pine needles at his feet, she wore a milky white gown that reflected moonlight and generated its own luminance, and she glared at him through the black circles of her eyes. "Why did you kill me?"

Shards of shame cut him. "Forgive me. I had no choice."

"Every human has free will."

"You were suffering. You were dying. I spared you."

"You cannot hide behind your false justification."

Cowering, he turned his head. "I know."

She furrowed her misty white brow. "How unusual for your kind. You truly despise yourself."

"Yes."

"You despise what you do."

"Yes."

"You have been condemned to doing more of that which you despise. No longer will you kill every fifty years, but you will kill with the blood moons."

"I know. It is terrible."

"You have broken the line of hunters. There are none to put an end to your misery."

As she vanished, he calculated the new burden. With a compressed cycle forcing him to take three tributes before a blood moon sacrifice, his survival would require an average of four homicides per year.

Forever.

CHAPTER 3

Six hundred and sixty-nine years later, Diane dreamt of a young woman burning on a crude woodland crucifix, blood pouring from her heart's puncture wound.

Time stopped, accelerated, and slowed again as the surreal nightmarish scene unfolded. The victim seemed distant, and then Diane was the victim. One moment, she was a sacrifice, then the next she was the savior.

A figure appeared in which an unseen wind flapped a milky gown over a female frame. The young woman, sickly and pierced at her death but now clothed in dignity and unblemished in the afterlife, called out in medieval Middle English. "Avenge me."

Diane understood the foreign words and responded in contemporary English. "Who are you?"

"We descend from the same line, the line of Nineveh."

"This can't be happening again. Not already. I just killed my second wraith yesterday."

The black pools of the ghost's eyes narrowed as her misty brow furrowed. "I need your help."

"Why me, again?"

"You are an empath. You know."

Diane had hated that answer when the other ghosts had said it, and she silently laughed at herself for asking the useless question. "Of course, I know. Another wraith to kill."

"Yes."

Though this apparition was a mirror image of the Maidens of Anduze and of Beit She'an, the empath sensed the apparition's individuality. "Who are you?"

"I am the Maiden of Yorkshire." The ghost's voice carried a

hint of cold venom, a toxin icier than those of her predecessors.

Diane sensed the ancient anger. "I can tell that you're furious."

"I am. It is a true feeling, although I know it is unbecoming."

"If someone ran a knife through your heart, I'd say it's very becoming."

"I was dying of the Black Plague when he killed me. I fear I redirect the anger of my sickness towards the one who stole only days from me. The life force within me was wasted."

Diane pictured skin welts shaped like rings around roses, pockets full of posies, and the ashes of burning bodies. "I'm sorry. I can't imagine dying so young."

The ghost nodded slowly. "I sense your true empathy. You are indeed an empath. I feel your love. Love is your power."

It had been her main power in the past, but armed with the enchanted twin of her first wraith's dagger, she'd learned and applied new techniques towards killing her second wraith when love alone had failed. "I am an empath. I have powers, but I'm finding they're only useful when I help people."

"Yes. You see that by the grace of divine wisdom."

The empath had started exploring her paranormal life by counseling people during tarot card readings, and her first instinct was to talk with the dead spirit about her feelings. "You sound angry and unsure about who to be mad at. Did you want to talk to me about what you went through?"

The ghost's head shook. "No. Avenge me."

Diane feared the conversation's direction. "I guess you're serious about that."

"Kill the one who killed me. You must face your third wraith."

Although she'd seen it coming, the edict stung with mortal fear. "Do I have a choice?"

As she leaked her anger, the apparition furrowed her brow, and her eyes swallowed the light of the empath's dream. "I've been denied passage since he killed me seven centuries ago. I need your help."

"But do I have a choice?"

"Yes. You always have free will."

Accustomed to visits from the latest sacrifice a wraith had murdered, Diane pursued the discrepancy of this maiden being an ancient victim. "When did you die?"

"I died the first day of July in the year of our Lord, one thousand three hundred and forty-nine."

Diane noticed another inconsistency. "I'm no math genius, but that's not a multiple of fifty years ago."

"He fell off his fifty-year cycle after he killed me. Now, he kills every blood moon."

In her dream state, the empath gained supernatural awareness of astronomy. "A blood moon is a total eclipse. That happens every six months to three years. He's killing hundreds of people."

The maiden trembled. "Since my death, he has murdered thousands. He kills one tribute under each of the three full moons preceding the sacrificial blood moon."

Equipped with keen math skills in her trancelike slumber, Diane let the death toll form in her mind. "Two thousand, four hundred and nine victims, counting tributes and sacrifices, since the end of his fifty-year killing cycle."

"Yes."

"How? How can one man kill so many?"

"He follows death and suffering. Where women are in misery and passing away, he strikes."

Diane envisioned him following plagues, famine, and wars around the world. "But how did this happen?"

"The prayer of a hunter was invoked upon him."

"Some prayer! What the heck did he pray for?"

"Fifty years before the wraith killed me, the elder of the hunter pair cut the savage with his enchanted blade and mingled their blood. He then prayed for the wraith's deliverance."

Diane found the outcome illogical, given the hunter's action. "What went wrong?"

"The hunter assumed the wraith wanted to kill, like every other savage of his ilk, and he prayed for him to find deliverance from that which tempted him. But the hunter failed to realize that his wraith was tempted to seek his own death, and the prayer spared him."

"A suicidal wraith?"

The ghost nodded. "This wraith wants to die, but he struggles to admit it to himself. And with the hunter's misdirected blessing and prayer, this savage is committed to bearing his burden as a killer."

"He's killed so many. How can anyone keep doing that?"

"Divine providence assures it. He draws strength from his dagger and its demon lord."

They all drew strength from their daggers and demon lords, but Diane recognized this as something different. "Where are his hunters?"

"The wraith broke the line when he defeated both hunters and took their enchanted dagger on the fourteenth day of July in the year of our Lord, one thousand two hundred and ninety-nine."

Diane recalled the power of the hunters' enchanted dagger, a bronze twin of a wraith's cursed weapon which had been paired to the savage's knife through a blessing. The blessing allowed the hunters' dagger to serve as a divining rod pointing towards the killer's trail. Without an enchanted blade, a hunter was helpless. "And nobody's hunted him since then?"

"Without the enchanted dagger as a guide, it has been hopeless. While it has been hopeless, a candidate from the line of hunters remains unborn."

A definition of her forthcoming task formed in the empath's mind. "If you say I need to help you, that means you believe I can find him."

"Yes."

Diane risked the direct question. "Do you know where he is?"

The maiden remained silent while the empath assumed she tapped into whatever divine lord governed the rules of her corporeal communications. "I cannot answer that."

"I can't just kick back with my dagger and expect to find him with magical powers, can I?"

"No. Beware the dagger he holds hostage. It gives him special powers."

The warning haunted Diane. "Can you give details?"

"I cannot answer that."

"Can you at least give me a hint of what I'm looking for?"

"Seek sadness and self-loathing."

Diane thought the combination would generate telepathic links with every person on the planet going through a failed romantic relationship. Desiring extra qualifiers, she applied her empathic powers of discernment. "What about compassion? If he's suicidal at his core, he must know he's doing evil things to the people he kills. That would suggest a hidden compassion."

"It is true. You see this with the insight of an empath."

Diane continued elucidating her line of logic. "He's got a self-awareness that the other wraiths didn't. I can't imagine being such an animal and realizing what I am. That's got to be traumatic."

"He rationalizes what he can, and his existence is suffering, but remember that he's a monster. You must destroy him."

"Down deep, he should want to be destroyed. If I can get him to see that, he'll see me as his savior, not his enemy."

"Ironically, yes. He tells himself he is the savior of his victims. But I cannot advise you how to destroy him. The approach is yours."

Diane pondered the combination of self-loathing, compassion, and sadness. To find the wraith, she needed more. He would have to embody a longstanding callousness to life itself. Otherwise, the man would have gone crazy killing so many. "I don't know how to find him, but I think I'll recognize him when I do."

The ghost's features became rugged. "You may find him sooner than you expect. He is in his killing cycle. If you tune yourself to his victims, you may link to them."

"I hate that! I don't know how to control that!"

"I cannot answer that."

"It wasn't a question."

"You are an empath. You know."

"Don't say that!"

The apparition drifted towards transparency. "I must leave."

Diane regretted getting emotional. "Wait. Will I see you again?"

"You are an empath. You know."

The empath awoke in the hunters' guest room, sat up in bed, and reached for her phone on the nightstand. It was one o'clock in the morning. She considered calling Liam for comfort, she considered grabbing her dagger and seeking the wraith, and she considered buying a plane ticket back home to escape the endless pursuit of savages.

After several breaths to calm herself, she allowed herself time to recover from the dream with the new maiden, and she placed her head back on her pillow.

Convincing herself she deserved a full night of rest, she fell into a deep sleep, unencumbered by paranormal visitors.

But her peaceful slumber turned into a violent vision.

CHAPTER 4

Ethan caressed the handle of the bronze dagger resting in the scabbard strapped against his thigh and hidden under his cargo shorts.

Stepping across the rickety wooden platform, his partner looked at the wraith's leg and spoke with the drawling American accent of English, the relief team's language. "I'm surprised our team leader lets you carry that around."

Ethan glanced at his watch station's partner and wondered why a young man would choose to work such a distasteful job. "You're still new here, Billy, but you'll notice that many of us carry utility knives. Mine just happens to be larger than others. This can come in handy if a rope or life vest or article of clothing needs cutting while a boat's sinking."

"I guess so. But I saw it in our tent at night. It's gold or some other precious metal, isn't it?"

"It's eighty-eight percent copper and twelve percent tin to be exact. If you're unfamiliar with what that is, that means it's bronze."

"Bronze. Isn't that going to rust in seawater?"

Ethan lied. "It's coated with a protective layer. An annealing process."

"Oh, cool. That's got to be worth a couple-three hundred bucks. Can I see it?"

The wraith showed the young man his back and walked to a window. "Perhaps I'll let you hold it after we spend more time together. For now, let's get serious about watching the seas for refugees."

"I'm sorry. You're right."

"Patience, young man."

"I suppose I guess it helps when you got lots of time."

The wraith shot his companion a suspicious glance. "What do you mean by that?"

Billy cleared his throat. "I mean that you've been here for months already, and you're on a six-month volunteer assignment. You must have lots of free time if you can do this for six months without having to earn a paycheck."

"I have money."

"Sorry, Ethan. I didn't mean to butt in to your business."

With his frequent hopping between fertile killing grounds, the wraith had used his true name with strangers for centuries. He'd arrived as a volunteer three months ahead of his first tribute to dissociate his arrival time with the homicide, and he knew when to leave a killing ground if suspicions arose about his murders. After killing two tributes, his crimes remained hidden. "Perhaps we'll be able to help people tonight."

The young man had shown up three days ago. "Do you think it's going to happen? I can't wait to see some action."

The danger and effort serving as a self-inflicted penance for his crimes, Ethan had risked his life twice since his arrival to save refugees from capsized boats. "Be careful what you wish for. There's a fine line between feeling good about volunteering and risking your own hide for complete strangers."

An hour later, after the sun had set and the Aegean Sea had become dark, Ethan gazed to the north and the city lights of Behram, Turkey. Turning east, he saw empty water and the dark stretch of a sparsely populated Turkish coastline.

His young partner in the small, rudimentary watch tower walked to the door, opened it, and let in the fresh, sultry sea air. "There's nothing out there. I'm going outside for a better look."

"Suit yourself, but don't complain to me if the wind chafes your cheeks."

Billy closed the door.

Alone, the wraith checked the time on his phone and calculated less than two hours until the end of his shift. When free, he would scour through the camp for the killing cycle's third tribute to his lording spirit.

After hours of observing normal sea traffic, primarily fishing vessels returning with their catches, his partner came back into shack. "I guess there won't be any refugees coming tonight."

"Apparently not."

"I'd like to see some."

"It's not a pretty sight. Overloaded dinghies that are barely worthy of bathtubs braving the open water."

"I just want to help people."

The wraith reflected. "We all want to help people, but nothing about this is glamourous. You've seen the camp, have you not?"

The young man swallowed. "Just once. It wasn't a pretty sight."

"No, it's not, but eventually, you grow accustomed to it."

Footsteps up the creaking wooden stairs turned the young man's head. "Looks like our relief's here."

The wraith saw two young people in volunteer vests climbing the steps to the small shack they called a watch tower. "That's the end of our shift. See you tomorrow, Billy."

As a Lighthouse Relief volunteer, the wraith had permission to drive a small truck with an enclosed cabin into the camp. As a wealthy man, he could purchase simple goods that refugees appreciated but had trouble finding without local assistance. Tonight, he brought cases of canned Pepsi products.

He drove to the gate, stopped, and greeted a familiar guard. "I thought I'd bring some good cheer to our guests."

The government worker put his hands on the truck's window frame. "It's good to see you again, Ethan. Got your ID?"

The wraith lifted the badge strapped around his neck. "Right here, as usual."

"Volunteers come and go. Sorry, but I always need to check."

"No rational man would enter this place without a good reason."

"I'm here because I'm paid to be. What's your excuse?"

Ethan snorted and looked out his windshield. "Redemption."

Driving by tents and temporary barracks-like huts of corrugated galvanized steel, the wraith saw few signs of human activity. Most refugees slept, many of them visible on blankets to exploit whatever cooling breeze passed through the camp. When he reached an intersection in the meandering path, he turned right and saw flames burning in a pit. He stopped the truck by the fire, saw three figures seated around it, and greeted the short, stocky man in Arabic. "How's business?"

"Ethan! What a nice surprise. It's been a week, has it not?"

"Almost a week."

The thickset man stood and stepped towards the back of the vehicle. "What do you have tonight?"

"I'll show you." The wraith got out of the vehicle and followed the curious man to the cargo hold. He opened the double doors, exposing his payload.

"Mountain Dew!"

"And three flavors of Pepsi. Forty cases."

"Thank you, Ethan." The man extended a thick palm.

The wraith accepted the handshake. "My pleasure. Come now. Let's get these into your shop."

The squatty man scoffed. "My shop? It's just a tent attached to a hut."

"Which serves as a marketplace for hundreds who appreciate it. And tomorrow, people with little hope will wake up to some nice gifts."

The man bent forward, lifted the top case, and heaved it atop his belly. "Hopefully these are just samples of better things to come for us all."

Ethan grabbed a case and followed the short man. "That will happen, if the government can ever process everyone."

"That's getting more frustrating every day. The talk of increased delays in the system is becoming more depressing."

"I've heard the same in the volunteer camp."

"It's almost like the nations of Europe are intentionally keeping us out." With the beverages between his extended arms and propped over his gut, the man walked towards his tent. "But let's talk about more encouraging things."

"Like cola products?"

The man snickered. "Yes, like cola products."

After helping deposit his gifts of carbonated sugar water, the wraith drove the truck deeper into the camp towards a circle where he could reverse direction. Seeking a life to offer his Master, he kept his desperate eyes open for a sign.

Outside a tent, wavy strands of hair flowing over a white tank top tee shirt caught his attention. A woman seated with her knees to her chin looked up with fear and hope.

He stopped the vehicle within earshot and called to her in the Syrian dialect of Arabic. "You're up late."

She spoke with gravelly sadness. "So are you."

"Yes. I was working."

"You were working, but not anymore. Why are you wasting your free time in this filth?"

Remembering his time constraints, he glanced upward at the full moon. He lowered his gaze, and under her grime and depression, he saw a radiant life. Revulsion consumed him when he accepted that hers was the life he'd snuff tonight, and his survival instincts compelled him to rationalize his crime. "Are you alone?"

Her tone turned cynical. "Do you see anyone else?"

"I mean here, in the camp."

She glanced at the mud. "I'm the only one from my family who escaped."

Knowing that his victim lacked mourners relieved the wraith. "Then it will be easier."

She took the bait. "What will be easier?"

He cast glances to verify their privacy and then lowered his voice. "Getting you to Macedonia."

Moonlight painted shadows over her eyes as she frowned.

"How can you make such a promise?"

"I've been here a long time. I have resources. I know people."

She scoffed. "I don't believe you. But let's say that I do. If you truly have such power, why me?"

"You said you were alone. It's so much easier to smuggle one than to smuggle families."

"Still, why me? There are so many people who escaped here alone."

"You're new, aren't you?"

She nodded. "I came with the latest boat. At least I think it was the latest boat. Five days ago."

"Then who else has more to gain? Someone who's been here a year already? No. Such a person is six months from being processed. I would be relieving only six months of pain, as opposed to you where I'd be removing almost two years of waiting, if I believe the latest rumors of long delays."

Her eyes sparkled with hope. "Of course, I'd want this, if you could do it. But I have no money."

"I have money. That's not the problem."

She rose to her feet and approached the truck. Of average height, she walked with a strong posture that revealed her alluring curves, even through the baggy, worn jeans flopping around her calves. When she stopped at his door, she leaned towards him, revealing a face of a woman in her early twenties. As she ran her eyes over him, her voice was a mix of anger and resignation. "Then would you demand sex?"

He snorted. "I'm saddened that you offer it and so quickly. It makes me think you had to offer it to get this far."

She shrugged and looked away. "I needed to survive."

His eyes narrowed. "Don't we all? But no. I do this freely."

"Why?"

His gut twisted with the ongoing charade. "Redemption. I assume you're facing a long road of misery and suffering if I don't help you."

"Look around you. Everyone here faces it."

He sought his rationalization. "But you are indeed miserable with little hope, are you not?"

Her shoulders slumped. "Of course, I am. Why do you think I can't sleep? I still have some fight left in me, but they all say that new arrivals like me will die before I ever get out of here."

Satisfied, he reached for the Taser by his hip. "May I show you pictures of those whom I've helped before you? You'll see women from this camp who I've taken to Thessaloniki."

"Thessaloniki?"

"The gateway to Macedonia and all of mainland Europe."

"Sure." She angled her head to see his hand.

Instead of producing the pictures he promised, he aimed the Taser at her chest and fired two leads. As she convulsed and fell, he tossed the weapon to the ground, opened the door, and sprang upon her. Hurrying, he yanked the cords from her shirt, lifted her mass, and marched to the back of his truck.

Dropping her into the cargo area, he scanned the bed for a plastic case. Finding it, he flipped it open, jammed the exposed hypodermic needle into her thigh, and pressed the tranquilizer into her bloodstream.

As she lay helpless, he climbed beside her, opened a backpack, and withdrew a body bag. He rolled her into it and zipped it shut except for a small slot for her breathing. After closing the door behind his victim, he darted around the quarter panel, recovered his Taser, and climbed into the driver's seat.

He drove through the camp to the exit and greeted the familiar guard. "Mission accomplished."

"You'll make many children happy, Ethan."

"And a few adults, I'm sure."

"Let me inspect your vehicle, and then I'll have you on your way."

"May I shake your hand first?"

The guard assumed a knowing, low tone. As he walked to the truck's window, he glanced at his fellow guard, who appeared ignorant. "Of course."

Ethan handed him a folded hundred-Euro bill as their palms met. "I appreciate the good work."

Without glancing at the cash, the guard pocketed it. "And I appreciate your volunteering."

Through the mirrors, the wraith watched the guard stride to the rear doors. He heard him open and close them.

As the man returned to the driver's seat, he murmured. "I didn't see anything unusual."

Ethan scoffed but said nothing.

Raising his voice for his companion to hear, the guard waved the wraith through. "You're clear, and thank you for your generous service to these suffering people."

As a wealthy man benefiting from centuries of compounded interest, Ethan had leased a private dock and a skiff near the camp. After driving to and parking on his secluded beach, he lifted the bag with the refugee over his shoulder and walked to the boat.

After lowering his victim into the vessel, he motored into the open water. When he felt the waves rocking and lifting him, he unzipped the bag and dragged his drugged tribute from it. Then he tackled his final preparatory task.

He reached for the rope running through a cinder block and tied it around her ankle.

CHAPTER 5

Helpless in her second visionary dream of the night, Diane lay on her back.

Flashes of white overcame her, and her world became a lucid life in another person's body, trapping her inside the unmoving flesh of a young woman.

Thoughts became images, images became words, words became thoughts. Minds merged in shared meaning, and Diane lost the distinction between herself and the other.

Immobilized on her back under a dark sky of magnificent starlight, she heard a man's heavy breathing as he hovered over the body she shared with a pending victim of violence.

The helpless woman issued her silent scream in their shared thoughts. "He's going to kill me!"

Diane had experienced links with wraith victims and knew how to respond. The woman's chances were slim, but the empath knew how to coach her. She responded in English, trusting her telepathic partner would understand. "I'm far away, but I can tell you what to do."

The man moved to the victim's face, revealing a demonic image of inhuman horror. Hollow dark sockets glared at the Diane-stranger tandem, and a reptilian tongue slithered through fangs as the man-beast tore open the woman's shirt.

Her compassionate instinct kicking in, the empath defined the first line of defense. "Protect your heart!"

Unwilling to move, the woman closed her eyes and protested with unspoken word's in Diane's mind. "This is too much. I've been through too much. I'm tired of fighting."

"What? You have to fight!"

An overwhelming futility issued from the young woman.

"What's the point? God wants me dead."

Diane became furious. "What the heck's wrong with you?"

"It's hopeless. It's miserable. I'd rather die quickly than suffer anymore." The young woman opened her eyes, looked at the stars, and slipped into a peaceful acceptance of her demise.

When Diane saw the starry sky again, she looked for clues to the woman's location but saw nothing other than heavenly bodies. She noticed a rocking suggesting the woman's presence in water. "Where are you?"

The woman's answer chilled the empath. "On my deathbed."

The evil monster appeared over her. "I'm sorry, but it's time."

While the woman's instincts compelled her to reach outward in defense, her resistance was a hopeless gesture. With a gentle stroke, the wraith brushed aside her hands and then slid a bronze tip down the shared symbiotic Diane-stranger body.

The savage pricked the exposed skin covering his victim's beating heart, marking his point of attack, and he grasped the knife's handle with both hands. White knuckles squeezed the weapon, and he lifted his torso behind the blade before driving it downward.

The empath woke from the link, clutched her chest, and noticed the stress her body had endured. A phantom pain plagued her heart, she was moist with sweat, and her lungs heaved for air.

After sitting and regaining her composure, she sprang from her bed and marched into the hallway. At the young hunter's door, she stopped and knocked. "Liam! Liam!" She heard groaning and footsteps.

When he opened the door, a tuft of hair rose on a canted angle from his head, and a reddened cheek suggested he'd been sleeping on his side. His tee shirt and shorts were ruffled, and behind puffy eye lids, he squinted. "What's wrong?"

She struggled to identify a starting point and blabbered. "He's killing. He just killed someone, a tribute, right now. I was with her in a link. It was horrible." Tears streamed down her cheeks, and she reached for him.

He offered a strong and caring shoulder. To his credit, he withheld the myriad questions that she assumed were swirling through his head.

In his arms, she gathered her strength to continue talking. "It's a new wraith. We have to stop him."

"But the order hasn't assigned us a new wraith. Not yet, anyway."

Satisfied she could stand on her own legs, she pushed back from him. "The order has no idea where he is. They don't have the enchanted dagger for tracking him. He has it."

Familiarity with her abilities allowed him to ask the specific question. "Did you learn this all in a dream?"

"A dream. A visit. A new maiden, but an old maiden. It's going to take time to explain."

"I'll say. As long as we're up, would you like some tea?"

Wanting his company, she agreed. "Yeah."

"Okay. Come on, then."

During the ten minutes during which he arranged the beverages' components and brought water in a kettle to a boil, she explained her two visions. "That's about all I can think of. Any questions? I mean, you probably have a ton of them."

He poured the hot water into her porcelain cup. His voice was calm, indicating his methodical thought process. "I do. Let's start with the threat analysis. This wraith kills three tributes under subsequent full moons, but only when the fourth full moon is a blood moon, under which he kills his sacrifice? And he does this every blood moon?"

"Yeah, that's right. I know I can be flaky at times, but when I get the info in a dream, it sticks pretty accurately."

"No, I don't doubt you. I'd say that there's a blood moon roughly every year, as close as six months apart but as far apart as three years?"

"That's my understanding, as I remember it from my vision."

"My astronomy isn't perfect, but that's close enough for the sake of argument. So, he's killing four women a year, roughly."

"Yeah, since the year thirteen forty-nine, and who knows how many he killed before that when he still had a fifty-year cycle."

He sat, sipped his tea, and lowered his cup. "Call it six hundred and seventy years at four women per year. That's almost two thousand, seven hundred, if my math is right."

"Yeah. It was closer to two thousand, four hundred and nine in my dream, but you were rounding up a lot, I think."

"I was. But still, that's an incredible amount of stabbing, even for a savage. Not that I'm going to be sympathetic, but it must be maddening. If he wasn't a madman when he started, he is now."

She feared contacting the wraith through a telepathic link, but she saw no other options for locating him. "I'm sure he's borderline insane, but I need to find him. There's no other way."

He lowered his gaze to his tea. "No, I guess not."

"He'll kill again. He'll kill every full moon until the lunar eclipse if I don't stop him."

"Hold on. We need to contact the order. Father and I technically shouldn't be involved until they give us their blessing, and you're not going after him alone."

She realized her thoughts had stopped short of determining her next step, with or without her hunter friends. "I don't know. Aren't they supposed to contact you?"

He shrugged. "Sure, I guess. But this is freakishly unusual. We'll have to ask Father when he's awake."

Her adrenaline levels rose. "If you and your dad can't help me, what should I do?"

"Nothing yet. Just relax. You're not taking on a wraith by yourself, not even telepathically."

"How do you know? You just said this is freakishly unusual. What if I'm supposed to get into his head and make him kill himself? What if that's my destiny for all the wraiths in the world from now on?"

"Then you would know, right? You're the empath, and that means you have discernment and prophetic powers." He sounded like a wise–or wiseass–ghost. But his words relaxed her.

"Yeah, I guess you're right."

He tipped back his teacup and then plopped it on the table. "Maybe tonight you were meant to just learn the information. Then we can work on a plan tomorrow, or later today, rather, after we get some more rest."

As she released her mind from analyzing the ghost's message, she recalled her episode with the tribute, and the tears started again.

"What's wrong?"

"It's hard dying with someone."

"I can only imagine. I'm sorry."

She flicked her wrist at him. "I told you to stop apologizing."

"I'm not apologizing, but I'm really sorry that you had to go through it again."

"Fine. Whatever. Just let me cry."

He stood and walked to the counter. "At least let me get you some tissues." Returning with a carton, he placed it beside her.

"Thanks." She wiped the moisture from her face, blew her nose, and extended the crumpled tissue towards him.

He accepted the used paper, which he cupped in both hands far from his face. "I'm really earning my 'Knight of the Order' title by carrying this snot-infested goo to the rubbish."

She frowned. "Is that supposed to be funny?"

"Yes."

She allowed a slight smile. "Okay, maybe it was a little bit."

After dumping the waste in the garbage and washing his hands in the sink, he grabbed the kettle, walked to her, and re-filled her tea.

"Thank you."

"You're quite welcome, my Lady of the Dagger." He refilled his tea, carried the water to the stove, and then stepped back to his seat.

"Maybe I should just get my dagger and try to contact him."

"No. Absolutely not. Not until we talk to Father. We need his counsel and probably the order's, too."

The pressure of needing to save lives weighed upon her. "But we have until the next moonrise until he kills again. We need to hurry."

"I know this is going to sound hypocritical, but you can't let that force you into moving too fast."

She snorted. "Says the guy who always wants to sprint after wraiths."

"I said it would sound hypocritical, but it's true."

Exhaling slowly, she agreed. "Yeah, I guess you're right. The sick thing in all this is that the victim hardly cared. If he's picking women who are really miserable or even suicidal…"

"From what you explained, that may be possible."

"Yeah, if he's doing that, then I could get trapped in some argument that this isn't worth the effort. It sounds horribly selfish, but what if it's not worth the risk to myself trying to save anyone?"

"That's a tough position. It stands against everything I believe in, and I thought it stood against everything you believed in, too."

"It does, at least I thought so. But now I'm not so sure. The only person who's asked me for help so far was a ghost who died forever ago. Am I supposed to help people who don't want my help? I'm confused. I hate this."

"I think you're just tired. It's still early in the morning. You should get some more rest."

As she wondered what surprises lurked in the ethereal world that found macabre ways to stalk her during her slumber, the concept of sleep frightened her. "I guess so, but I'm not sure I can."

He stood, cleared the table, and placed the cups in the sink. "Come on. You have to try."

"Okay." She followed him up the stairs and stopped at her door.

He hugged her. "We'll figure this out."

In the short time she'd known him, she'd developed a deep appreciation for him as a protector, a crime-fighting partner, and as a friend. As she broke the embrace, she wondered how much more he could mean to her. "I know. I appreciate your help."

"Well, good night."

"Wait."

"What?"

She was embarrassed to ask, but she had to. "Could you sit beside my bed while I fall asleep?"

A quizzical look overtook his face, but his tone was compassionate. "Sure."

Without a word, she entered her room and slid into the sheets.

He followed her into her chambers and pulled an armchair from the window to the side of her bed. "Would you like me to say anything? Perhaps a bedtime story?"

"Only if you know one about a crazy wraith that's killed thousands of women that has a happy ending."

"Can't say that I do. At least not yet."

"Not yet. That's encouraging enough. Just be really quiet and think safe thoughts for me."

"Okay."

Within minutes, she fell asleep.

CHAPTER 6

Liam watched the empath enter deep, rhythmic breathing, and then he crept from her room.

He walked down the hallway to the master bedroom, stopped in front of the door, and questioned if he should wake his father. Absorbing the impact of Diane's news, he decided in favor of interrupting the elder hunter's sleep.

After several loud knocks, he heard the knob click open.

Wearing striped pajamas, his father opened the door and sounded groggy. "Yes, lad. What is it?"

"Diane had two visions tonight. There's a new wraith."

Shadows formed on the elder hunter's face. "Good gracious. How could she know about this before the order?"

"That's what I was going to ask you."

"We'll have to call them immediately."

His father's urgency surprised him. "Immediately?"

"This is a grave matter. The order has an emergency phone line that's always staffed."

The young hunter could only wonder about the daily operations of the still-mysterious order. "Okay. There's a lot to explain. Perhaps over tea?"

In the kitchen, Liam refilled the kettle and explained the details while boiling the water.

His father sat in the seat Diane had occupied fifteen minutes earlier. "This is dire. He kills four women with every blood moon?"

"Yes. She was certain of that."

"That's how many thousands of victims?"

"Probably around twenty-five hundred after you account for

those he killed on his fifty-year cycle."

"That's extreme. I can't imagine that any human has stabbed so many with his own hand."

"Probably not."

"It almost makes me wonder if we should capture him alive. A savage like that would be a valuable psychological case study of a serial killer."

"The concept of capturing a wraith has never crossed my mind."

His father waived away the idea. "Bah, ignore me. I'm still waking up and just thinking out loud. Whatever our mission may be, if there's to be any mission at all, it will be a decision from within the order."

"Well, do you think we'll have a mission?"

The elder hunter sipped tea and then lowered his cup. "It's time to make the call and find out." He lifted his cell phone and tapped a number from memory.

Liam wondered if or when his father would bequeath him the phone number he'd just dialed.

The elder hunter spoke into his phone. "It's Connor. Yes. Apparently, our empath was visited in the night by an apparition who tasked her with hunting a wraith. That's right. Yes. Yes. And then she had a telepathic link with a tribute immediately afterwards to confirm a kill. Yes, just this morning. Less than an hour ago."

Liam whispered across the table. "Mention the dagger. The wraith has the blessed dagger."

Connor lifted his palm and nodded. "No, we don't have any idea of the location. Identity? Uh... we know he kills one tribute every full moon for three moons in a row before a blood moon, and then he takes his sacrifice under the blood moon. Yes. Every blood moon. I know that's an unprecedented lunar frequency. That's why I felt it worth calling immediately."

"Father, the dagger."

The elder hunter frowned and nodded. "Would it help to know that the wraith has had our enchanted dagger in his possession for centuries?" Connor fell silent as his listener digested the question. Then the phone issued forth a response, which the hunter relayed to his son. "The missing dagger identifies the wraith. They know which one he is."

"What does that mean for us?"

His father raised a finger as he listened to his phone, and then he replied. "Yes. Yes. Of course. Thank you." He placed his phone on the table.

"What did they say?"

"This wraith has been lost to us for more than seven hundred years. The man I spoke to didn't have the authority to order a mission, but he'll have confirmation from the order's council by midday."

Liam had never heard of a council within the order, but he wasn't surprised to learn of it. "What's he expect from the council?"

"A mission to hunt down and kill this wraith."

"We didn't even yet have the ceremony for retiring the dagger of the last wraith."

"We will in good time, but it's just ceremonial. There's nothing empowering about it, unless there's an enchanted dagger changing possession, which obviously can't happen in this case."

Remembering the retirement ceremony of the dagger of the first wraith he'd defeated, the young hunter saw his father's point. "It's just happening so fast–again."

"This is truly abnormal."

Liam's head was becoming clouded with facts, conjectures, and ideas. "Everything about the last thirty minutes of my life has been abnormal, but it's been an epic half hour. Can you be more specific?"

"Our rapid and continued successes are one factor the order has no experience managing."

The young hunter had expected a different answer. "That's the first thing that came to your mind in this?"

"Remember that we may never understand which events are

the causes and which are the effects. Because we saved Diane, she joined our team. But even before we saved her, she saved us. So, is our empath a cause, an effect, or both? Is she becoming a huntress on our team because we're seeing unprecedented success, or are we seeing unprecedented success because she's becoming a member of our team?"

"I don't know. I can't even say if the answer matters."

"It may not, but these are the things the council members will discuss as they reach their decision. Remember that Diane's still a sensitive topic for the order. Because we rescued her, nobody's comfortable with putting her at risk."

Liam was more concerned about how to track and kill his prey, and he needed the empath to do it. "But we wouldn't have caught our first wraith without her, we wouldn't have caught our second wraith without her, and we sure as hell can't even hope to find our third wraith without her."

"I agree, but let the order do what it must."

The frustrated hunter stepped away from the table and walked to the stove. He returned to his father's side with the kettle and poured steaming water into a cup. After refilling his own tea, he carried the water to the burner and then strode back to his seat. "For the sake of argument, what if the order says Diane can't help us?"

Connor inhaled through his nose while collecting his thoughts. "That's an excellent question. Without her, we'd have no way of finding the wraith, and we'd be at a tremendous disadvantage."

"I'd say we'd be bloody well screwed. There's a reason this wraith has eluded the order for seven hundred years. We don't have the bloody dagger for tracking him."

"Careful before jumping to conclusions. Diane has revealed the man's killing cycle. He's the worst savage we've faced, at least in terms of bloodshed. That alone could be all the supernatural insight we need. There's bound to be a pattern to his murders we could follow and predict."

Liam agreed. "You have a point. There's something vulnerable about needing to commit murder on a frequent and predictable schedule. I understand that limits his ability to run or hide, but then again, the world is a huge place to search when you lack the first clue, which we don't have without the blessed dagger or Diane."

"I admit it would be a challenge without Diane, but you know how I hesitate to place her in danger. You saw how close she came to getting hurt in Istanbul."

Three days ago, the young hunter had been mortified watching the empath lose ground in a knife fight against a superior opponent. A clean line of fire to the wraith's head from a friendly rifle had saved her, but Liam feared placing the woman he suspected he loved in danger. "Maybe she doesn't have to ever see this wraith. Maybe she can attack him telepathically. He doesn't sound as strong mentally as the last one."

"You're overthinking this. Let the order dictate the scope of our mission, and then we can formulate a plan."

Liam sipped from his tea. "I'll do my best."

"Now that we've shared this news with the appropriate people, perhaps it's best that we get back to our beds." Connor stood, making his suggestion a command.

Conceding, the young hunter got up and cleared the table. "I'm not sure I'll be able to sleep."

"The lessons I taught you about quieting your mind to focus while hunting also apply to sleeping. Go through your imagery exercises and see how they serve you."

"You're going to be unconscious in five minutes, aren't you?"

The elder hunter shrugged. "I certainly hope so."

"I'll follow your advice."

Lying in his bed, Liam tried to picture a gentle stream, but thoughts of a new hunt disturbed him. He groped for answers about the new mission he hoped the order would define before the next sunset.

Who was his enemy? Who was his team? Did the wraith want to die? How would he find his prey?

Find his prey.

A fan of science and technology, the young hunter envisioned data flowing over a global map. Where were the world's disenfranchised young women? Where were the wraith's targets? Could he move ahead of him and ambush him? Without Diane's help, the answer seemed at best difficult and distant.

Could Diane help?

She'd seen the savage through a tribute's eyes, but he appeared a demon to the empath, like every other wraith. And the forlorn, surrendering victim had been unable or unwilling to share information about her location.

But Diane had lived through the experience, and it was emblazoned in her memory.

An idea struck Liam like lightning, igniting hope. He sat up, threw off his covers, and marched towards the hallway. But he stopped before opening his door. Rethinking his timing, he decided to honor Diane's circadian rhythm, and he backtracked to his bed.

Crawling under the sheet with confidence in his new idea, he found his way to peaceful thoughts and a restful sleep.

CHAPTER 7

Liam woke up early and energized, and he raced through his morning routine. As the first dweller within the house to reach the kitchen, he greeted the housekeeper who'd arrived during his morning shower. "Good morning, Agnes. Can I help you get breakfast ready?"

"No, Mister Liam. But if you want to get started before the others, you can cut the bread."

Hungry and anxious about his idea, he moved to the cutting board on the counter beside the stocky housekeeper and drove a thick knife into the brown bread. After turning half the loaf into slices, he tossed a piece onto a plate before stuffing half of it in his mouth. Chewing, he ran up the stairs to retrieve his laptop and a tablet computer. When he came back down the steps, he yelled into the kitchen. "I'm going to read in the den. I'll join the others at the table when they come down."

"Okay, Mister Liam. Remember to pick up your plate."

Since his father insisted on the hunters cleaning after themselves, Liam left his computers on a coffee table and raced into the kitchen. He popped the rest of the bread slice into his mouth and then whisked the plate into the dishwasher. While chewing, he mumbled his muffled apology. "Sorry."

"It's okay. See you soon." Selected by the order for her vow of secrecy of anything she would overhear, Agnes had raised him like a surrogate mother. "You seem nervous today."

"I can't fool you. I'm excited because I need to talk to Diane about something really important."

"She'll be down soon. I hear people upstairs."

He kissed her ruddy cheek and marched back to his computer. While awaiting the arrival to breakfast of his father and their three guests, which included Diane, her grandmother, and her brother, Liam scanned astronomical web sites to test his theory, and he liked what he saw.

In support of his idea, the stars were metaphorically aligned in their literal, physical divergence.

When the stairs creaked, the young hunter's hopes arose in testing his theory with Diane.

But Connor appeared at the bottom of the steps. "Good morning, lad. How'd you sleep?"

"Fine, actually. How about you?"

"I was out cold within five minutes, as you predicted."

"I didn't need much longer myself."

"Oh, good. You managed your relaxation techniques."

"No, sir. I came up with a great idea, and then I was able to sleep like a baby."

Connor sat on the couch opposite his son. "Well, do tell."

Liam's confidence seeped into his voice. "I can figure out where the wraith is with Diane's help."

The elder's tone became imposing. "You know that's not authorized yet, and it may never be."

"No, Father, that's not what I meant. She doesn't have to do anything except remember what she's already done."

Connor frowned. "But she already told you everything. Is there something you thought of that she's omitted?"

"Yes. Well, sort of. It's going to take time to explain."

Footsteps on the creaking stairs caught Liam's attention, and he looked up at the empath.

Diane's smile illuminated the room. "Good morning, gentlemen."

"You seem chipper, young lady."

"I'm not letting last night get me down. I'm going to look at it as an opportunity to follow the path I need to follow."

Unable to contain himself, Liam jumped from his seat, darted to Diane, and cupped her shoulders. "I have an idea we need to try."

Shocked, she looked over his shoulder for his father to rescue her.

"Slow down, lad. Let's get some breakfast into our systems before we burden our friend."

The young hunter scrambled for a thought to preserve his dignity. "Well, since Josh and Nana are still asleep, I thought we'd use the time before they arrive for breakfast."

"Nonsense, lad. They're perfectly aware of the house rules. If you're not in the kitchen by seven, we start without you. Let them have their rest."

Liam released Diane. "Of course, Father. We can have a nice breakfast and talk about everything."

Sitting with the empath and the elder hunter at the kitchen table, Liam watched Agnes lay out a breakfast of bacon, sausages, black pudding, poached eggs, fried potato wedges, and brown bread. He sipped a robust tea that he always appreciated, no matter how often he drank it.

After Diane swallowed a bite of sliced melon wedges, which she'd requested specially, she gave Liam his opening. "So, what's so urgent that you couldn't wait to tell me?"

He swallowed an enormous hunk of sausage. "I think I can use your memory to guide you through an exercise where we can figure out where the wraith is."

Her face went blank. "I thought I told you everything."

"You did, sort of. But there's one detail we can recreate that neither of us thought about that can give us the location."

Connor powered through his final bites of a potato wedge and aimed his fork at his son's nose. "Enough with the dramatic flair, lad. Spit it out."

Liam raised his palm and offered a quick bow in concession. "Yes, Father. We'll use astronomy to generate a celestial fix."

The elder hunter pursed his lips. "Well, I suppose that could work in theory, but Diane would have to literally paint the night sky she saw with every celestial body positioned at its proper place. I think that's asking a bit much."

Liam had expected the challenge. "That's what I feared at

first, but that's the approach when you're looking at the night sky and trying to figure out where you are. What if instead, I could show you pictures of night skies, and you picked ones that looked like your memory?"

Diane interjected. "Um, I'm right here, guys. You don't need to have another one of your testosterone-driven theoretical arguments. Tell me what you want, and I'll see if I can help."

The young hunter pursued his opening. "I'll show you computer-generated pictures of the night sky as it was exactly when you had your telepathic link with the tribute. You won't know where in the world the sky is being seen from, but I will."

Connor scowled while tearing a strip of bacon in half. "This might work, but it'll take some luck and a nearly photographic memory on Diane's part."

"I can remember a lot from these episodes."

The elder hunter shrugged. "Well, then. Far be it from me to doubt our empath. Why not give it a go after breakfast?"

After their meal, Liam sat on the coffee table and looked over the empath reclining on the couch. He verified the image in a tablet and extended the computer over her face.

"What am I looking at?"

It was a view of the night sky as seen from Damascus, Syria at the time of her vision. Liam had picked Syria as a starting point based upon its continued warring after the collapse of the Islamic State. "It shows the stars as seen from the ground somewhere in the world at the time of your vision."

"I don't get it."

"Does that look anything like the position the stars were in during your vision?"

"I don't know what I'm looking at."

"Do you see the north, south, east, and west symbols?"

"Yeah?"

"Well, north would be at the north horizon, south at the south horizon, et cetera."

"I get it, but it doesn't look familiar."

Liam withdrew the laptop, put his finger over the image on its screen and angled it towards Diane. "Okay, do you see this constellation?"

"Yeah?"

"It's the Northern Cross. Real simple, and pretty much alone in the sky. You see how its top star is in the northeast here? That means if the tribute was lying on the ground in this location, you would remember the Northern Cross in the same place in the sky."

Sitting behind Liam, his father interrupted. "But she may not have seen the horizon while lying on her back in a boat."

The young hunter glared at his screen. "What about the Big Dipper? It's in the northwest, but the end of the handle starts more overhead than by the horizon."

"I didn't see the Big Dipper."

"Are you sure you'd recognize the Big Dipper?"

"It's like one of only three constellations I do recognize. Big Dipper, Little Dipper, Orion, or at least his belt. That's about it."

Ruling out Syria for Diane's exclusion of the Big Dipper, Liam put the tablet in his lap and called up a new area, Baghdad, Iraq. Since Diane's vision had occurred at fifteen minutes after one o'clock in the morning local time, he moved the Iraqi sky three hours ahead to coincide with Irish time. He studied the constellations and then extended the screen over Diane. "There's no Big Dipper here, but you can see the Little Dipper to the north."

"Lying down isn't helping." She sat up, grabbed the tablet from him, and studied the image. She pointed at a random spot in the hunters' home that aligned with her memory of the constellation's position. "The Little Dipper was to my right. This is close, but not quite right. It was tilted differently."

Liam took the tablet and rotated the sky to align with the empath's pointing. "That means your head was facing roughly southwest, while your feet were facing roughly northeast. This should be easier to see now." He gave her the computer.

"Yeah, that's a lot better."

The young hunter envisioned the fine-tuning. "From your

perspective, should I stand the Little Dipper more on its spoon end, or should I take it the other way?"

"More on its spoon end."

Liam qualified his challenge. "I need to ask if you're sure, because your memory's impressive."

"I'm sure. I can't tell you why my memory's so clear about this, other than it was traumatic." A tear streamed down her cheek.

The young hunter turned to the elder. "Can you get her tissues, please?"

Connor darted to the kitchen and returned with a carton.

Diane wiped her tear and blew her nose. "Remembering this is painful."

While checking locations he'd considered as possibilities for the wraith's recent killing grounds, Liam offered his condolences. "We can slow down, if you'd like. I can't imagine how hard this is."

"No, let's keep going."

From his mental list, he picked a region with oppression that had been under a night sky with the Little Dipper. He dialed in Istanbul, Turkey. "Try this."

She stared at the image. "That's better, but the Little Dipper still needs more tilting."

Liam angled his head to see her view. "We're on to something with this location. Let's see if we can tighten it up." He called up Athens, Greece and solicited the empath's feedback.

"That Little Dipper looks pretty good where it is. Real good."

He craned his neck and scanned the image for confirmation. "What about the Northern Cross? You must have seen it since it's right overhead."

"Yeah, I saw it. It looks good, too."

He pointed. "That's odd. It's almost perfectly lined up like a crucifix in the sky as you, I mean as she was facing."

"I know. I'm trying not to overthink that."

He shook his head and then pointed. "No, don't bother. Let's do one more check. Do you see that elaborate constellation to the east?"

"Yeah."

"That's Pegasus. I don't know how people get a winged horse out of that, but there's a lot of stars in it. How do they look to you?"

"It looks right. It feels right. Maybe just a little off."

"I think we're within a few hundred miles of the attack."

"It still doesn't feel perfect."

Liam took the tablet and tried an adjustment to Izmir, Turkey, on the Aegean Sea, and then he put the image in front of her.

"That's the best, I think."

"Try toggling between the last two."

She whipped the images back and forth, shifting the sky in tiny jumps. "It's hard to tell, but I like the latest one the best."

"That's as close as I can get with major cities."

"Then it's between the last two, closer to the last one." She gave him the tablet. "Where is it?"

"Between Athens, Greece and Izmir, Turkey." Liam considered fertile grounds for a serial killer. "I'll confirm this in recent news, but I suspect he's attacking refugees in Greece. They get bottlenecked on the islands before they reach the mainland."

"Okay. So, where do we go?"

"I'm not sure yet. We need better precision. I think it's time we go rent the use of our local planetarium."

An hour later, Liam stood beside the planetarium operator. "Try moving the ground point a bit to the west."

The balding operator wore the bulk of his hair in a long ponytail and spoke with a slow and relaxed tone that made the young hunter suspect he'd eaten marijuana brownies for breakfast. "How far west you want it?"

"Move to the center of the island of Lesbos."

"Sure thing." The operator tapped keys, and the projected night sky rotated across the room's overhead dome. "How's that, man?"

The young hunter addressed the planetarium's sole seated observer. "How's that, Diane?"

"That's the best so far, but it's not quite right."

His ponytail swinging, the operator turned towards Liam. "Has she got a photographic memory or something?"

"Or something, yes. Let's go back east into the water right at the midpoint between Lesbos and the Turkish coast."

"Sure, man. Whatever you want."

After a motor whirred and relays clicked, Liam called out. "How's that?"

"That's too far. Move the Northern Cross back a little bit."

"She knows her stuff, man."

"You have no idea. Go west and stop a mile off the coast of Lesbos."

The planetarium's sky shifted, and Diane called out. "That's good. It's the best so far."

Liam tried fine tuning. "Go north ten miles."

"Okay, man."

Relays clicked on and off in rapid succession with the tiny astronomical shift. After the sky settled, the hunter called out. "Take a look, and then we'll move it again. I want a better or worse between this location and the next."

The empath's voice carried impatience. "How exact does this need to be?"

"Just humor me." Speaking softly, Liam instructed the operator. "Go twenty miles south." Relays clicked again, and the hunter called out. "Is this better or worse."

"Better."

"Take it another ten miles south." The operator and the projector's motor obliged. "How's that, Diane?"

Her voice conveyed her exasperation. "That's it. If we keep doing this, I'm going to go crazy."

"That's good enough. Good job, Diane."

The ponytail swung again. "What's all this about anyway?"

Liam conjured a fabrication but left it unsaid, recalling that a Knight of the Order should avoid lies. "I'm sorry, but I can't say."

"Ooh, spooky, man. Okay, whatever."

"Come on, Diane. We're done."

CHAPTER 8

In the hunters' den, Diane flopped onto a couch. "I can't believe this is happening."

Reclining into a leather chair across the coffee table, Liam seemed energized. "Me neither. It's amazing, isn't it? I trained my entire life to defeat one wraith, and now I'm going to beat my third."

The empath sighed. "Aren't you getting a little ahead of yourself?"

"Well, yeah. Sure. But what's the point in planning for failure?"

She shrugged. "Eh. Good point. I'm just tired. At least I think I'm tired. Those visions were draining, and then you made me remember the last thing an innocent woman saw before she died, and you did it over and over."

"Sorry."

"No, you're not."

"No, I'm not. Not really. I mean, I'm sorry you had to go through it, but you had to go through it."

Despite her protestations, an energy buzzed within her. "I'll be fine. I just need some time to chill."

Through Connor's office door, she heard the elder hunter raise his voice. "Tomorrow?"

Liam craned his neck towards his father's study. "I think he's talking to the order."

Diane's heart raced knowing a group of secret strangers discussed her fate. "What do you think's going to happen?"

"They must give us a mission to hunt down this wraith. That's what we do."

"Yeah. But what about me?"

The young hunter's glare disquieted her with its callousness. She'd hoped to see a growing spark of loving affection from him, but he was businesslike in objectifying her. "You're a necessary asset. They'd be fools to make us leave you behind."

She whispered to herself. "How romantic."

"What?"

"Nothing."

As the door to Connor's study creaked open and the elder hunter's boots clapped the hardwood floor, Liam sprang to his feet. "What's the news?"

Connor cut slow strides underneath the game heads mounted against the walls while lowering his phone into his pocket. He stopped and stood between Diane and Liam. "I just heard from the order. Unfortunately, there's no answer yet on the mission."

"Then what's tomorrow, Father? I couldn't help but overhear you say something was happening tomorrow."

"We're traveling to Rome."

Liam frowned. "But the wraith's in Greece. His last kill was off the coast of Lesbos. Diane and I just spent all morning figuring that out."

"I don't doubt you, but we've been summoned to the council of the order."

The news stirred conflicting emotions. "That's all well and good, but we have work to do. We've got less than four weeks until he kills again."

The elder hunter raised his voice. "And it's no business of yours what he does until so ordered."

"The order said nothing, then?"

"Quite the contrary. The order said plenty. The council's conflicted, which is why we're joining them tomorrow."

Diane expected her excitement to sway Liam into perking up about the trip. "Ooh, I've never been. Can Nana and Josh come, too?"

A smile cut the sternness covering Connor's face. "Yes, they can come."

Seeming to accept his fate of visiting Rome before getting anywhere near a wraith, Liam pried for information. "If I'm going to meet them tomorrow, can you finally tell me who they are?"

The elder hunter scrunched his face in a stern glare. "You'll know the public name of the order soon enough, but we'll be ushered to the secret council through unidentifiable passageways."

Liam rolled his eyes. "So, even after we meet the council, I won't know who they are?"

"Not even close, lad. You'll learn a lot by virtue of the environs and the proceedings, but the visit won't even give you a quarter of the answer of who they are."

"Well, can you at least tell me where we're going?"

"The street is in the downtown of Rome, Via dei Conditti."

The next afternoon, Diane's head spun with tourist ideas as she followed Josh and Nana out of a taxi's back seat. "Can we go to the Colosseum first?"

Her brother walked with his tablet in front of his face. "The emperor Vespasian started building it two years after he destroyed the Temple in Jerusalem."

Waddling against decades of orthopedic problems, the Chaldean grandmother, the matriarch of Diane's Iraqi-Christian-descended family, struggled to keep pace with the hunters. "He was a busy emperor."

Leading the group, Connor stifled the banter. "Everything depends on what we learn from the council." Stopping in front of a building spanning the entire block, the elder hunter tapped a code into a lock and pushed open a door.

When Diane followed him into the space, the lobby seemed sterile against her expectations. A lone steward in a pinstriped suit stood behind a counter and greeted the arrivals with an Italian accent. "Welcome ladies and gentlemen. Friar Don is expecting you. Please sit."

With her colleagues, Diane sank into leather armchairs and

looked at the elder hunter. "Were you expecting a 'Friar Don'?"

"No, but I know him, and apparently, he was expecting us."

Within two minutes, an elevator opened, revealing a lean man in his early sixties. Above his black robe with a white eight-pointed cross, he wore a strained expression. His accent was British. "Greetings, all. I'm Friar Don." He shook hands with each member of the team, brought them into the elevator, and then tapped a code into a keypad.

Diane's stomach moved upward. "We're going down?"

Friar Don nodded. "Matters of grave security are dealt with in our lower levels. I think you'll find our security measures quite modern and effective. Steel-reinforced doors, security cameras, motion alarms. We spared no expense to protect our privacy."

Although she understood the mortal implications of their visit, the empath challenged the mood. "Oh, that sounds serious."

"I don't mean to be so formal. I'm normally much more up-beat with visitors, but the sentiment among the council members concerning the matter at hand is solemn."

The elevator stopped, and the friar led the entourage into a subterranean chamber spanning the area of a two-car garage. Leather sofas formed a square in the room's center, but other than places to sit and rest, the area lacked a purpose beyond that of a junction.

A door on each wall offered exits, and the friar led the group around the seating area to the far portal. He tapped a code and then pushed open the heavy door. The next space was a long hallway leading underneath adjacent buildings. Several turns through locked security points reminded Diane of the group's secrecy.

In a final room with a seating area, the friar aimed his palm at couches. "Please sit. Excuse me a moment. I will return shortly." He tapped a code into a keypad, pushed open a massy oaken door, and disappeared behind it.

Walking off nervous energy, Diane strolled along a wall. "This is a danged secretive group."

The young hunter appeared beside her. "The inner sanctum is. The public-facing part of it is the oldest chivalric order still in existence."

"And you're one of its knights."

"Only because you're one of its ladies, or dames, rather."

"I'm picking up a lot of cool titles with you."

Still wearing his upper arm cast from bullet wounds received while stopping the Michigan wraith, Liam flicked back his fingers. "Whatever. Don't get too wrapped up in all the pomp and pageantry. We're only third-class royalty anyway."

"What's that mean? Am I a newbie on probation?"

He shrugged. "I haven't paid too much attention to it, really."

"How many wraiths do we need to kill to get some rank around here?"

"It's not that important. In fact, your role's only honorary."

She turned to him and frowned. "Why?"

"You never took any vows or made any promises to the order, did you?"

"Well, no."

"I did, long ago, and I don't think you'd want to do it for yourself. It was all about poverty, chastity, and obedience."

Recalling her brother's astute observation that chastity and celibacy were different, she challenged the first virtue. "Poverty? You're anything but poor. You and Connor have everything you need."

"Yeah, we do. Stuff we need to do our work. But the order owns everything and only lets us use it for our work. You also didn't see any luxury goods in our home."

She scanned her memory. The hunters had the best technology, modern weapons, and a housekeeper. "People in poverty don't have housekeepers."

"She's practically family, and we need her. You've seen how busy we are. We're always training."

"It still doesn't meet my definition of poverty."

The wooden door swung open, revealing the friar. "The council is ready for you. Please enter the sanctum."

Diane followed Connor and Liam through the doorway and saw a room resembling a law court except for its shadowy semi-circular alcove where she expected a judge's bench. The dim lighting from candles illuminated the sloping square-shaped floor upon which she stood. As she followed her colleagues down a central aisle between rows of empty benches, she questioned if the seating area served observers of trials, religious worshipers, or both. "I thought they were ready and waiting for us?"

Liam twisted to her and spoke at low volume. "They were ready and waiting for us to enter this room–so that we could wait for them. Protocol, you know."

"I'm not sure I like protocol. I'm not sure I'm going to like this council much at all."

CHAPTER 9

Liam was astounded to have reached the bowels of the order without having provided a shred of evidence about his identification. His father's knowledge of the entry code to the keypad on the street sufficed to generate their welcome. "Father?"

Connor raised a hushing hand. "Silence, lad. Remember your oath of obedience."

Beside Liam's right shoulder, Diane protested. "I didn't take any oaths. Can someone please explain why we're standing in an underground courtroom with bad lighting?"

The black-robed friar faced his guests. "Yes, the proceedings. The council entered the sanctum before you arrived and has been preparing in their antechamber behind their bench. Witnesses for the hearing will be Connor Brady, Liam Brady, and Diane Yousif. Please sit behind this desk next to me, where I will represent you. Linda Gulla and Joshua Yousif will be observing. Please sit in the first row behind the witnesses."

Liam sat, leaned towards the empath, and whispered. "Linda?"

"Nana's real name is Awatif, but she picked an American name when she came here from Iraq."

"Huh. I like it."

"It worked for her business selling dresses. Her clients liked it." Diane scanned the room. "What's this all about? I was expecting something more friendly and casual."

"I think we're on trial, or something close to it. Whatever's going on, the order doesn't do anything casually."

The friar stepped in front of the desk. "Please wait in reverent silence while I summon the council." He turned and marched up the aisle towards the entrance.

Honoring his oath, Liam sat in stillness while listening to the oaken door swing open behind him. Murmuring accompanied the subtle shift in air pressure, and then multiple slow footsteps headed towards him.

Friar Don appeared first in the corner of his eye, and then another man in a similar black cloak. The two friars sat on opposite sides of the aisle, suggesting they represented contradicting poles of an argument.

A third friar in black carried a metal staff upon which stood a bronze casting of the order's eight-point cross. He planted the shaft into an invisible hole in the floor, and then faced the room's occupants. "All rise for the Council of Paranormal Activities."

While standing, Liam mentally explored the name of those who'd summoned him. A secret paranormal council within the order kept the identity of his full brotherhood a mystery, frustrating him.

Diane seemed more optimistic. "They have a cool name. Maybe this won't suck."

Leaving the staff in the room's shadowy center, the third friar stepped aside.

A rectangle of bright light cracked the darkness in the chamber's front, and then human silhouettes passed through the doorway. As the council members stood in a semicircle, the arcing bench before them became discernible in its blackness. Then the seventh member entered, closing the door behind him and returning the space to the dim candlelight.

Continuing the pomp, the third friar, who stood beside a wooden desk with his back to the wall, addressed the congregation in Latin. "I declare this special hearing of the Paranormal Council open. Friar Lucio, Knight of Justice, and chair of this council, presiding."

His memory of the language rusty, Liam paid keen attention.

In a soft but confident voice, Friar Lucio also spoke Latin. "Connor Brady, approach the council."

The elder hunter stepped from behind the witness bench and

John R Monteith

strode to the center of the semicircle.

Still standing with the council, the chairman issued his next order. "Turn your back to the council."

As Connor faced his audience, the third friar marched beside him and faced the seven members.

Friar Lucio issued his next command. "Friar Francesco, reveal the cursed daggers."

Liam's pulse raced as he suspected his proximity to the knives he'd retired from wraiths.

Friar Francesco walked to a short stone column that rose to his waist in the shadows in front of the council's semicircular bench. He withdrew a large metal key from his pocket and stuck it into the stone. Twisting the latch, he unlocked the small vault and then flipped back a creaking iron hatch. "The empty vault reminds us the first demon prowls the world. May God rebuke him, we humbly pray, and guide us in returning this savage to Hell." He then closed and locked the hatch.

When Francesco finished his announcement, the council member standing nearest the vault sat behind the bench.

The friar followed the arcing bench to another vault and opened it. "The empty vault reminds us the second demon prowls the world. May God rebuke him, we humbly pray, and guide us in returning this savage to Hell."

The next council member sat.

When the friar reached the third vault, he made a new announcement. "The retired cursed dagger of the third demon reminds us of deeds of exemplary virtue. May God bless Connor and Liam Brady, Knights of Honor, for enacting God's will upon the savage."

Behind the desk, the third council member remained standing.

The friar continued. "The retired cursed dagger of the fourth demon reminds us of deeds of exemplary virtue. May God bless Konrad and Heinrich Staufer, Deceased Knights of Honor, for enacting God's will upon the savage."

Located in the council's center, its chairman remained standing.

At the fifth stubby column, the friar announced the elusive wraith. "The empty vault reminds us the fifth demon prowls the world. May God rebuke him, we humbly pray, and guide us in returning this savage to Hell."

The fifth member sat.

Blending with the shadows, the friar's cloak moved to the sixth column. "The retired cursed dagger of the sixth demon reminds us of deeds of exemplary virtue. May God bless Connor and Liam Brady, Knights of Honor, for enacting God's will upon the savage."

The sixth member remained standing.

Then the friar reached the final column. "The empty vault reminds us the seventh demon prowls the world. May God rebuke him, we humbly pray, and guide us in returning this savage to Hell."

As the seventh council member sat, the friar marched across the room. "Connor Brady, face the council and see the retired daggers."

Obedient, the elder hunter turned.

A standing member uttered indistinct phrases. Surprising Liam, a red aura rose in front of the friar from the vault atop the column. "Upon invocation, the cursed dagger glows in his sight. This man is a hunter of wraiths, descended from the Tribe of Naphtali, and ordained to represent this council in battle against the enemy." As the glow receded, it yielded blackness over the column.

The chairman then summoned magic to the dagger in front of him, which glowed. He declared Connor a descendent of the Tribe of Naphtali.

The final standing member repeated the test, bringing sanguine light to the dagger in the vault before him. Then he also declared the elder hunter's ordainment to represent the council in battle.

The chairman raised his voice. "Based upon your vision bringing light to the cursed daggers, I hereby identify you as a wraith hunter. Based upon oaths you have sworn and virtues that have been bestowed upon you, this chair recognizes you as Connor Brady and proclaims your testimony truthful. Be seated."

As the elder hunter returned to his seat, he whispered. "Whatever you do, keep your eyes on the glowing dagger. Don't look away until it goes dark again."

The chairman summoned the young hunter. "Liam Brady, approach the council."

He took his father's place before the seven men and saw the knives laying behind plexiglass on forty-five-degree angles. As the first standing member uttered his phrases, Liam discerned the words as a blessing upon the cursed dagger. While he glared at the knife, it glowed red, and he felt an evil spirit within the bronze protesting the prayer imposed upon it. He wanted to close his eyes and turn from the knife's suffering, but it ended as quickly as it rose.

"Upon invocation, the cursed dagger glows in his sight. This man is a hunter of wraiths, descended from the Tribe of Naphtali, and ordained to represent this council in battle against the enemy." The first standing council member sat.

Liam repeated the examination of the remaining two daggers, sending the final members into their chairs.

The chairman raised his voice. "Based upon your vision bringing light to the cursed daggers, I hereby identify you as a wraith hunter. Based upon oaths you have sworn and virtues that have been bestowed upon you, this chair recognizes you as Liam Brady and proclaims your testimony truthful. Be seated."

The young hunter walked to his seat.

Standing, the chairman called out. "Diane Yousif, please stand."

The empath obeyed.

"Connor Brady, do you recognize this person as a dame of the order?"

The elder hunter stood. "I do, Master Chairman."

"Be seated, Connor Brady. Liam Brady, do you recognize this person as a dame of the order?"

Relieved his father had provided an example, Liam stood. "I do, Master Chairman."

"Be seated, Liam Brady. Be seated, Diane Yousif."

His head spinning with discoveries of his order and his brotherhood, Liam sat. Questions about the group that he feared would remain unanswered swam laps in his head. Just as he thought his body would snap with the rigid discipline he placed upon it to remain motionless, overhead lights bathed the room in whiteness.

The chairman stood and said his first words in Italian-accented English. "That takes care of matters of ritual. Welcome everyone. We have important matters to discuss."

CHAPTER 10

Diane whispered to Liam. "That was wild."

"Tell me about it. I didn't know the cursed daggers could glow red at all... just like ours."

Sensing multiple emotions from the hunters and the council members, she noticed her empathic radar spinning out of control. "I have no idea what's about to happen."

"It must be tough, being mortal like the rest of us."

She backhanded his upper arm, which resisted her smack like stone. "Not funny."

The chairman halted their exchange. "We've never faced the option of hunting a wraith without possessing the twin of his cursed dagger. However, we have a dame of the order who claims a telepathic connection to a long-lost wraith. Given her recent achievements in assisting our present hunters with retiring two daggers, we must view her testimony with the utmost seriousness. Friar Don will argue in favor of aggression. Friar Giovanni will argue in favor of passivity. Friar Francesco will serve as scribe. We begin with Friar Don's opening statement."

Standing, the black-robed cleric-turned-attorney faced the council, whose faces revealed the cracks and sagging skin of age under the artificial lighting. "Per the assignment to their line, Connor and Liam Brady were hunting the sixth wraith last year, which they tracked to the United States. There, they met the virgin and her family–"

Before temperance could stop her, Diane squawked. "Empath!" In an uncomfortable silence, she felt eyes glaring at her, but since she'd committed to her protest, she finished it. "I'm 'the empath'. I'm not 'the virgin'. Please keep my sex life out of this."

From behind the center of the bench, Friar Lucio nodded. "Friar Francesco, please strike the last sentence from the record and note that henceforth, we will no longer refer to Miss Yousif as 'the virgin'. She may, however, be referred to as 'the empath'."

Her pulse still throbbing from the potential faux pas, Diane looked to the chairman. "Thank you, your honor. Mister Chairman."

The old man gave a smile the empath found endearing. "It's 'Master Chairman' if you wish, or just 'Friar Lucio' is fine. Very well, continue, Friar Don."

"There, in the United States, they met the... Miss Yousif and her family. The reports of both hunters credit Miss Yousif with telepathic abilities, dialogues with supernatural entities through visitations, and divine control of the enchanted twin to the sixth wraith's dagger, which she now possesses."

Having expected to part with the blade at a security check point, Diane kept it in her purse. The order seemed to trust her with the weapon she hated parting with.

Friar Don continued. "Days after playing a critical role in defeating the sixth wraith, Miss Yousif entered into a mission helping Connor and Liam Brady defeat the third wraith in Istanbul. In doing so, she demonstrated enhanced powers of telepathy, to include possessing living human souls, which is credited to a divine union with her dagger."

She disliked hearing her control of others' minds labeled as "possessing" for its demonic connotation, but she remained quiet.

"Throughout her short but remarkable history aiding Connor and Liam Brady, she has also used information from supernatural entities which has proven reliable. I therefore urge the council to consider Miss Yousif's contribution to be a divine gift which must be accepted and acted upon in retiring the fifth wraith."

"Thank you, Friar Don. Be seated. Friar Giovanni, your opening statement."

Shorter and stockier than Friar Don, Friar Giovanni spoke

with a voice that floated up and down with the extra syllables of his Italian accent. "I concede the empath's contributions in defeating two wraiths, since the evidence is before us. The question of hunting the fifth wraith, the only wraith who possesses the twin of his cursed dagger, is about prophecy. When he broke our hunting line and took its enchanted dagger, he entered a life of impunity. We had never before and never since have lost an enchanted dagger, and this grave defeat has kept the hunting line broken for centuries."

Diane shot a glare at Liam to see if he knew the wraith's history.

Catching her from the corner of his eye, he turned to her, shrugged, and shook his head.

The portly, balding friar continued. "But God sent an angel to this very chamber one hundred and seventy years ago who promised a new hunter to replenish the fifth line. Divine providence dictates that we must await the new hunter, while prudence dictates that we preserve Connor and Liam Brady for the second line, which is broken but for which we have the enchanted dagger."

"Thank you, Friar Giovanni. Be seated. Friar Don, Friar Giovanni has offered two challenges. You may rebut the first now."

Friar Don stood and addressed the bench. "The prophecy of a new hunter for the fifth line is well known, but it's not well understood. It's quite possible that Connor Brady or Liam Brady fulfill the prophecy. Like many miracles, our angelic prophecy is subject to interpretation. If there's the remotest possibility that one of these hunters fulfills the prophecy, we owe them the chance to prove it."

Seeing a smug look on the young hunter's face, Diane pinched his thigh under the table and whispered. "Don't let it go to your head."

He whispered back. "Ouch. Don't."

"Thank you, Friar Don. Friar Giovanni, your counterpoint?"

The portly man stood. "There are no signs relating to Connor Brady or Liam Brady suggesting that they fulfill the prophecy.

True, we don't always enjoy the luxury of signs, but can any council member confidently risk the lives of two esteemed hunters on the distant probability that the angel foretold of them? These men have already defied incredible odds by defeating two wraiths. The probability of them fulfilling a prophecy calling upon them to battle a third is infinitesimal."

"Thank you, Friar Giovanni. Friar Don, you may rebut the second challenge."

"Father Giovanni says prudence dictates that we preserve Connor and Liam Brady for the second line, but this assumes they will perish if they hunt the fifth wraith. We have not groomed and supported hunters for missions of suicide. Quite the contrary, nine out of ten hunts fail to bring hunter and wraith together in combat. And when we meet the enemy in combat, are we not successful six times out of ten, across all lines throughout our history?"

Believing she could find the wraith, the one the council labeled as their fifth of seven, Diane held her silence since she assumed she'd expended her goodwill during the protest of her virginity. But she would find him. Somehow. And that meant forty percent odds that pursuing the new wraith would bring death to Connor, Liam, or herself.

"Thank you, Friar Don. Friar Giovanni, your counterpoint?"

"We have four wraiths at large and only three active lines of hunters. It's a simple matter of mathematics. We must apply the lines where the lines are equipped to succeed. The second wraith has nobody hunting him, and the Brady line must remain intact. True, this team has achieved unprecedented success, but the fifth wraith poses an unprecedented danger. He has both daggers, he's lived for more than a thousand years, and he mocks us with his existence. Any sign the empath has that would lead our hunters to him could as easily be a trap as an opportunity."

As Giovanni placed his sizable buttocks into his chair, the chairman opened his arms. "You have both made strong cases about our opportunity with the fifth wraith. The council will now probe further with direct testimony from the witnesses.

Connor Brady, please tell the council your opinion of hunting the fifth wraith and how you arrived at it."

The elder hunter stood. "As an aging man who's already lived a full life, I have no fears for my own safety. However, I fear for my son and for Miss Yousif. My concern for Liam is obvious, as he's my son, but in the short time I've known Miss Yousif, I've come to consider her like a daughter. After my failure in Anduze, I trained fifty years to save her life, and doing so has made me overprotective of her. I cannot help that. These two young people have much to offer, but not if we bring about their deaths by rushing them into disadvantaged combat."

Diane liked Connor calling her his daughter, but she disliked his overprotective caution.

"Thank you, Connor Brady. Be seated. Liam Brady, please tell the council your opinion of hunting the fifth wraith and how you arrived at it."

The young hunter stood. "I'm at risk of the sin of pride, but I must state my confidence in myself and our team. My father and I with Miss Yousif and her two family members standing behind us have killed two wraiths together. The results we've achieved are legendary, and I believe it would be unwise to stop us from stopping a monster. As for the lack of an enchanted dagger, I say we have the Lady of the Dagger. Diane's amazing when she uses hers. She'll find a way to overcome our shortcomings and put us face to face with a monster we need to stop."

"Thank you, Liam Brady. Be seated. Diane Yousif, please tell the council your opinion of hunting the fifth wraith and how you arrived at it."

As she pushed her chair back, her mind blanked, which made her susceptible to her startle response during her brother's outburst.

"Oh, why is everyone so stupid?"

Diane snapped her jaw over her shoulder. "Josh!" She turned back to the judge. "I'm sorry, Friar Lucio."

Apparently aware of her brother's autism, he shook his head and raised his palm. "It is quite alright. If we need a recess to calm your brother, we can take one."

"Let me talk to him." She twisted her torso to see her sibling. "You were behaving so well. Why are you interrupting now, Josh?"

He looked at his tablet computer.

"Josh? Will you please talk to me?"

He looked at a corner of the ceiling. "This is so boring."

"I'm sorry you find this boring. I actually think it's very exciting."

"No."

"No, Josh? Why not?"

"It's not exciting. Everyone's just talking about nothing."

"It's not nothing to me. It's about killing another wraith."

Undeterred, her brother raised his voice. "I know that. I'm not stupid. Everyone else here is stupid."

"Okay, Josh, that's enough name-calling."

"But it's true!"

The chairman called out. "Would you like a recess, Miss Yousif?"

She snapped her head to Lucio, shook it, and then looked back to Josh. "Why's it true that everyone's stupid, Josh?"

He looked to the other corner of the ceiling.

"Josh, why is it true that everyone is stupid?

"Because it's easy."

"What's easy, Josh?"

Silence.

"What's so easy to see, Josh?"

"You're the new hunter the angel was talking about. Your name means 'huntress'."

Startled, Diane turned around slowly, but instead of seeing the council she saw white haze and a human form floating within it. In a moment occurring outside the bounds of sidereal time, she watched a female form materialize from the mist.

With an unseen wind flapping a milky gown over her, the Maiden of Yorkshire called out in medieval Middle English. "Your brother speaks the truth."

"What?"

"It is by the grace of his perception that I am here."

"Josh brought you here?"

"At this moment, but it is not my first visit to this place."

Diane's eyes opened wide in wonder. "No!"

"I am the angel of whom they speak, the one who prophesized a new hunter."

"But you're not an angel."

"I appeared as such to the eyes of their predecessors."

"It can't be. I'm not a hunter. I'm an empath."

"An empath can hunt, as you already have."

"But I would've known this was coming because I'm an empath."

"No empath sees all futures."

Fear struck Diane's core. "I need to face mortal danger again, against the toughest wraith they know nothing about?"

"Yes. Avenge me."

"Will the council even let me?"

Revealing a cloudy smile, the maiden cocked her head. "Friar Lucio cheated in his golf game three days ago. He failed to record a stroke in the woods on the thirteenth hole, and he failed to log his fourth put on the seventeenth hole. If he challenges you, remind him." The ghost disappeared, and time restarted for Diane.

Friar Lucio cleared his throat. "Well, given the opinion of Joshua Yousif with respect to the prophecy, Diane Yousif please rise and state your opinion."

She sprang to her feet. "He's right. I am the hunter, or the huntress, of your prophecy. Since you guys seem to get it about how my powers work, I'm going to just spit it out. Friar Lucio, you played golf three days ago, and for whatever reason, you didn't tell the truth about your strokes."

He raised his eyebrows and blushed. "Well, that's impressive. Friar Marco and I were indeed part of a foursome, and... um... you say I did what?"

"Cheated."

The man two chairs down from Friar Lucio turned his jaw towards him. "Could it be that you're in need of confession from the outcome of our golf game, my friend?"

His voice gravelly and distant, Friar Lucio kept his eyes on Diane. "I refuse to answer on the grounds that I want to hear Miss Yousif condemn me with every detail she knows."

"Fine. You dropped a stroke on the thirteenth in the woods and again on the seventeenth on the green. You need to work on your putting game."

As he stood, the friar opened his eyes wide. "It's true. All of it. This is incredible. Yes. Yes. I cheated!"

Two seats away, a councilman protested. "Two strokes? And you claimed to have beaten me by one! Shame on you Lucio! Do you repent?"

"I do."

"Well? Go on. Finish it."

Friar Lucio aimed his gaze upward. "O my God, I am heartily sorry for having offended Thee, and I detest all my sins because of Thy just punishments, but most of all because they offend Thee, my God, Who art all-good and deserving of all my love. I firmly resolve, with the help of Thy grace, to sin no more and to avoid the near occasions of sin."

Friar Marco recited a rote incantation. "God, the Father of mercies, through the death and resurrection of his Son has reconciled the world to himself and sent the Holy Spirit among us for the forgiveness of sins; through the ministry of the Church may God give you pardon and peace, and I absolve you from your sins in the name of the Father, and of the Son, and of the Holy Spirit."

"Thank you, Friar Marco."

"Not so fast, my friend. You have penance. You will do the dishes for a month straight!"

"Shame on me. I'll do the dishes indeed. But forgive me for cheating. You know how I abhor the dishes, with my hands getting so chafed and cracked."

"Why didn't you say so? We could wager something else."

"We will, my old friend, after I make amends. But first, shame on us all for doubting her. I move that we move ahead to a final vote. All in favor of aggression towards the fifth wraith, allowing Miss Yousif to participate as she sees fit?"

Seven hands went up.

"The motion is carried. Connor Brady, Liam Brady, and Diane Yousif come forth for our blessing on this mission. Let us assure ourselves that God is with you all."

CHAPTER 11

Ethan lay in bed staring at the bottom of the upper bunk. The rustling sheets above him worked in concert with his shame in thwarting his attempt to sleep. "What's wrong, Billy?"

The young American from Alabama sounded tired. "I can't sleep. Jet lag."

The wraith scanned the darkness of the volunteers' bunkroom for motion but saw nobody awake. Sleeping men occupied all beds except for the empty bunks of those who stood watch looking for foundering refugee vessels. "I'm having trouble sleeping, too."

"Why? You've been here practically forever."

Ethan snorted. "I have my reasons."

"Well, here we go again. Seems like we've been here before."

Ever since the eager American had arrived as his new companion, Ethan had taken a liking to the youngster. He considered him a nice change from his prior comrade, who'd been secretive and reserved. "You need to sleep, my new friend. Tomorrow's a busy day." They were scheduled to repair a crumbling temporary home in the camp.

"Yup, I know. I get blisters pretty easy if I'm not careful. What if I get them tomorrow?"

"I'll get you a salve and proper gloves. I know where to find them. I'll get some moleskin, too, if it's really bad. Also remember to take a relaxed grip on the hammer. Let the tool do the work."

"Shucks, I guess I'll be okay, Ethan. I don't know what I'd do without you?"

"I'm sure someone will help you if I don't. That's what we're all about here. I just happen to be the senior guy they paired you with."

"Well, I still appreciate it, this being my first time away from home, and all."

The wraith threw off his sheets, placed his feet on the cool floor, and stood in the humid air. Resting his arms on the side of the upper bunk, he saw the youngster's profile. "This is your first time away from home?"

"Well, yeah. People in my town don't travel much."

"But here you are."

Billy waved his fingers dismissively. "My parents are pretty well-to-do, seeing how Daddy runs the biggest Century-21 in the whole county."

"He's the broker?"

"Yeah, and my mom's the top agent. Go figure. Anyway, they didn't want no spoiled brat taking over the business. So, it was either three years of volunteering in tough places, or else I had to join the marines. Now, my cousin's a marine, and they're good people, but I ain't cut out for that."

"Three years volunteering? Not all here, I assume?"

"Nah, this is my first job."

Despite his immortality, Ethan suffered deep human emotions and questioned if he had become overly sensitive during the centuries. He felt pity and compassion for his colleague. "I see why this is difficult for you."

"Yeah. Maybe you can get my mind off it. You got another one of those Middle Age stories on you?"

"I have many."

"Anything to get my mind off home. I miss everyone."

"Alright, then. I'll tell you another one about the evil wizard with the enchanted daggers."

"He's kind of creepy, but I like him. Go ahead."

The wraith adjusted his weight across his bare feet. "It was April thirtieth, in the year one thousand three hundred and fifty-two. He'd just killed a maiden under a blood moon."

"Remind me what that is."

"It's a total eclipse. It happens about once a year on average, but it had been almost three years since his last... atrocity." Speaking about his past gave Ethan a temporary reprieve from his shame. "He'd been killing for centuries, but this time, he got lazy."

"He kills to stay immortal, right?"

"Right. Why else would a man kill innocent strangers?"

"There's all kind of sick and messed up people out there."

"Our wizard is sick and messed up, regardless of his motivations. Nobody can kill so many people without losing either their humanity or their sanity."

The youngster lifted his torso, propped himself on his elbow, and looked at Ethan. "Which is it, for our wizard? Did he lose his sanity or his humanity?"

The wraith was unsure which he'd lost, although he suspected centuries of serial murders had taken portions of each. "Let me finish the story, and you can be the judge."

Billy rolled onto his back. "Okay. Sorry, Ethan."

"The wizard got sloppy and didn't think about night patrols. The Black Plague was still ravaging Europe, and he thought he could kill a sick woman like he always had. But the plague was just starting to slow, and the Sheriff of Yorkshire was trying to restore order with increased law enforcement. After so many people had died, there was chaos as the survivors sorted out how to handle the gaps in land ownership and open jobs."

"And people complain about modern times."

"Many thought it was the end, but the wizard knew better. He had magic and knew he could live forever, as long as he killed innocent women and avoided harm from accidents or combat. But as he was walking out of the forest after coldly murdering a sick maiden and burning her body, three of the sheriff's men on horseback met him. One of them aimed a crossbow at him, one of them rode towards the fire's flickering lights, and the leader ordered him to surrender."

Billy scoffed. "Little did they know they were messing with a wizard."

"He warned them. He told them to leave him alone for their

own safety, but since he was armed with only two daggers, they thought he was crazy."

"Two? You said he only had one in your last story."

Ethan's prior tale to the homesick American had been about an earlier kill before he'd captured the twin dagger from the hunters. "I know. This is the first time he'd ever carried two daggers. One was gifted to him long ago by the spirit that kept him alive. The other he'd won by defeating two fellow wizards who had a dagger like his, only they used it against him."

"Until he took it from them."

"Until he killed them and took it from them. He'd been afraid to use it, but the spirit of the first dagger encouraged him to carry it on the night of the sacrifice, as a warning... a premonition."

The American snorted. "He's got a pretty sharp spirit guide."

Ethan looked away as he recalled the battle with the sheriff's men. The pain lingered in his heart with the suffering he internalized from all his victims.

"What's wrong? Keep going."

"The wizard didn't know it yet, but he was still young. However, he thought himself old, and the burdens of life were weighing on him already. He dared the men to shoot him. At first, they refused, saying he deserved a fair trial, but when the scout returned from the forest and described the homicide, the men were ready to kill him. There he stood, holding two ancient daggers, and he lifted one to his ear as if to throw it, praying for crossbow bolts to end his misery."

"Why didn't he just kill himself?"

Ethan scoffed. "You make it sound easy. Have you ever tried?"

Billy rolled his jaw towards the wraith. "Well, no."

"Don't. Your life's already short enough, comparatively. Think of living hundreds of years, knowing you're a monster, and that you could live hundreds or even thousands of years more."

"Yeah. I get it. Like you said, you'd lose your humanity or your sanity, I reckon."

"The wizard dared the men to attack him, and two of them shot their crossbows. The bolts were well aimed, but the wizard's magic was too strong." Ethan paused while remembering the power of his lording spirit protecting him and condemning him to ongoing homicides. "His arms and hands moved like lightening, shifting the daggers into the paths of the incoming bolts. He deflected them, and then he again begged the men to leave."

"I would've run after seeing a guy knock away two arrows."

"They must've considered it mere trickery because all three of them drew their swords and dismounted. Then he made quick work of them. Imagine it, one man with two ancient bronze knives defeating three men with swords."

"That's magic for you."

The wraith considered it magic with a curse. "The wizard had to leave the county and start his life over. He was immortal, but he was scared and lonely. It's never easy to restart. So, it's okay that you're a bit homesick."

"You're good at making up stories. Did you come up with these while you were digging your own dagger out of the dirt somewhere in Ancient Greece?"

Ethan kept the hunters' captured dagger locked in a box, which was secured under his lockable bunk. As far as his volunteer companions knew, he had a solitary knife.

"Babylon, Billy. Mesopotamia."

"It's almost like you were there."

"How do you know I wasn't?"

The American scoffed. "Huh. Reincarnation. Daddy says that's a bunch of bunk, but he's a blue-blooded American Baptist. I say, you got to keep an open mind to everything."

"That's right, my friend. Just keep your mind open and stop worrying. After all, what's the worst that could happen? Death?" Ethan returned to his bunk and half-whispered his suicidal conclusion. "And if you were like the wizard, you'd welcome the end."

CHAPTER 12

The next morning, Liam glanced at the seats of the Colosseum while a tour guide droned on about the structure's history. The young hunter's thoughts twirled in all directions except those leading to Rome's tourist attractions.

Beside him, Diane nudged the cast over his upper arm. "Where's your mind?"

His bullet wounds were itchy, as he imagined the healing process after being punctured by metal rounds would feel. Their slow mending contrasted the deep cut of his other arm, which had undergone a miraculous recovery at the end of the empath's enchanted and self-cauterized dagger. "I can't enjoy this while there's a wraith out there."

"If he's planning his next attack in Lesbos, we'll find him. If he isn't, a day or two of chilling in Rome isn't going to matter. You need to relax. You're too high strung."

In silence, he accepted her judgment as true.

Since his father had shown him Rome during his childhood, Liam was finding the day hopping between sites uninspiring. While the elder hunter seemed to enjoy pointing out details that Josh called out from memory and from his tablet, the younger hunter's frontal cortex twisted itself around the problem of the wraith.

Under the vaulted ceilings of Saint Peter's Basilica, he tried to admire the architecture of the transept where the halls of the cross-shaped building met at right angles, but his mind wandered. Lacking an enchanted twin of the savage's cursed dagger, he needed Diane's empathic power to find the killer, but she was a neophyte in her art. Her skills offered many paths, but each option risked warning the wraith or leaving Diane in a coma-like state for days.

Behind him, Josh called out. "St. Peter's Baldachin is a large Baroque sculpted bronze canopy. It's technically called a ciborium or baldachin, but all my references call it a baldachin."

"Huh? Oh, yeah. Nice." Liam looked at the high altar before him, and then he returned within himself while strolling through the church.

When they entered the Sistine Chapel, he lumbered by frescoes and paintings of famous origins, but art held little value to him. He preferred function over form. In front of Michelangelo's Creation of Adam, where God extended his finger from a cloud to his naked, reclining creature. He snorted. "Wouldn't his exposed willy be considered profane nudity today?"

Diane stood by his side, right where he liked her and where she managed to always be. "Nobody minds naked statues, though. Here, we'll make a statue. I'll play God and you play Adam. Just take off your clothes." She giggled as she leaned back and extended her fingertip.

"I'm not showing as much as my skivvies in here, much less my bum and my willy."

"You're no fun."

Exploring her ludicrous lack of balance, he pushed his finger into hers. To both his dismay and his amusement, the perturbation to her stance sent her tipping backwards. "Bloody... Diane!"

She thrust her arms forward and collapsed to her hip, and her purse spilled on the floor. Atop her concealed belongings, her dagger clicked across stone and tapped the sole of a tourist toddler's walking shoes.

Before Liam could race to the knife, the empath crawled to it and clutched it. He grabbed the sleeve covering her nearest arm to lift her, but his hands caressed her bare skin. His mind went blank, and he stood in paralyzed awe, in a trance. Seeing everyone in the room in frozen timelessness, he glared at her.

With her knife in her other hand, she remained on the ground. Though she stayed still, he heard her voice. "Don't move."

He answered within his mind. "Bloody hell. I can't move a muscle. What's happening?"

"This is kind of what it's like in my visions and telepathic links, but it's never been so clear. Yeah. Clear. I'm not sure what else to call it."

"Are you in my head, or am I in yours? This is different than when you tried to make me pick my nose."

"I don't know. I think we're in a shared trance."

He likened the experience to a dream. Everything remained in perfect stillness–except the dagger. "Look. It's moving. Can you see it?"

Frozen, her eyes faced enough towards the floor to give her a line of sight to her knife. "You're right. It's moving in my hand. I can't stop it. I can't do anything except hold it."

"What do we do?"

"I don't know. I was going to ask you the same thing."

"How the hell should I know? The dagger's obviously doing this, and you're the Lady of the Dagger."

"Nobody calls me that except you."

"Father and Josh do."

"Besides them, nobody else does."

"That's not the point. We can't just slip out of time in the Sistine Chapel and slip back in with things having moved. The Vatican's a place where people happen to believe in miracles– and demonology, for that matter. They'll take notice if witnesses see us teleporting ourselves, or a dagger, or anything across the room."

She remained a statue while chastising him in his head. "Oh, for God's sake, stop worrying. The hand is quicker than the eye. Anyone who sees the dagger rotate at the speed of light won't believe what they see, and nobody's going to even see it."

Mentally grunting, he agreed. "Just make sure we don't move anything else."

"Like we can. I can't move a muscle. Can you?"

He realized he wasn't breathing. "Well, no."

"Stop worrying!"

Her prodding helped him accept the risk. "Okay, the dagger's moving. I'll live with that. What does it mean, though?"

"If I could look at you, you'd feel like an idiot."

"That happens a lot when you look at me, actually."

"Ugh. Don't play the martyr. Poor Liam."

"I wasn't. It's just that you're so damned simple."

"Simple? You mean like a dumb ass?"

"That's not what I meant."

"What did you mean?"

He put some thought into his damage control. "I meant that you're quick to call something black or white, when it's really gray and needs more analysis."

"Oh, thanks, Mister Deep Thoughts. Have you ever heard of analysis paralysis?"

Ignoring her jab, he saw the dagger steady almost ninety degrees from the direction it had pointed before he'd touched her. "Look. It stopped."

Her wrist stopped with it.

The world around him recommenced its normal pace, and his chest expanded with air. "Don't move. I'll get a picture." Holding her with one hand, he used the other to whip out his phone and take a snapshot of the dagger. With the right-angled lines of the floor serving as a grid, he expected to reconstruct an approximation of the weapon's final orientation. "Okay. I got it."

She tucked the weapon into her purse and let him pull her to her feet. "Thanks."

"Are you okay?"

"Yeah, just a sore hip. You get used to it when you're a klutz."

"I didn't mean to push you over. I was just playing around."

"I know. I should've been more careful the way I leaned."

He moved close to her, inhaling the scent of her intoxicating perfume. For a moment, his desire for her broke through the stratosphere before he could calm himself with thoughts of his purpose. "Maybe this was a divine accident. If this was what I think it was, your dagger just pointed to the wraith."

"My dagger with you and me touching it became a substitute for the missing enchanted dagger."

"It's not really missing. We know he's got it. Or at least he had it, and he's a fool if he lost it."

"A thousand years is a long time to keep something safe."

"He's lived for a thousand years, but he's only had it for about seven hundred. Anyway, I get your point. But it's a good question if he lost it or buried it or whatever. Did your dagger just point to the site of his last kill, or did it point towards the missing enchanted dagger?"

She shrugged. "In case you're not listening, which you stink at, I'm as clueless about this as you are."

"I listen!"

She rolled her eyes. "I guess you're not that bad, for a man."

"Get back to the question. It's important. I'm pretty sure this is pointing towards Lesbos."

"How can you know?"

"I'm just estimating, but I'd be surprised if it isn't. Look at the sun through the windows up there. The sun's roughly to the south. That means the knife's pointing roughly east."

"You're such a boy scout."

"Get serious. It's really three questions, because if your dagger points to the enchanted twin of his cursed dagger, and he's lost that twin, then what just happened only helps us recover the twin."

"But that's still a good thing."

He nodded. "Absolutely. I won't deny it. If it pointed to the site of the last kill, then we know how to play by those rules. But if it pointed to the twin, and he has the dagger, then your dagger will take us right to him, and we've just stumbled upon the most powerful tool we've ever had to hunt any wraith."

CHAPTER 13

Alone in the beach shack, Ethan held his breath as his domineering spirit terrified him with an epiphany. Silent for seven hundred and nineteen years, the hunting line that had once sought him had been reborn. "No, Master."

The wordless epiphany continued. Yes, descendants of the Tribe of Naphtali sought him.

He burst through the door of the watch station, raced down its steps, and ran down the path leading to his quarters.

Behind him, Billy yelled. "Where are you going? We just started our shift."

Terrified, Ethan ignored his American colleague and jogged to the tent that housed the male volunteers. Under the canopy, standing fans blew tepid air over him which cooled the sweat running over his skin.

When he reached his bunk, he pulled his tiny safe from under the bed and worked its combination. Opening the steel door, he slumped his shoulders when he saw the enchanted weapon he'd taken from the hunters six hundred and sixty-nine years ago. Confused about his Master's warning, he locked the safe, slid it under his bed, and walked back to his post.

The American greeted him with a scowl. "What was that all about?"

Ethan formulated a lie. "I... needed to use the facilities."

"You had to take a shit?"

The wraith shrugged. "Let's leave it at that."

"Damn, that was quite a clip you were running at."

Disoriented from his hasty jog and the news from his lording spirit, Ethan lumbered up the creaky wood steps and passed his colleague. "Yes, it was. Let's just get back to work."

"Okay. Don't run off and leave me alone like that."

Alone in the watch shack, Ethan gathered his thoughts. He questioned if he'd misunderstood his Master, but then a visitation erased all doubts.

To assure him of his new horror, the ghost appeared in front of him. Floating above the moist planks, she wore a milky white gown that reflected the morning sunlight, and she stared at him through black circles. Her soft, fuzzy features seemed haughty. "Why did you kill me?"

Her presence haunted him, but he believed he deserved her torment. "As I've told you for all these years, I had no choice."

"Every human has free will."

"I spared you from needless suffering."

"Your continued false justification delays the inevitable."

Her words had characterized a new threat. "What's that? What's inevitable?"

"Your acceptance of the truth."

Scared, he looked away. "I'm afraid. I know of what you speak."

She cocked her head. "Yes, the hunters. You know of their revival." Her tone was teasing, like he'd glimpsed the truth she'd threatened, but he'd overlooked the hidden meat of it.

"Stop with your torment. I beg you."

Her misty white brow furrowed. "Your begging me for mercy is justice. Even if I would will it, I cannot."

He resigned himself to his anguish. "Continue then. Do what you must."

"You know they are coming for you."

"Yes. It is shocking news."

"Did you think the line would remain broken forever?"

"What else was I to think?"

"Divine fate has peculiar ways of surprising us."

"I trust you enjoy the toll their rebirth reaps from my soul."

More animated than she'd been during her hundreds of prior visits, she sneered. "The pain in your heart is justice, but it pales in comparison to the destiny the hunters portend."

He spat his anger. "What would you have done in my stead? Offered immortality... able to feed upon doomed lives... alleviating suffering. Could you have resisted the temptation?"

"I resisted the temptation to sicken my family when faced with imminent death. I passed my test, but I am stranded here because of you!" Her brow cast paranormal shadows from unseen light sources over her darkening eyes.

"You will pass. You must. You burden my conscience."

"Your conscience is dubious and irrelevant. You are an aberration born of wickedness."

"No."

"Yes. You love no one but yourself, and that is not love. This has corrupted you."

Based upon past visions with the ghost he'd created, he knew her words were meant to torment him, but with the renewed hunting line, his perspective changed. Faced with destruction, he found himself questioning his existence. He brooded over the meaning of his lengthy life, and the introspective analysis sickened him.

She furrowed her brow. "You are heeding my words."

Realization struck him. He was a monster. "Yes."

"Amazing. The threat of death has changed you."

"Yes. I can bear it no longer. Can you not see that I have detested what I am for too long?"

"Yes."

"What am I to do?"

Her facial features relaxed. "This is unexpected. Do you seek guidance... from me?"

"Yes!"

"Do you desire deliverance? Perhaps forgiveness?"

"I seek redemption. I seek justice. I seek any end other than the life I live."

"Is this truly your desire?"

"Yes!"

"You no longer justify yourself with claims of alleviating the suffering of your victims?"

"No, I do not."

"Then the end you seek is open to you. Beware the hunters."

As she vanished, he fell to his knees, unsheathed his dagger, and held it in both hands. "What must I do, Master?"

His domineering spirit issued the unspoken answer. He would have to defeat the hunters.

"Can I not simply avoid them?"

No, he could not. His killing was too frequent to escape a re-born line, and his overseeing spirit needed his wraith to carry out a mission of vengeance. A huntress had joined the hunters, bringing their number to three. Much as his Master disliked the men who sought his wraith, the spirit despised the female who had sullied his past.

"I will face them, Master." His words were misleading since he would welcome defeat more readily than victory. He rose to his feet and put away his dagger.

From his patrol around the watch shack's exterior, Billy entered the small space. "Who were you talking to?"

Quickly, Ethan lifted his cell phone. "I was on speakerphone."

"Was it anyone interesting?"

"She's a very old... acquaintance."

"She's a 'she', huh? Got yourself a girl back home?"

"More like a stalker."

"Well, shucks, Ethan. You don't always got to answer the phone. I had me a girl in high school who wouldn't stop pestering me until I wore her down by ignoring her. Took a little guts to let the cell phone ring or to walk by her at school, but I did it."

"Excuse me, Billy." He brushed by the young American and into the sultry air. Behind him, the door clicked open.

Billy sounded meek. "I didn't mean to offend you."

His thoughts consumed in pending mortal combat, the wraith ignored him.

"I'm sorry if I offended you. Are you okay?"

Ethan lied. "I'm fine. Just let me be alone."

"Okay." The American retreated into the shack.

As solitude amplified his fear, Ethan lowered his gaze to the beach and watched the gentle waves lap the shore in rhythm with the mix of negative emotions washing over his soul. The more he reflected upon his fate, the heavier his depression weighed upon him.

Attempting to distract himself from his uncertain fate, he pulled his ball cap to the bridge of his nose to shade his eyes from the rising sun, and he scanned the water for overloaded dinghies and other small vessels carrying refugees from mainland Turkey.

The thought of desperate, frightened, and hopeless refugees reminded him of the thousand years of misery he'd seen in the world, a misery which had embedded itself within his heart. His life had devolved over the millennium into a hollow and meaningless labor of survival, and his instincts drove him to remain alive.

The threat of death from the hunters set his thoughts in new directions. Caressing the knife at his thigh, he wondered if he had the courage to use it on himself.

He withdrew it from its sheath, clutched its handle with both hands, and aimed the tip at his heart. Pulling as hard as he could, he punctured his tee shirt and sliced the skin between his ribs. As his nerves sent pain signals to his brain, and as he felt his heart's rhythmic pumping against his dagger, he gave up.

Glaring at the blade, he hoped to recover his dignity and find a simpler way to accomplish the task. He lowered the bronze edge against his wrist and slashed, but the shallow cut missed his vulnerable veins. Trying again, he redoubled his effort to bring forth a deadly flow, but his second attempt created another superficial wound.

"Damn it."

He lifted his wrist to his mouth and sucked away the trickling fruits of his failures. The coppery taste mocked his attempts, which in retrospect were pathetic gestures.

Although he struggled to drain the life from his flesh, he thought of a new way to commit suicide–relative to his cursed existence. He hoped that ridding himself of the dagger would free him from his Master and allow him to die within a normal human lifespan.

He marched down the stairs and onto the shore. Laboring against the dirt, he strode towards the water. Standing at the edge of the waves lapping against the grass and reeds below him, he pinched the blade between his thumb and index finger, lifted it behind his head, and cast it into the surf. "Good bye, Master."

He turned his back to the water and started towards the watch station. His fleeting moment of triumphant euphoria yielded to the horror of his lost immortality. Though he'd demanded mortality, now that he'd declared it, he was afraid to die.

A jolt knocked his jaw and sent him sideways. Pain rose from the skin above his neck, and he palpated the side of his face. Blood covered his fingertips. Wondering what had cut him, he saw dirt shoot up from the footpath between himself and the shack, and then a blur of bronze traced a line from the ground to his sticky hand.

Sporting the blood from his jawline on its tip, his dagger rested in his palm. Shocked, he looked back to the sea to verify his solitude, but he saw a small circle of boiling water with fire and rising smoke, as if gasoline burned on the surface. In awe, he stared until the water swallowed the eerie vision and left him in the early morning solitude.

He looked at the shack for confirmation of his vision, but some distant vessel held the American's glare in a different direction.

Ethan then gazed at his knife and exclaimed his terror in a single-word whisper. "Master?"

The answer came in a silent flash. His lording spirit had rejected his resignation, and he would remain a savage killer with a destiny of engaging in mortal combat with the hunters.

CHAPTER 14

An atmosphere of intense scrutiny filled the subterranean courtroom as Diane followed Friar Don down its central corridor. Standing under the bright lights where Connor and Liam had stated their cases days ago before the council, a tall, broad-shouldered man studied her. But instead of him making her feel uncomfortable, she sensed he was an ally.

When they reached the witness bench, Friar Don introduced the stranger. "Miss Diane Yousif, this is Jean-Paul Diop, one of our knights from Senegal."

She thought he appeared shy of fifty, his smooth dark brown skin showing small cracks forming around his eyes. A scar reminiscent of a slashing wound ran down his cheek from his left eye to his jaw. "Pleased to meet you, Jean-Paul."

As he took her hand in a strong but gentle grip, he spoke with an accent hinting of the relaxed French heard in Western Africa. "The pleasure is mine, Miss Yousif."

Touching him invoked a deep spiritual connection, buried and dormant but ready to wield great power if awoken. She knew immediately what he was. "You're a wraith hunter."

Above six feet in height, the African hunter nodded. "I am. It's remarkable that you can tell."

Friar Don stepped in front of the bench. "Jean-Paul is fifty years old, and after the passing of his father fourteen years ago, he is the elder of his line. We pray for the birth of his son soon to deliver him his heir."

Diane eyed the African again. "You've hunted a wraith already?"

"Twenty-five years ago." With a hint of pride, he pointed to his scar. "And he gave me this to remember him."

The empath's curiosity overcame her, and she wanted to know every detail about his experience with a wraith. A quick debate raged in her head about asking him, but she took the black cloak moving towards the bench as an indication to remain quiet.

Friar Don carried the metal staff upon which stood a bronze casting of the order's eight-point cross. He planted it into the floor and then faced the room, which included only Diane and the African hunter. "All rise for the Council of Paranormal Activities."

As the council entered the room from its front door, Diane wondered why she'd been summoned without Connor or Liam and why a third hunter from a different line stood beside her. Impatient by nature, she clenched her jaw to withhold her questions inside her head.

Friar Don stepped to the center of the arc, waited for the seven members to find their seats, and then addressed the elder knights. "Esteemed members of the Council of Paranormal Activities, we are gathered to investigate the episode of enlightenment shared yesterday between Miss Diane Yousif, Honorary Dame of Honor, and Liam Brady, Knight of Honor. Before you stand Miss Yousif and Jean-Paul Diop, Knight of Honor. I begin the session with the verification of identity of Jean-Paul Diop."

From his central chair, Friar Lucio spoke in the voice Diane still found endearing. "The abridged version of verification of identity will suffice. Use only the dagger before me."

"As you wish, Master Chairman." His thin frame moving swiftly under his black cloak, Friar Don stepped forward and unlatched the hatch covering the dagger. Iron hinges groaned as he flipped open the lid, and then he stepped away.

Friar Lucio called Jean-Paul to the bench, and with the hunter's gaze present, the chairman summoned magic to the exposed blade, which glowed. "Upon invocation, the cursed dagger glows in his sight. This man is a hunter of wraiths, descended from the Tribe of Naphtali, and ordained to represent this council in battle against the enemy." As the glow receded, it yielded blackness over the column. "Be seated, everyone."

Friar Don moved to the column and sealed the dagger under its hatch. He then followed Jean-Paul to the witness bench.

Seated beside Diane, the hunter whispered. "No matter how many times I visit the council, I always feel like an alien."

"I'm glad it's not just me. How many times have you been here?"

"This is my third time. They try to keep the younger hunters away during their training. So, I didn't even know about this until I was twenty-five years old."

Seated behind the semicircular bench, Friar Lucio addressed the small audience. "Friar Don, please give your opening statement."

The friar stood. "Yesterday while touring the Sistine Chapel, Miss Yousif lost her balance and fell to the floor. Her dagger fell from her purse, and when she grabbed it, Liam Brady grabbed her, creating a paranormal trance which they shared. While they were within the trance, the dagger rotated in Miss Yousif's hand and settled on a bearing which Liam Brady later estimated at one-zero-zero degrees. This bearing aligns with Miss Yousif's visions of the sixth wraith's last tribute near Lesbos, Greece, on June the twenty-eighth. We are here today to understand this shared trance through discussion and experimentation."

The chairman's endearing voice set Diane in motion. "Miss Yousif, do you agree with Friar Don's statement?"

"I do."

"Very well, then. Please bring your dagger with you and approach the bench."

After withdrawing the blade from her purse, she walked to the center of the semicircle, revealing the lines of age, whitening hair, and bald spots of the council members.

Despite his age and rank, Friar Lucio maintained his air of courtesy. "Miss Yousif, the first experiment we'd like to conduct is to attempt to repeat the trance with a hunter from a different line. Ergo, we have summoned Jean-Paul Diop. Do you agree to reattempt the trance with this hunter whom you've just met?"

She saw no harm in it. "I do."

"Please hold the dagger on the ground as you did in the Sistine Chapel."

"I was actually sitting on the floor when it happened. I fell."

"Friar Don, can you acquire a blanket for Miss Yousif to recreate the scenario?"

"Don't bother. If I can handle the germs of a tourist spot, I can handle whatever germs are still alive down here."

"Very well, Miss Yousif. As you wish. Please." He gestured to the ground.

She sat on her hip, rolled to her side, and extended the knife on the ground. Glancing at etchings in the stone, she noticed a strange pattern on the floor.

Friar Lucio seemed to grasp her confusion. "What you're looking at, Miss Yousif, is a compass. The direction of true north points to me, while the direction of true south points down the aisle."

"That's pretty cool."

"Cool is an adequate description. It's been there for centuries. Jean-Paul, approach the bench and hold Miss Yousif as if helping her to her feet, but let her stay on the ground."

As commanded, the guest hunter obliged and squeezed her arm with tempered strength.

She felt nothing abnormal. "It's not happening."

The hunter confirmed her experience. "I also notice nothing."

A random member of council spoke. "Can you both close your eyes?"

She tried it. "Still nothing."

"Me neither."

Another random voice. "Is the dagger moving at all?"

Loosening her grip, she sought active evidence of the blade's will, but it was silent. "No. It's doing nothing."

Friar Lucio's tone betrayed his disappointment. "This is unfortunate. We're gaining no insights. We'll be forced to speculate."

Another council member speculated. "What if Jean-Paul thinks of his last battle with the wraith?"

"I will try." The hunter closed his eyes. "I sense nothing."

"Me neither." Diane wanted to help. "Maybe there's something about the Sistine Chapel being holy ground?"

The chairman grunted. "This, too, is holy ground."

"Then I can't think of any way to make this happen again without Liam. Um, can I get up now?"

"Yes, yes, of course. Please, be seated, Miss Yousif."

With impressive ease, the hunter helped her up, and she walked to her seat. She was surprised as she looked back at the hunter who remained before the council.

Friar Lucio stood. "Thank you for your service, Jean-Paul Diop, Knight of Honor. God willing, I'll enjoy seeing your son presented to you soon."

The hunter nodded. "You honor me with your goodwill, Master Chairman. I welcome the day."

"You are dismissed. Friar Don, please escort Jean-Paul out of the building."

Following the friar, the hunter turned and strode up the aisle. He offered a cordial nod to Diane as he passed, and then as mysteriously as he'd appeared, he slipped away.

Still standing, the chairman addressed Diane and his council. "We're waiting for Connor and Liam Brady to arrive. I declare a ten-minute recess. When we come back, we'll see what sense we can make of this."

CHAPTER 15

Liam followed his father and Friar Don into the subterranean courtroom. At the chamber's far end, several council members stood in front of their benches in animated discussions. Alone, Diane sat behind the witness bench.

Her eyes glimmered when she saw him, and she waved.

He brushed by his father and joined her. "What'd I miss?"

"Nobody swore me to secrecy, but I don't feel like telling you."

"I know the gist of what you were doing, but I'm never supposed to meet another hunter."

"Somehow, I know that. I also know that I'm not supposed to tell you anything about him."

Beside Liam, his father interjected. "Her empathic powers serve her well. It's indeed true that she cannot tell us. If she were to try, she would not find the words. Divine providence dictates that the hunters of separate lines remain ignorant of each other."

"You guys didn't pass him on the way out?"

Friar Don answered. "I stashed Connor and Liam in a waiting room off the beaten path, so to speak. And Connor's correct, we don't need to instruct witnesses who've met hunters from multiple lines. Fate has prevented anyone from revealing clues of the identities of one line to members of the other."

The supernatural laws rang true with Liam. "I wanted to ask her, but I knew I shouldn't, and I doubted I could if I tried."

"It's a mystery, but it's proven, nonetheless." Friar Don faced the council and raised his voice. "Is the council ready to reconvene?"

His question sent the members into motion walking around

the end of their arced bench to their places. From the central seat of the seven, the chairman brought order to the room. "Be seated everyone. Let us reconvene with a summary of our earlier session. Friar Don…"

"With Miss Yousif and a hunter of a different line, we attempted to recreate the trance that Miss Yousif and Liam Brady shared. We were unable to recreate any sort of unnatural phenomenon."

Mixed emotions flowed through Liam, and as he questioned how he should feel, he settled on 'special'. He was something special to Diane–so he hoped–until Friar Don issued a challenge.

"We will now attempt to reproduce the trance with Connor Brady and Miss Yousif."

Liam watched in helpless silence as the chairman summoned his father and the empath, his empath. "Miss Yousif, please bring your dagger and approach the bench."

Her blade in hand, she walked to the center of the semicircle. "On the ground again?"

Friar Lucio sounded too affectionate for Liam's liking. "Yes, please. Just like last time."

The empath sprawled on the ground.

"Connor Brady, approach the bench and hold Miss Yousif as if helping her to stand, but let her stay where she is."

As his father walked to Diane, Liam burned his eyes on the blade. The elder hunter reached for the empath, and the dagger shot immediately to the east. Liam grew envious of his father's touching of Diane and of its paranormal effect.

The chairman sprang to his feet with energy Liam had considered impossible for the older man. "The dagger moved."

Diane released the dagger and stood. "That was really slow."

Connor frowned. "It seemed no slower than what Liam and I have seen with enchanted daggers."

"It was slow compared to what Liam and I had."

Her words soothed the young hunter and reduced his envy.

Friar Lucio sat. "That's interesting, but we'll see if you experience the speed you expect with Liam here in these chambers.

But first, Connor, please note the bearing."

"One-zero-zero. It's the same one that Liam noted in the chapel."

"Excellent. Connor, be seated. Miss Yousif, I'll have to ask you to grab your dagger and feign falling to the ground one more time."

"It's okay. I'm getting used to it."

"Liam Brady, approach the bench and hold Miss Yousif as you did yesterday, but let her stay on the ground."

Although he and Diane had repeated the phenomenon three times the prior evening, the young hunter was eager to demonstrate his special bond with the empath in the confines of the sanctum. He trotted towards her but slowed when he realized he portrayed an embarrassing exuberance.

She lifted her arm and made contact with his fingers.

When their flesh touched, they became frozen in time, but he could speak into her mind. "What did you mean it was slower with my father?"

"It took forever. He's adorable, but he's boring. I don't know what to talk to him about."

The dagger passed through its midpoint of its expected rotation. "This time together when the world stops for us goes by too fast for me." He felt like a dork after letting the words escape.

"That's sweet, but the part where we can't move is creepy."

Hearing her call his clumsy reveal of affection 'sweet', he wanted to rip himself out of the paralyzing trance and slap his face against his palm. To save what dignity he could, he diverted her attention towards the knife. "It's almost there."

Several more seconds of trance time concluded the dagger's movement, and the world returned to normalcy. She tugged him, reminding him to lift her.

He helped her up and then shot a nervous glance at the chairman. "Was it the same as with my father from your perspective?"

"Yes. Exactly."

Diane folded her arms. "It was a lot faster for me, though. At least ten times faster, maybe more."

"Thank you, Miss Yousif. Liam, please note the final direction of the dagger." The chairman sat and leaned back. "What could this mean?" After blank stares, he aimed his palm towards the witness bench and looked at Diane and Liam. "Be seated."

When he returned to his seat, the young hunter mulled over the chairman's unanswered question. To him, the difference in perceived speeds of the trance meant he was unique to Diane, and the observation consumed him. He was special to her.

One council member speculated. "Could the difference be a matter of Miss Yousif's perspective?"

The chairman responded. "That's a difficult question, since all time in her trance is subject to her perspective. Perhaps we should hear from the hunters. Connor Brady, can you estimate in seconds or minutes how you would measure the duration of your trance?"

"Perhaps five to ten minutes."

"Thank you, Connor. Liam Brady?"

"Thirty seconds, I'd say."

"Thank you, Liam. Apparently, the hunters agree that there's a temporal difference."

Liam noted the equivalent tactical value of his father's union with Diane and his, given that the dagger produced the same real-world result, but he kept that observation a secret. He groped for a cause of the difference. "Could it be genetic? I'm a biological cousin of my father, but I'm not his offspring. My DNA could be a lot closer to Diane's than his."

Friar Lucio raised his eyebrows. "That's a possibility worth assessing. Friar Don, please get a saliva sample from Miss Yousif after our proceedings so that we can have her DNA."

"Of course, Master Chairman."

Liam recalled that the order had recorded his DNA before he was old enough to remember it.

Another member called out. "Could it be a factor of age?" The comment begat soft laughter from his aged colleagues.

Diane blurted out her epiphany. "It's love. Love is the power of an empath."

Friar Lucio cocked his head. "Connor Brady did say during our prior session that he perceived you as a daughter. Do you see him and love him as a father?"

She shared a glance with Connor. "Yes."

The chairman's tone was assertive. "The Greeks would call this *storge*, or familiar love. It's a strong human relation. But there are stronger bonds. Miss Yousif, your insight has taken our conversation in a surprising direction, and I must ask if you love Liam Brady."

Her eyes paralyzed the young hunter. "Yes."

"And you, Liam Brady. Do you love Miss Yousif?"

His heart pounded his chest. Exposed and ambushed, he kept his gaze upon hers while he forced his hasty answer. "Yes."

Friar Lucio became pensive. "This is most unexpected. If I am to hypothesize an answer, I would estimate that our young people share an intense love. The Greeks would call it *ludus*, or the playful love of lovers. If true, I must question how a knight pledged to chastity and divinely protected from unchaste temptations has engaged in such a bond."

Diane corrected the friar. "It's *agape*. Maybe it's both *ludus* and *agape*. But during our last mission, I had to adopt a selfless love for him to save him."

Thankful he could stay quiet, Liam felt his innards melt into hot jelly while his heart fluttered. How did she love him, and what did it mean?

The chairman summarized his quandary. "*Agape*, you say? If love is the power of the empath, and if love has an impact on the shared trance, then we have a working theory. I can only warn you to protect and nurture these bonds between yourselves, because this is the strongest advantage you have over your enemy."

CHAPTER 16

One thousand years ago, a teenaged voyager walked on a cart path in the county of Essex. On the dawn of his adulthood, he strolled towards his desired destiny.

Though he missed the sheep-herding family he left behind, he enjoyed a young man's levity of a hopeful heart and an unburdened back. Carrying a skin of water, a knife, and a pouch of coins at the hip of his tunic, he intended to join a mendicant order of friars with whom he could serve his fellow man.

As the afternoon heat receded on the first day of his three-day southward trek, he entered a hamlet and walked to its tavern. Brushing dust off his front, he pushed open an oaken door and walked to a counter.

A ruddy-faced man with grayish white hair and beard greeted him with a smile. "Welcome weary traveler. Do you seek accommodations?"

Lacking the funds for an overnight stay, the voyager intended to sleep in the woods. "No, sir. Just sustenance."

The smile on the tavern's apparent owner shrank with the lost opportunity for lodging income. "I have a meal with rye bread, ale, and pottage of barley, leeks, and fava beans for six pence."

As he reached for his pouch, the young man shared his exuberance. "Money will soon no longer matter to me. I'm joining the Hospitallers of Rochester."

"Never heard of them."

The voyager slapped six coins on the counter. "I was sure their work had reached you here. They tend to the sick and the poor."

"Rochester's a two-day walk. Perhaps they're a bit far away to reach us here."

Budding energy flowed through the young man. "Then I will open their arms wider! None will want for sustenance and care after I join them."

The inn keeper chuckled. "I like your youthful ways." He pushed two coins across the counter. "Four pence is enough for your supper today."

The voyager beamed with pride as he pushed the pennies back to the inn keeper. "I am called to a destiny of charity, sir, and I mean giving–not taking. I shall pay for my supper."

After satiating his hunger, the young man departed the inn and took to the dirt road. As the sun set, he hailed a traveler on foot who approached from the opposite direction. "Hail, fellow! What tidings from the south?"

The stranger wore a tunic of grayish undyed wool. "God save ye, fellow." As he approached, his sandy blonde hair appeared disheveled over a round face. He stopped and offered tidings. "To the south there are strange occurrences. A farmhouse outside Tidwalditun went ablaze under the full moon before dawn, and there's talk of the sheriff's men afoot."

The voyager estimated the distance to the village of Tidwalditun at three leagues down this path. "The sheriff's men? How unusual. What laws have been violated?"

"I met a traveler on the other side of the village as I walked north. He claimed landownership and privilege as a man of standing in the county. He rode a steed and wore a tunic of fine linens. So, I won't doubt him. He spoke of the farmhouse burned to ashes and of the sheriff's men on horseback, but he cast doubt upon the riders."

"How so?"

"The sheriff's men were few–only two–but abnormally well-armed. Full chain with helms, crossbows, and long swords, and their steeds wore flanchards. He said the riders claimed to the villagers to be sheriff's men, but as witnesses described their equipment, he suspected they were from beyond Essex. Possibly men in employment of the governor, or even the king himself."

"Did you not visit Tidwalditun?"

Shooting paranoid glances at the trees lining either side of the road, the stranger lowered his voice. "No. I took great pains to walk a long path through the woods around it, for the traveler convinced me of the devil's work. He spoke of a missing maiden... whispers of murder... and under a full moon. I say the village is cursed."

The voyager respected the supernatural and heeded the warning. "I shall avoid Tidwalditun. I thank ye for the tidings."

"God save ye, and be sure to make camp tonight far from that dark village."

Hastening his pace, the young man walked southward towards Tidwalditun. When he saw its church's steeple rising above the trees, an ominous anxiety rose in his stomach, and he veered into the woods. The circuitous path added hours to his journey, but he sensed that avoiding the village warranted the inconvenience.

Stopping periodically to climb trees and locate the steeple, he followed a crude semicircle around the village. As dusk consumed the forest, he took a last fix on the church and judged himself three-quarters through his detour. With moonlight breaking through the branches above him, he forged onward through the forest.

Several furlongs later, the cursed population center was at his back and a clearing ahead marked the road. As he drew inspiration from the path to quicken his pace, a horse's whinny stopped him. He scanned the darkness between pine trunks but saw stillness.

Curiosity compelled him towards the suspected animal, and he crept deeper in the wild. "Hail! Is someone there?" Stepping farther from the road, he snapped twigs under his feet, and the horse called again. He changed direction towards the sound, and then he spied the standing animal's silhouette. "I say, is someone there?"

Met with silence, he approached the steed and discerned a saddle on its back. A competent rider from his father's teaching, he wondered if divine providence had gifted him the animal. "You look strong and swift, but where's your master?"

While debating if he should take the steed, he circled and inspected it. When he reached its flank, a human groan surprised him. He called out as he turned. "Hail! Who's there?"

A feeble man groaned in desperation. "Water."

The voyager moved towards the voice. "I cannot see you. Where are you, good fellow?"

"Here."

The young man saw his first chance to help a stranger in need. He walked beside the fallen rider who reclined against a pine, and he noticed a crossbow bolt protruding from the stranger's side. Kneeling beside him, he offered his water skin. "Here. Drink."

Holding the water with one hand, the man gulped.

The young man saw another bolt protruding from the back of the stranger's lame arm. "You're hurt. What can I do for you?"

After downing his fill, the man lowered the skin. "Nothing, lad. It is my end."

"No. It's but one arrow in your belly. Men can survive such wounds." The village suddenly seemed less cursed when it offered the injured man comfort. "I will help you mount your steed, and I will take you to Tidwalditun."

The fallen rider closed his eyes as he drifted into unconsciousness.

"Sir! Sir!"

Half-opened lids exposed the wounded man's dilating pupils. "I've been run through."

An examination of the stranger's stomach revealed unblemished chainmail.

"My other side."

The voyager rose to his feet, stepped around the man, and knelt again. Blood oozed from the fabric exposed between gaps in the armor's metal links. He felt helpless as knew he was comforting a dying man. "I see."

"What's wrong, lad? Never seen a man die?"

"I have not."

The fallen rider scoffed. "It was a curse."

"A curse caused this?"

"No, lad. Mortal hands did this to me. They finally caught me. How cruel a fate to desire immortality only to have it snuffed. My life was a curse. This world is a curse."

Unsure how a doomed man should behave on his deathbed, the voyager refused to let him die with a heavy heart. "You must see this life as a blessing. You must pass into the next with an unburdened heart."

Spitting blood, the fallen rider gave out a laugh that degraded into a hoarse cough. After he recovered his breathing, he looked the young man in the eye. "Do you really believe life is a blessing?"

"I do."

"Perhaps for you, it will be." Wheezing accompanied labored breaths. "Take… my sheath. Do not touch the weapon."

The voyager grabbed the long scabbard that held a sword by the man's hip.

"No… inside my leg."

Under the tunic, a strap held a shorter sheath around the rider's thigh, and moonlight glimmered on a bronze handle. "You want your dagger?"

"No… you hold it."

The young man unbuckled the strap and lifted the sheathed weapon. "What shall I do with it?"

"Are you ready to learn for yourself… if life is a blessing or a curse?"

"I already know the answer. It is a blessing."

"Then God save ye. The dagger… is yours."

"Why's it special?"

"It will call to you… I know not when…. tomorrow… years from now, but it will call out."

The voyager's heart raced with anticipation. "What will it

say?"

"It will promise... immortality."

The young man considered the dying rider delirious and assumed a patronizing tone. "Very well then, sir. I thank you for the gift."

Grabbing with the strength impossible for a dying man, the stranger clutched the voyager's hand and stared into his eyes. "Do not take this gift... lightly. It will... change you."

"I do not understand."

"Your name, lad?"

"Ethan."

"Ethan, remember... only now as I die... can I see. The dagger... is a blessing... and a curse. When you accept it... as your destiny... only then... can you touch it."

"I fear no destiny." Ethan withdrew the dagger, and every nerve in his flesh burst into unseen flames. Succumbing to excruciating pain, he collapsed and lost consciousness. When he awoke, the knife remained in his hand, innocuous, but the stranger who had gifted him his blessed curse lay dead.

An unseen horse neighed from the direction of the village, and the bronze weapon called out a wordless warning. Two dangerous men on steeds hunted him.

"Why me? I've done nothing but comfort a dying man."

The silent answer terrified him. The hunters sought him not for his deeds, but for his being. Possessing the dagger had transformed him into something savage.

"No! I reject this fate!" He extended his arm to drop the weapon, but his fingers formed a vice. "I reject this! I reject this evil!"

A conscious spirit within the dagger corrected him. Fate had united him with the weapon, and the bond was unbreakable.

Fearing his pursuers and guided by a divine power within the bronze blade, Ethan trotted to the dead man's steed, mounted it, and escaped into the forest.

CHAPTER 17

Diane sat in the back of a minivan taxi worrying about her colleagues' reactions to her exposing of their loving bonds. As she'd stood in front of the council, the idea of love dictating the power of the shared trances had overcome her, and she'd blurted out her epiphany before having processed it. Now, an awkward stillness consumed the vehicle's occupants as it took them from the order to their hotel.

Her brother's random observation cut the silence. "It's faster to go through Turkey."

In the front passenger seat, the elder hunter twisted to see the team behind him. "Do you mean to get to Lesbos, Josh?"

"Yes."

"I agree, but we don't have contacts in Turkey who can help us transport our weapons. We need to use our contacts in Greece to get to Lesbos with all our possessions."

The young hunter spoke for the first time since leaving the council's chamber. "Don't we need to fly home for our gear?"

"Nonsense. It's all being shipped to Athens. The order respects our sense of urgency and took care of it. We'll inventory everything when we get there, and we can have a second shipment sent if anything was forgotten."

After the vehicle made several turns, the Colosseum moved by Diane's window, reminding her that her short, part-time vacation in Rome was ending, and she wondered if her outburst in the council's sanctum would cause her to leave her dignity in Italy's capital city.

In the seat beside her, Nana spoke in hushed tones of Aramaic. "Why's everyone so quiet?"

Diane answered in the language of her lineage. "I admitted in the council that I love Connor and Liam."

The grandmother frowned. "What? You just yelled it out in front of everyone?"

"I had to. My dagger moves when I touch a hunter I love, but not when I touch a hunter who's a stranger. It was important to the conversation, but I think I messed up the delivery."

"It doesn't work at all with a stranger?"

"No."

"How do you know that?"

"I tried it with one in the courtroom. They brought a hunter in from far away, and we did an experiment, but nothing happened."

"So, it's because you and Liam are in love."

Diane snapped defensively. "It worked with Connor, too!" After raising her voice and speaking familiar names within her otherwise secret code of Aramaic, the empath blushed while the quiet people in the minivan looked at her. She lowered her voice and continued, avoiding names. "It worked with the father, too, but much, much slower."

Nana gave a knowing nod and folded her arms.

Her grandmother's gesture annoyed her, but Diane was relieved to end the conversation. The uncomfortable silence endured for the remainder of the taxi ride, and the empath welcomed her chance to race to the solitude of her hotel room.

But Connor slowed her for a few steps while he announced the next step of the team's logistics. "Everyone meet in the lobby in two hours sharp. We'll fly to Athens and then eat dinner there. The rest of the day is dedicated to travel. Mind your belongings, keep in touch with each other, and remember to watch the time."

As she emptied the contents of her hotel room's drawers into her suitcase, Diane hoped for and feared a possible visit from Liam. After confessing their love for each other in public, they'd ignored each other, and she wanted closure.

Her heart leapt into her throat when she heard a knock on the door. She ran to it and opened it.

Connor stood before her. "May I come in?"

Disappointed, she acquiesced. "Sure."

"May we talk about what we learned in the council?"

She flipped her wrist backwards. "What's there to talk about? I made a fool of myself and dragged Liam down with me."

"No, you recognized an important distinction and educated your teammates. We now know that either Liam or I can empower your dagger when assisting you, but Liam's the proper choice whenever we have a choice."

"I guess. But I still feel like an idiot."

"Nobody would agree with that assessment. I'm sure that as an empath you have feelings and emotions flowing through you like a river. I can't imagine what it's like."

She sat on the edge of the bed. "It's hard. Sometimes I can't tell intuition from divine insights from false hope. But sometimes I can, and I just knew in the council meeting that our teamwork with my dagger was about love."

"Of course, I'm thrilled that you see me as a father. I've hardly known you for a month, but it seems like we were destined to adopt each other."

Unsure if intuition or hope motivated her, she agreed. She sprang from the bed and hugged him. He smelled like cologne and an aging man. "I agree."

As they separated, Connor looked at her with gentle eyes. "This may be easy for us to declare each other as family, but I'm afraid we have a delicate matter to address between you and Liam."

She dropped her buttocks back onto the bed. "No kidding. He hasn't said a word to me since then."

"He's hardly said a word to anyone."

"Did I screw this up?"

"That depends what 'this' is. As long as we're being candid, we need to address this elephant in the room."

"I think I was pretty clear in front of a bunch of strangers."

He walked to an armchair and sat. "If you'll excuse the mixing of metaphors, I believe you only exposed the tip of the iceberg."

She lowered her face into her palms. "Ugh."

"Don't despair. I'm not sure if I should share this, but it's only my opinion, to which I'm entitled, but I believe that my son is enamored with you."

Thoughts scrambled throughout her head, muting each other with their growing cacophony. Her heart fluttered, tears welled in her eyes, and she shook her hands.

Connor marched across the room, grabbed a handful of tissues, and brought them to her. "Here you go, young lady."

She wiped her eyes and blew her nose. "This isn't fair."

"Love never is, so they say. I unfortunately have little experience in the area, given my vows."

"That's the problem. What about Liam's vows?"

"I checked with the council, and it turns out that there's a provision allowing marriage."

Diane remembered her brother predicting it days earlier. "You don't sound too optimistic."

"Perhaps I'm a pessimistic old man, but it's a difficult mountain to climb. Oh dear, I've just used a third metaphor in as many minutes. Nevertheless, there are several criteria, and the most challenging is the number of hunting lines. For a hunter to marry, it's assumed that his future as a hunter is in jeopardy, and there must therefore be more hunting lines than active wraiths to allow it."

She recalled her discoveries with the council. "There are four wraiths out there and only three lines."

"I know, dear. That's why I'm less than optimistic. But understand the council's position. You wouldn't give up a third of your police force knowing that you'd have half as many cop partnerships as killers."

Her mood plummeted as she learned the rules. "I guess not."

"And even if they could relinquish a hunting line, there's no promise that Liam would be the one allowed to marry. He'd be competing with two other hunters for the privilege, and therein lies a complex debate which hasn't been seen for eight hundred years."

Sadness enveloped her, and tears trickled. "It's not fair."

He handed her fresh tissues. "I know it's not. Here you are risking your life for others, and the framework in which you operate prevents you from following your heart. The sacrifices you make are deeper than just risking your life."

She blew her nose and dropped the crumpled tissues onto the comforter. "What can I do?"

"I think you need to be honest with Liam. The uphill climb you face will be impossible unless you and he agree on your goals and support each other."

"Goals? Am I supposed to write down a laundry list of mission objectives about falling in love?"

"Not at all, my dear. What I meant was marriage. Although it seems distant and impossible now, it's nonetheless a possibility."

"I haven't thought it through that far since it always seemed taboo. Now you're saying it's a given that we both want it?"

He sighed. "Except for possibly Nana, I'm best suited to offer you advice. I believe marriage is what you both need, since it's the only outcome that can spare you both from horrible heartache. The only foolish thing you could do, young lady, is ignore it."

CHAPTER 18

The next day, Liam awoke and questioned his whereabouts. He grabbed his phone and noted the time as six o'clock in the morning. Recovering from a murky dream in which he'd fired rifle rounds that ricocheted off a distant enemy, he remembered he was in an airport hotel in Athens, Greece.

He slogged through his morning routine, recovering from and still digesting his prior day's confession of love for Diane. The public acknowledgement left him drained, but it also lifted a weight from him. While showering, he likened himself to a thin mist, rivaling the empath's ghosts in substance.

After putting on his clothes, he took the elevator to the lobby and smelled the diverse offerings of a buffet. Hotel guests filled several other tables, but the young hunter was the only member of his team at breakfast. He piled meats, eggs, bread, and gravy on a plate and added a steaming cup of coffee to his serving tray, sat at a small table, and started devouring his food.

As he gulped a bite of sausage, motion at the dining area's entrance caught his attention. His heart fluttered as Diane approached him in jeans and a blouse. Her eyes met his, trapping him, and he felt compelled to speak his first direct words to her since the council. "Good morning."

"Hi." She stopped behind the chair at the opposite side of his table. Appearing uncertain how to behave, she looked at him blankly. After several seconds that irked him, she announced her intentions. "I'll get some food and join you."

Ideas raced through his mind grasping for something smart to say before she returned, but he could only conclude his social buffoonery. Anxiety quelled his appetite, and he nibbled on a biscuit while watching her load her plate and then sit.

She dipped a slice of ripe green melon into a cup of yogurt, lifted it, and bit into it. Looking away while she chewed, she seemed unreceptive to a conversation.

Hoping he'd escape without revisiting the issue of their love, he risked a mouthful of eggs.

While he chewed, she looked at him. "Pretty crazy stuff yesterday, huh?"

A pit formed in his stomach, and he nodded and grunted while powering through the eggs that had become tasteless in his panic.

"I didn't mean to blurt it out."

Unsure if he was allowed to keep eating, he swallowed and lowered his fork to the plate. "I know you didn't. You did it because of who and what you are, and I can't blame you for it."

"Thanks, I think."

"No problem."

She swallowed another bite of yogurt-covered melon. "It's funny. The last time we were in Athens we didn't even get to stay overnight. Now, we're here for just one night and we're going to get rushed out of here again this morning."

He shrugged. "I guess so."

"We're going to miss cool touristy stuff again. This sucks."

"I admit I wasn't thinking about it."

"What were you thinking about?"

"Nothing."

"So, your mind was a complete blank?"

"I am a man with meat in front of him, after all."

"Good point." She ate another bite of melon. "Back to yesterday. I think we need to talk about it."

"Okay."

"You have to say more than 'okay'."

"Okay."

She rolled her eyes. "Ugh."

"Sorry."

"Stop apologizing when you don't mean it."

"I did mean it, sort of. It's a rough patch for both of us, and I'm sorry you have to go through it."

"I'll allow that."

"Oh, you'll allow it? I wasn't aware that you were in charge."

"I'm the woman. That means I'm in charge."

Somehow, he knew she was right, but he had to fight back. "In charge of what?"

She spread her arms. "This. Us."

"So, we're an 'us' now?"

"After yesterday, we need to deal with it. It wasn't exactly a dream come true when we professed our love for each other in a courtroom, but it beats hiding from it."

"Yeah, I guess hiding from it isn't an option."

"So, what do we do?"

"You're the woman. I thought you were in charge."

She lowered her forehead into her palm. "Of all the men I could find in the world, I get the typical caveman."

"What's that supposed to mean?"

"You're supposed to take charge and lead and be romantic, but you have to read my cues to do and say things I want."

His father had failed to prepare him for this. "I guess that will take time to learn."

She lifted her head. "At least you're willing to learn. That ranks you in the top half of your kind."

"My kind? You think being a guy is easy? Women want us to be strong and masculine and gentle and compassionate. It's like you want two opposites jammed into one person."

She smiled and clapped. "Yay! You got it."

"You want the bloody impossible!"

"Would you prefer pre-menstrual syndrome and child birth?"

"I... um... would not. But this still isn't easy for me. There's nothing normal about my situation, and my lady has a... you know what... made of bronze that does... well, I can't say what it does while people can hear."

"Oh, I'm your lady now?"

"I don't know. I have rules I need to sort through with the order."

She pointed at him. "No, buddy. You have rules you need to sort through with me, first."

Although her insistence on reviewing their relationship's rubrics contradicted her prior command for him to take charge as the man, he welcomed the opportunity to define clear instructions. "That makes sense. I guess that gives us a chance to pick up right where we left off yesterday. Let's explore your rules."

"They're our rules, not my rules."

"Fine. Our rules." He tried to take charge. "Let's figure out what we want from each other."

Her gaze lifted towards the ceiling in thought. "Um... well. Crap, you're right. Everything we could talk about is going to be dictated by your annoying order. It's like we have no free will in this."

"We have some. It's limited to one pretty straightforward decision, though. Marriage. Everything we could do to advance our relationship has to be an investment in figuring out if we want to get married or not."

"Is that your idea of a proposal?"

"No, but we need to talk about it as if I'm going to propose to you eventually."

"That sounds so crazy. Can't we just hang out and get to know each other like normal people?"

"Do you mean before or after we hunt down and kill our third immortal serial killer?"

Her head returned to her palm. "Why's this so complicated?"

"It's complicated because we have special destinies. I was born into my fate and raised from a baby to do what I'm doing. You're still figuring out who you are and what you can do, but you were born as something special."

She smiled and blushed. "See, you can be romantic."

Somehow, he'd earned credit for something he'd said, but he lacked the first clue on why she'd rewarded him. But he wasn't going to admit his ignorance. "Who said I couldn't be romantic?"

"Me."

"How do you know, when I haven't tried?"

"It's not romantic if you have to try. It's just supposed to happen."

"Maybe in fairy tales, but I'm a real man."

She guffawed. "You forgot to pound your chest."

"I mean I'm not a fairy tale. I'm real flesh and bones." He pointed at the cast over his arm.

"I know that. Did you forget that I healed a cut in your artery?"

"No, I remember. My point is that I come with flaws and blemishes."

"But you still have to be romantic."

"What the hell does that mean? You just said I was romantic when I said you were something special, but I was stating a simple fact. How is a fact romantic?"

"It's the way you said it. I knew you meant it."

"Of course, I did."

"Well, at least we have that going for us."

He reflected upon the rapid pseudo-courtship they'd endured under life-threatening duress involving mortal combat. "You know, we professed our love for each other in public before talking about it in private. Now, we're talking about marriage pretty much because we have to, but we've never been on a proper date."

"Oh. And what do you consider a proper date?"

Since supernatural intervention had insulated him from temptation, he'd enjoyed social dances and group events with friends for his past dates. He'd never tried a true date with a woman he cared for. "Dinner and a show."

"A show? On Lesbos, the epicenter of theater life?"

"Okay, dinner and a romantic walk."

"That's better."

"So, what sort of cuisine do you like?"

"Now that's a great question to ask a woman you want to get to know. You're getting the hang of this."

"I've hardly seen you pick food just for yourself, other than the fruits you eat for breakfast. Other than that, you've been picking big meals for everyone. I'd like to know what you like when it's just for you."

"You and me."

"Have you seen me eat? Can you picture anything I don't like?"

"That's true. You have no taste buds. Me? I like seafood."

"That should be doable in Lesbos. I'll make reservations for tonight."

She cocked her head. "How can you make reservations when you don't know our plans for today yet?"

"I'm going to let Father know that we need some time alone where we aren't involved in warfare."

She lifted her nose. "Good for you. If you can stand up to him and schedule us a date, I'll consider it a very romantic gesture."

CHAPTER 19

Diane laughed at herself as she strained to lift her suitcase into the Jeep Renegade. "Liam!"

The young hunter darted to her, took her luggage, and tossed it into the hatchback.

The soreness in her shoulders subsided. "Thanks. My arms are so scrawny."

"No problem."

She leaned into his ear. "Did you talk to your dad yet?"

"About our date?"

She nodded.

"I haven't had the chance. I've been too busy with everything."

"What 'everything'? Just ask him."

He frowned. "Two SUVs don't just roll up to a Greek hotel with our weapons in them without effort. He's been busy getting the cars while I was inventorying our equipment and inspecting it for damage."

"Inspecting what?"

He became sarcastic. "Oh, I don't know. A few important things like night vision goggles, tactical body armor suits, rifles, suppressors, concussion grenades, fragmentation grenades, riot guns, shotguns, pistols–".

"Fine! I get it. But don't you keep all that stuff packed and ready for action all the time?"

"Yeah, but the wrong time to find out you're missing equipment, or that something was broken in transit, is when you're on an island getting ready for combat."

She recalled having seen him clean his weapons with a hypnotic fervor, and she respected his diligent attachment to them, although she didn't understand it.

A man with a dark jacket and beige pants stepped from the trailing of two black Renegades. He wore dark sunglasses, leather gloves, and a black tee shirt. As he walked towards Liam, he maintained a cold expression under his cropped hair.

Diane thought he looked like a handsome, muscular, and well-groomed thug.

From the other Jeep, Connor stepped from the driver's seat and announced the stranger's arrival. "This is Thomas Smith. He's a contractor in the order's employ."

Impeding her view of the newcomer, the young hunter stepped to him and extended his hand. "Liam Brady."

Framed in a Londoner's accent, the contractor's voice was deep and strong. "Tom Smith."

"And this is Diane."

She extended her hand. "Diane Yousif."

His eyes hidden behind his glasses, the contractor was mysterious while wrapping leather around her fingers. "So, this is the Diane I've heard so much about."

"Me?"

"They told me about your powers, although they were purposely vague. I'm hoping I get a chance to see you demonstrate some of your skills in action."

Liam sounded jealous. "You'll see what you can when and if you can. She's not a sideshow."

Unfazed, the contractor countered. "I meant no offense, but one can hope."

The discussion reminded Diane of a missed step. "Crap. We forgot something."

Seemingly offended by the challenge to the completeness of his planning, Liam sounded defensive. "What'd I miss?"

"A directional reading with my dagger."

The young hunter shrugged. "I'm not sure it's necessary. No matter where it points, our next stop is Lesbos to look for clues."

Part of her wanted to show off to the handsome contractor.

Although she felt no attraction to the rugged man, she wanted to use his presence to tease her possible future fiancé. "But we should at least verify where it points."

"Sure. Let's do it. Grab your dagger and take my hand."

"Here?"

"Why not? It happens instantaneously for all witnesses except you and me."

The elder hunter interrupted. "Nonsense. Wait until you're in the car and do it at a traffic light."

Liam lifted his keys from his pocket. "Let's go then. I'm driving the trail Jeep, right?"

"Correct, lad. I'll drive with Tom. You take Diane, Josh, and Nana. Let's get moving before we miss the ferry."

Diane found the passenger seat comfortable and the ride smooth for an SUV. At the first red stoplight, she pulled her dagger from her purse and held it over the console. "Are you ready?"

In the driver's seat, Liam glanced at her hand. "Sure. Point it at me."

She aimed the blade at him, and she felt a tingle as he clasped her wrist. Time stopped, and she froze in a trance with him. "Can you hear me?"

Motionless, he responded in her mind. "Yes. Watch the dagger."

"It's moving just like always."

"And it's heading towards Lesbos. That's good."

The dagger stopped, and time recommenced.

From the back seat, Nana called out. "That was amazing. I saw your dagger move like a flash."

Since her blade's movement provided the only clue about their wraith, Diane prayed it pointed them towards the one they hunted instead of some false, unknown target.

Upon reaching the ferry, Liam aimed the car behind his father's onto the cargo hold. He parked the Jeep and shut off the engine.

Before opening her door, Diane gave the young hunter a sideways glance. "Now's a good time to talk to your father."

"About what?"

Reminding him of their evening's date, she glared at him, thinking she'd explode if he missed the clue of her frustrated stare.

He got it. "Oh, okay. I will."

She opened her door and walked to the nearest weather deck with her family. "Can you handle the stairs, Nana?"

"Yeah, yeah. We go up."

Diane led Josh and her grandmother to the ship's highest passenger deck, and she pushed through other travelers to procure a spot by the railing. Behind her, a tall superstructure housed the bridge and upper decks for the crew's use. Spanning piers and shipping channels over the central port of Piraeus, dozens of large passenger vessels catered to tourists from the Athens metropolitan area to the Aegean Sea and distant Greek possessions.

Standing behind her with his face in his tablet, her brother announced the local trivia. "Piraeus is the second-largest port in the world for passenger traffic."

"Cool. It looks busy."

"It's important in Greek history. It used to be connected to Athens by a really long wall, but the Romans destroyed it in the first century BC."

"That's interesting, Josh."

He changed subjects. "This ferry's going to arrive in Mytilene nine hours and fifty-three minutes from now."

Diane didn't recognize the destination. "What's Mytilene, Josh?"

"It's the capital of Lesbos and its main port. It's 'Mytilene' in English but '*Mytilini*' in Greek."

"That's good to know, Josh. I'll remember that."

"I'm going to listen to how the natives say it. I bet they use the Greek and English pronunciation since they get so many tourists."

"You're probably right."

The ship's whistle blew a long blast, signaling its divorcing from the pier, and then the low, densely populated hills surrounding the harbor slid across the horizon.

She saw movement in the corner of her eye, turned her head, and saw Liam approaching through a crowd. As he reached her side, her grandmother grabbed her brother's arm and escorted him away.

The young hunter greeted the empath. "They ran off fast."

"I think Nana figured we wanted to be alone."

"She's got good instincts."

"What's going on?"

"What do you mean? We're on our way to Lesbos."

"I mean with the new guy. Why's he here?"

"He's our contact for getting the cars and arranging our equipment's arrival."

"I figured that much out, but that's all taken care of. Why's he still here?"

"He's got all the connections on Lesbos. He's networked in with the government, the volunteers, the coast guard, the police, and even the refugees."

"So, what is he? Some sort of missionary?"

Liam shrugged. "Something like that. I get the sense from watching him that he's got Special Forces or martial arts training. I wouldn't want to mess with him."

"You? The he-man stud? Afraid?"

"Respectful. I'm a wise he-man stud, and I pick my battles. Fortunately, Tom's an ally of the order."

She remembered the pesky supernatural and strictly enforced rule precluding the seeking of outside help in hunting wraiths. "Did he volunteer or get volunteered to help us?"

"I asked Father about it, and no. He's been commissioned to help us find our way around the island. We'll definitely need his help getting into the camps, but I can't ask him to take up arms against our target."

"But it could happen if he volunteers or by accident?"

"Well, yeah. Anyone can help by accident if they're in the right place at the right time."

"More like the wrong place and time."

"It'll probably depend on what we find when we chase down the spot where your dagger's pointing. Just in case we stumble upon our target, I'll brief him on what to do."

"You might want to do that during this ferry ride."

"Maybe, if I can get some privacy with him."

"I hope you do. You're busy tonight."

"How can you be so sure?"

"Because a he-man stud asked me out on a date."

He rubbed his nape and sounded defeated. "Oh, yeah. About that. I... uh... talked to Father."

"If he said no, I'll deal with him."

Liam smiled. "Just kidding. He's fine with it. I've made reservations for eight o'clock at the Marina Yacht Club. We'll head straight over when we arrive. So, save up an appetite, and get ready for a spectacular view and good company tonight."

CHAPTER 20

Ethan moved through a daze during his watch. The few ships dotting the seas offered him minimal distractions from his pending and forced death match against the rekindled hunting line.

The young American noticed. "What's eating you, Ethan?"

"Nothing."

"You ain't your normal friendly self."

"I don't want to talk about it."

"Suit yourself."

Turning his attention to the water, the wraith saw a speck on the southeastern horizon. He grabbed binoculars from a hook on the wall and examined the new vessel. It was a dinghy with people seated around its edge. "If you want to make yourself useful, keep an eye on them."

The American picked up the nearest optics and pressed them against his face. "Finally, my chance to help."

"Do you remember what to do?"

Billy lowered his binoculars. "I think so. I need to call the coast guard."

"Right. What are you going to tell them?"

The American scrunched his eyes shut. "I forget. Wait... no. Oh, God. Help me, Ethan."

"Coordinates of our watch tower, type of vessel you see, number of refugees on it, and bearing and range from our watch tower."

"I don't know all that!"

"They know we're guessing. So, make your guess."

"Well, our coordinates are written right here." The American pointed to a laminated placard showing the instructions Ethan was drilling into him.

The wraith appreciated the momentary distraction from his brooding over his fate and continued teaching his colleague. "Correct. Keep going."

"It's a dinghy?"

"Correct."

"The people are too far away to count. It's a blur."

"You always guess fifty for a dinghy until you know better."

"Okay. I don't have any idea of the range."

"From our height above sea level in this watch shack, the range to the horizon's eight miles. Since we didn't see them come over the horizon, they'd already passed it when I saw them. Guess six and a half miles."

"Okay. Um... bearing." Billy stepped to a compass mounted on a table and eyed the direction to the refugees. "I'd say about one-two-five."

"Good enough. Call it in."

"What if they don't speak English? I don't speak Greek!"

"They have an English speaker available all the time."

The American lifted a cell phone to his face and called the local coast guard.

While Ethan eavesdropped to assure the accuracy of his colleague's report, he watched the incoming vessel through his binoculars. The sight terrified him.

The boat rolled clockwise, sending passengers over the side, and splashes filled the water. As the vessel showed him its width, he sighed in relief knowing it was smaller than most. Few people, if any, would be pinned underneath, but the risk of yet another group of drowned victims was real. "Billy! It's capsizing!"

"What?"

"Rolling over. Find out how fast the coast guard can get to them."

The American went through a quick verbal exchange on his phone. "The coast guard says they don't have anything close to help. All their ships are busy with a cruise ship that caught fire to the south. They can only spare a helicopter, but even it's not ready yet, and it won't help them all. They're looking for nearby ships on radar to assist."

The coincidence of a cruise ship fire and a dinghy flipping over on his watch struck Ethan as anything but a coincidence. His Master was taunting him.

"Now they say the closest ship that's agreed to help is a fishing boat eleven miles away from the refugees, but it only has a max speed of nineteen knots."

Accepting his fate, the wraith grunted.

"What's that mean, Ethan?"

"It means we're going out there."

Billy raised his voice and pointed. "In that?"

The wraith glanced at the twenty-seven-foot cuddy cabin utility boat his volunteer organization kept lashed to a small pier. "Yes, in that."

"We can't fit them all in there."

Ethan grabbed the boat's keys from a table and pushed open the shack's door. "We won't take them all. Just the wounded, elderly, women, and children. So, are you going to follow me, or did you forget why you came to this island?"

Behind Ethan, the two-hundred-and-thirty-horse-power Mercury outboard motor revved with urgency. Standing at the wheel, he aimed the bow towards the capsized vessel. Salt spray hit his face as the small ship bobbed over successive waves.

Beside him, the American yelled over the wind. "Are you sure this is necessary?"

Ethan nodded.

"Shit. If my life depended on it, I'd swim six miles."

The wraith shouted back. "They're exhausted and hungry. Some of them are elderly, invalid, or sick, and very few of them have life jackets."

"I guess you're right."

Ethan nudged the throttle forward, pushing the engine to the redline. "Spread out the spare lifejackets across the deck."

"When did you learn to drive a boat?"

The wraith reflected on his last century of life of leisure as a wealthy man, which included time for boating sport. "I've had a lot of free time."

As the first bobbing head approached, the American pointed and called out. "I see someone!"

Ethan slowed the boat to a three-knot crawl, and the wind died. "Is he swimming or drowning?"

"He looks okay. I don't know if he saw us, but he's still swimming to land like a champ. He looks like he'll make it on his own."

"He must be a strong swimmer. That's why he's the closest to land." Ethan nudged the throttle forward and accelerated the boat to six knots. He then saw a group of six swimmers. He aimed towards them and then drifted to them. Recalling the Syrian dialect of Arabic, he called out. "Are you all okay?"

Several thumbs went up.

"You're five miles away. Can you swim it?"

More thumbs. One man claimed they were all fit swimmers and would be fine. The main group by the inverted dinghy needed help more than they did.

Ethan forged ahead to the mass of refugees who had opted to stay together near their upside-down boat. As he saw the whites of the nearest person's eyes, he idled the engine and drifted.

Billy stepped to the vessel's ledge and looked down at the immersed man. "What now?"

"He looks fatigued. Throw him a jacket."

The American heaved an orange vest over the side.

As Ethan gave the boat a gentle reverse nudge, it stopped within speaking range of the bobbing group. But when they saw him stop, they started swimming towards him, and he attempted to scream in Arabic over their splashing. "Women, children, injured, elderly!"

Whipping the water white, the horde of swimmers approached.

"Women, children, injured, and elderly only!"

"They're not listening, Ethan. What do we do?"

"I'll keep shouting at them." He screamed. "Stay back except for women, children, injured, and the elderly!"

The first able-bodied man reached the boat and climbed its hull. Then another followed him, and then another. As the horde arrived, their white-knuckled grips angled the boat downwards.

Wide-eyed, the American yelled. "Do we help them up or kick them away?"

"There's too many of them. Come with me." Ethan led Billy to the boat's rising railing. "Sit and lean as far back as you can to balance us against capsizing."

The American obeyed him.

Ethan saw the successful refugees helping climbers into the boat, exacerbating their list to port. "No, come here and balance the boat."

A few refugees came to him, but the vessel's dangerous angle increased as more swimmers clutched it.

The wraith heard a female voice behind him, causing him to turn. He saw a lone woman with a lifejacket drifting away from his boat. From the wrinkled skin and worried eyes poking out from under her hijab, he knew she was old and desperate. He jumped into the water and swam to her.

Her weak voice was tinny on the water's surface. "Help!"

Having attempted to volunteer himself free of his guilt for decades, Ethan had learned rescue swimming as part of his training. When he reached the distressed woman, he spun her back to him, reached his arm around her neck, and used his three free limbs to paddle to the boat.

She squirmed, jerked her arms, and became heavy in his arm.

He pulled her upward and kicked, bringing the boat's white hull within reach. But the woman's increasing weight became undeniable, and he turned to see her lifejacket two strokes away in their small wake as she slipped below the waves. Grunting, he yanked her up and accelerated his pace.

Her face reappeared above the surface, and she gasped.

He gave a lunging kick and pushed her towards Billy's waiting arm. But the boat's curved side rose, lifting the American's arm beyond reach of the refugee woman. Then a wave pushed Ethan under the hull as its listing ceased and reversed. While the boat rolled towards the wraith, a new wave hoisted him head-first into the white fiberglass.

Pain shot through his skull, and his world went blank. His final thought before losing consciousness was a dark desire to drown and escape the malicious spirit that dominated him.

CHAPTER 21

As he stared at the stunning young lady across the table, Liam forgot she was an enchanted killer.

Diane wore a black sleeveless dress that showed her smooth, tanned skin. Despite her claim of scrawniness, her arms provided sufficient lines to frame the elegant strength to her torso. Although she lacked upper body bulk, her cardiovascular routine on an elliptical machine had toned her shoulders.

"Why'd you call your arms scrawny? I think they're fine."

"You mean while loading the luggage? I was trying to sound pathetic so you'd help me."

"Ah, effort and reward, conditioning me to relieve you of future labor, I assume. Well played."

She smiled. "Of course."

"Did you ever think I'd help out just because I like you?"

She looked at the window which gave a scintillating view of coastal nightlife and seaborne lights of docked or lazily moving vessels of Mytilene. "All you've ever done is try to save my life, which is great, but what happens when there's no more dragons to slay?"

"There'll always be dragons."

"But if we're going to become anything together, we need to see what our lives could be like in between the battles."

He understood. "Like taking heavy things out of your hands, opening doors for you, or reminding you how beautiful you are."

She blushed, and mascara accentuated her long lashes as she batted them. "That's a great start. There's hope for you yet."

"I'd like to consider myself a fast learner."

"Don't get a big head. You've still got a lot of rough edges, caveman."

He leaned over the tablecloth and lowered his voice. "Well, I am a trained killer. Doesn't that handicap earn me a little patience from you while I try to become Mister Romantic Sensitive Guy?"

"You have no idea how patient I've been."

Her impact on him had been like a stampede in its magnitude and quickness. From nowhere, she'd ambushed his emotions, and he was a willing hostage.

She stood. "Excuse me while I powder my nose."

Having enjoyed divine protection from desire, he lacked the self-governing will to avoid ogling her as she walked away. Her tall, thin frame and long dark hair trailing down her back commanded his gaze. She reminded him of a model, but she had respectable real-world curves, which created heated sensations within him.

A waiter appeared with a tray of entrees, rescuing him from the mesmerizing trap of the empath's allure. The server lowered plates to the table and spoke with a Greek accent. "Planked salmon for the lady, and grilled porterhouse for you, sir."

After the waiter departed, Liam's mind gravitated towards the hunt. Although the evening with Diane was enchanting, it was an ephemeral respite from his purpose. The idea of enjoying a normal life with a beautiful wife seemed fake, like the fading memory of a forgotten dream.

Regardless, he needed to force a decision, despite his distant odds of enacting it in reality.

Did he want to marry Diane?

Ignoring the herculean hurdles of killing killers, earning the council's permission, and expecting permanent celibacy during the first twenty-five years of his existence, he needed to determine if he desired a lifetime with a woman he'd met two full moons ago.

She returned and sat. "What's wrong?"

"What do you mean?"

"There's a steak in front of you, and you're not inhaling it."

He lied, trying to hide his doubt about their united future. "I was just waiting for you."

The empath gave no hint of detecting the deceit. "That was nice of you." She stabbed her fork into her salmon.

"No points for being romantic?"

"That wasn't romantic. That was polite. And no, you can't have any of my salmon."

He scowled. "I didn't ask."

"But you've been staring at it long enough, and I know you. You're already eating it subconsciously."

Upon a moment of reflection, he agreed. "Can't say that you're wrong, but I'll stick to my steak."

"Good idea. I have my dagger in my purse, you know. So, keep your hands off my food unless you want to lose a finger, buddy."

"Let's talk about anything but daggers tonight."

"Sure, I'll give it a shot. What do you have in mind?"

His heartbeat accelerated as he sought a topic of mutual interest and realized he was groping. "I don't really know where to start. I guess, how about music?"

She looked to the ceiling while formulating her answer and then turned her large brown eyes to him. "I like rap and alternative."

"That's an odd mix, isn't it?"

"Yeah, my friends say my tastes are eclectic, but I think they're just being nice. I call it weird. How about you?"

"Me? It depends on what I'm doing. I like old rock when I'm driving, but I like classical when I'm studying."

"That makes sense."

"Well, rap and alternative aren't too odd a mix if you think about it." He was familiar with her styles of music from hearing songs during car rides with friends. "The lyrics usually are attempts to express a message, and the music tries to invoke the right emotion behind the message, like anger, futility, hope, or whatever."

She shrugged. "Yeah, that sounds okay. I thought I was just weird about it, but you made it make sense."

"I charge two hundred quid an hour for talk therapy, and I round up. So, keep talking to get your money's worth."

Her face lit up. "That was cute, but what's a quid?"

"It's slang for one British pound sterling."

"Oh. Got it."

"But you missed the second layer of humor in that. I'm from Ireland, which uses the Euro, but I thought it sounded better if I charged you in quid."

"Ha ha, funny man. What else do you think's wrong with me?"

"Nice try, but I'm not falling for that. You said your musical tastes were odd, not me. I proved they were logically connected."

She swallowed a bite of salmon and washed it down with her glass of Riesling. "If opposites attract, we're in great shape. I'm all about feelings, and you're all about logic."

"And I'm all about muscles while you're all about scrawny."

She scowled and covered her bare upper arms with her palms. "Hey! I can call them scrawny. You can't."

He swallowed a savory chunk of steak and let a smile break through his straight face. "I'm kidding. You work out a lot. We both take fitness seriously. A healthy mind requires a healthy body."

"I do believe in heart health."

"Whether you believe it or not, taking care of your heart is important. You don't have to believe in magnetism or gravity either, but they're facts you can't ignore, even though you can't see them."

She lowered her hands towards the table, grabbed her fork, and carved a bite of salmon. "There's another opposite. You're all factual, but I'm all about feelings."

He grunted. "Maybe, but I see feelings as facts. So, we may be closer together on that front than you think."

She gave him a blank stare.

"I mean, they exist and have measurable and predictable effects."

"Um, yeah. We're opposites."

"What? I'm finding common ground for our perspectives."

"Feelings are supposed to be felt, not analyzed."

"Feelings are always felt, by definition. But if they're not analyzed, you become their puppet."

"So, you're calling me a puppet?"

As the conversation turned against him, he redirected her accusation. "Not at all. I'd say it's the opposite. You're a puppet master when you use people's feelings against them."

"I don't use other people's feelings like puppet strings."

He stuck another savory morsel of steak into his mouth, chewed it, and swallowed. "You've explained it to me several times, but it's so experiential that I can't know what it's like when you, you know… do your thing." He avoided using the word 'telepathy' in public.

"Feelings guide me sometimes, but I can't use them as weapons."

"Huh. And here I was thinking every woman on the planet did that against men for fun."

"Maybe you're not as smart as I thought."

"You think I'm smart?"

"Not anymore."

Though he knew the empath was joking, he feared a grain of truth hiding behind humor. "What if I can think of something else we have in common?"

"Okay. Go on."

"We both like to read."

She seemed warm to the observation. "That's true."

"We live in a world where people have the attention spans of tired puppies, watching video snippets of idiotic things, but you and I both respect that learning anything worth learning takes an investment of time and that reading is the most efficient way to digest information."

She swallowed her bite of salmon and then wiped her mouth. "Maybe there is hope for you. I agree. I like reading about marketing for my homework, even though everyone else in my classes complains about the workload. And I also think anything worth doing for leisure requires an investment in time, which is why I like to read books for fun."

"For example?"

"Harry Potter. Hunger Games. Divergent. Maze Runner."

"Actually, I read Hunger Games. I thought it was awesome. Cruel, but awesome." He considered mentioning that he'd seen most of the other series as movie adaptations, but he wanted to keep his momentum as a fellow reader.

"How demented do you have to be to force children to kill each other for sport?"

"It's sickening, but we know the depths of darkness of the human soul. We've both seen it."

She looked at him with disappointment. "You were doing so well until you brought it back to our... unique connection."

He took the strong hint that he needed to stick with subjects of conversation beyond hunting wraiths. "I get it, but you also can't pretend it's not real. It is real, and it'll always be a part of us."

"But since you keep bringing it up, you're dwelling on it."

"Okay. I can't lie to you. Guilty as charged. It's hard to get my mind off it, even in front of a vision as lovely as you."

She groaned. "The words were romantic, but your delivery was horrible."

During an extended silence, he put his energies into devouring his steak. But with his attention aimed at satiating his hunger, her beauty across the table kept calling him. He tried to pretend otherwise, but he sensed a missing piece of his heart with her name on it. Decades of divine protection against his need for companionship from the farer gender seemed to evaporate in her presence.

She tipped back her wineglass and then returned it to the tablecloth. "You've gone quiet."

"Just thinking."

"Dare I ask about what?"

During the introspective moments during which he'd consumed half a pound of meat, he'd made his decision. He realized he needed Diane as a companion, and nothing short of marriage would suffice. "Nothing interesting. Just some boring guy stuff you wouldn't understand."

CHAPTER 22

After last night's dinner date, Diane knew Liam loved her. Being an empath made it unambiguous, but the harder question was determining how she felt about him.

The young hunter was right. Feelings were facts as invisible as gravity and magnetism, and they were powerful. Hers were doing laps around her heart, confusing her.

A knock on her hotel door got her attention.

"Coming." With her purse over her shoulder, she walked to the door and opened it.

Her potential future father-in-law greeted her. "Good morning." He lifted a polystyrene cup. "Coffee?"

"No, thanks. I had enough at breakfast."

"Are you ready, then?"

She took the hint. He was visiting her room because she was the lagging member of the day's hunting party. "Can we first check on Josh and Nana on the way out?"

"Of course."

She thought about opening her purse to verify her dagger's presence inside, but she could feel it. She entered the hallway, led Connor to her grandmother's room, and knocked.

As the door opened, it revealed Nana. "Hello."

"Are you all set with Josh today?"

"Yes, I'll take him to the beach."

Diane had verified earlier in the morning that her younger brother's tablet contained enough books to hold his interest until she saw him again. "Okay. Have fun."

Nana stared as if into an abyss. "You be careful."

"I'll be fine. I have three big strong men protecting me."

"I've seen this before. You know I know what you're facing.

You make sure to come back to me alive."

Diane hugged her grandmother and then followed the elder hunter into the morning's humid air and the waiting SUV. Liam sat in the driver's seat with Tom beside him.

Connor opened a door to the Jeep's back seat for the empath, who climbed into the vehicle. Her potential father-in-law then circled the Renegade, entered from its far side, and sat next to her.

Liam's eyes appeared in the rearview mirror. "Everyone ready?"

Connor answered. "Let's get moving. We need some bearing separation from the hotel to get a fix on where we're going."

"Anywhere in particular, Father?"

"Head north a few miles towards Tom's apartment."

The view from the moving SUV included public buildings and private houses–mansions aligned side-by-side as they hid in plain sight–of neoclassical design, with pastel-colored walls and orange roofs. With its impressive dome reflecting golden sunlight, the church of Saint Therapon stood out above neighboring structures as a landmark. At a stylish café, old men played cards at a sidewalk table while tourists dressed in designer European garb wrapped fingers with glittering rings around five-dollar drinks.

After covering several blocks, Liam pulled the vehicle to the side of the road and parked. "Let's get a bearing." He twisted and extended his hand into the back seat. "Father, get a GPS compass ready, please."

Connor reached into the cargo compartment and pulled out the requested electronics. "It's on and calibrated already."

Diane withdrew her dagger from her purse and pushed it towards the young hunter.

He grabbed her wrist, time stopped, and he spoke into her mind. "I hope you enjoyed last night."

She watched the dagger rotating. "I did, thanks. We'll have to do it more often."

"This island's a great place to relax and see ancient architecture."

"You mean when it's not overrun by refugees."

"They're harmless. It's our target I'm worried about."

"I hope you're not really worried."

"I'm trained to defeat him, but I can't help but think I'm pushing my luck by taking on a third wraith."

"Are you afraid?"

"I'm the right amount of afraid. Fearlessness at this point would be arrogance. I respect him for breaking our line long ago and for whatever powers he's gained over a thousand years."

She wanted to let him know he had help. "I'll be with you."

The dagger settled, and as time restarted its normal cadence, Liam stared at the blade. "This doesn't make sense. It's pointing at Moria."

Diane sealed her dagger within her purse. "Isn't that a big refugee camp?"

"Yeah, it pointed there last night, too, but I assumed it was really pointing in front of it or beyond it."

Tom interjected his local knowledge. "It's the biggest camp. Moria was initially established as a temporary measure to house no more than two thousand people. Now it's got close to six thousand."

She found the numbers alarming. "Why's it so overcrowded?"

"Intentional bureaucracy. The nations of Europe are sending a message to the refugees and to the nations that help them reach the Greek islands, mainly Turkey. They're saying you're no longer welcome, which leaves Lesbos with a big problem. But the people of Lesbos and volunteers from abroad have helped ease the strain."

"I know this is going to sound selfish, but I was hoping to avoid dealing with refugees. My heart goes out to them. I feel their sadness. It's consuming the island."

Liam answered. "I don't know if that's selfish or just practical for our mission. If their sadness overwhelms your senses, you could lose your ability to track the wraith."

"I don't think that's a risk, at least not yet. I feel okay."

Tom pointed ahead. "My apartment's a couple blocks that way. We can get a final bearing there and suit up."

Liam drove the Renegade through tight roads until Tom tapped his phone to open a garage on a one-way street. After pulling into the enclosed space and shutting off the Jeep's engine, Liam helped his father carry huge canvass equipment bags up narrow stairs to their liaison's quarters.

The bachelor's loft was simple and decluttered. A few chairs, a sofa, an island in front of a small kitchen, a computer work area, a large-screen television, and a hammock in the corner.

As he lowered a bag to the laminated wood flooring, the young hunter described it. "Your apartment's a thing of beauty, like one big man cave."

"It works for me. I have no time for toys other than what you see."

Connor placed his bag next to the one his son had carried. "Let's get another bearing to be certain."

Diane walked to the kitchen island and placed her dagger on it. "Come here, Liam."

The young hunter pulled the GPS module from a bag, stepped to her side, and clasped her wrist. As time stopped, he spoke in her mind. "I can't wait until we figure out what this is pointing to."

"I'm surprised I don't know. I thought it would be part of being an empath, but apparently not." The dagger settled, and the world began moving again.

Liam eyed the bearing. "That's still Moria."

The disconnect that had been bothering Diane since the prior bearing struck her. "But my vision of the last victim was in the water. There's no bodies of water in Moria."

Connor frowned. "No, there aren't." Defying his age, he stooped with ease and rummaged through a bag. He pulled out a laminated map and a felt-tip marker. He then sprang back to his feet, walked to the kitchen island, and flattened the map.

Liam took the marker and dabbed dots on the three locations where he'd entered the trance with Diane–the hotel, the street, and the apartment. He freehanded the three lines of bearing the dagger had revealed. As with most fixes, they failed to define a point, but they formed a small triangle in the camp. "Yeah. That's dry land behind the walls of Moria."

Diane resisted the conclusion. "He can't be a refugee."

Connor countered. "Why not? It's a smart disguise if he believes his next sacrifice is also a refugee."

Liam countered his father's counter. "But he's got to have all the money in the world after centuries. If he needs to get into a refugee camp, he could bribe his way in or pay a smuggler to help him. I can't see him suffering with those who have nothing, especially when he could end up trapped there and separated from his sacrifice."

Connor nodded. "Your last point is valid. The risk of being trapped in what amounts to a prison for refugees would be a grave risk for him."

"That could ruin him completely. Something's not making sense, Father."

"This is why when logic no longer helps us, we abandon analysis and embrace field work. Let's study some finer maps of Moria, suit up, and get ready for tracking and hunting."

CHAPTER 23

Letting Tom drive, Liam sat in the back seat. He wanted to spare Diane from the lethargy of trances with his father, and so he made himself free to engage her to update their tracking.

Beside him, the empath squirmed. She unbuttoned her windbreaker, revealing the straps of her body armor. "This is uncomfortable."

"That must be heavy for you." He'd triple-checked her protective gear in the apartment, but he doted on her with another inspection, reaching around her torso and checking the straps for pinching and tightness. The dagger was poised for action in a sheath on her leg. "It's all fitting you correctly."

"I didn't like wearing armor last time, but I'll be fine."

"Tom, can you crank up the air conditioning?"

The order's liaison protested. "It's not really that hot."

"But it's humid, and she looks uncomfortable."

"The temperature's fine. I'm fine. Liam's just overreacting."

Agreeing with her assessment, the young hunter remained silent as the Jeep slowed and the windshield revealed the approaching gate into Moria.

The order's liaison stopped the vehicle, rolled down his window, and spoke in Greek. A uniformed guard replied, and a quick conversation rose and then ended. Tom updated the team in English. "I need to pull us to the side and await our police escort." He accelerated the Renegade to a crawl, moved it to a patch of gravel, and then parked.

Recalling the divine laws governing his purpose, Liam warned the liaison. "We can't ask them to help us hunt."

Tom looked over his shoulder at Liam. "The order warned me of that. I'll make it clear that they need to stay out of our way.

It may be touchy, though, if this gets hot. You can't ask a cop to look the other way if a gunfight breaks out."

Liam became anxious. "Are they really necessary? Why invite them at all?"

"I've been here for a couple years, and I haven't found a way to bring weapons into the camp without the local police. I've gone in armed with a pistol a few times looking for criminals, and the cops have been necessary and helpful."

Liam wasn't ready to drop the argument. "Can't they just give you a stamp of approval? Let you and your friends in to take care of business?"

"I would love to, but it's not happening. Look at us. Four commandoes in unmarked body armor, and three of us will be carrying assault rifles and shotguns. We'd set off a panicked stampede before reaching the middle of the camp, unless we have a police escort."

Liam sighed and accepted the facts, but the risk remained real. "We don't know what we're going to find or how it's going to go down, but we need to talk this through before we pull outsiders into a battle with a wraith."

Connor interjected his wisdom. "There are too many variables to discuss contingencies for everything. We'll instead set up ground rules for our police escort. The obvious preferred tendency is to minimize their involvement."

Tom shrugged. "I can have them set up a perimeter and focus exclusively on crowd control, but again, you can't expect them to ignore gunfire if it happens."

Accepting the rules, Liam questioned the assumptions. "That's a risk we'll have to accept. What are you going to tell them about our business?"

"I'll tell them that we're going after a suspect wanted for murder in Syria. Sometimes, criminals sneak into camps, even coming on the boats claiming to be refugees."

"How do you normally fit into such a scenario? How can you explain us?"

"I established myself first as a volunteer, with support from the order. I spend a lot of time in the camp hammering nails, rolling duct tape around stuff, and picking up garbage. When I pick up a weapon, which is rare, it's viewed as an extension of cleaning up around here. I become a bounty hunter picking up dangerous scum who hide here to escape justice, and I take out the human trash. Today, you're here as an extension of my bounty-hunting role."

Liam respected the man's efforts. "That's good groundwork, but won't our firepower make the police nervous?"

The liaison reached into the Jeep's console and withdrew a large wad of cash. "This'll help calm them. They respect me, but they expect a financial gesture of appreciation to look the other way."

Fifteen minutes later, an SUV with police markings parked next to the Renegade, and Tom glared at it. "That's them. I recognize the driver. Stay here." He stepped from the vehicle, walked to the cops, and propped his hands against the driver's door. After handshakes, nods, and the exchange of cash and a handheld radio, he returned to the Jeep and sat. "I'll drive behind them, but they'll go wherever I tell them. I told them where we triangulated our latest fix. So, we'll head straight there unless we get better intelligence along the way."

Liam sought refined data. "Let's get a fix now." He reached into the canvas bag behind his seat for the GPS compass module and a laminated map of the camp.

Tom shrugged. "Sure."

Diane withdrew her dagger, leaned sideways, and pressed it against the floor.

Liam put the compass next to the knife and then took the empath's wrist. After the blade rotated and settled, time returned to normal, and the young hunter measured the direction. "Shit. It's off."

His father twisted in the passenger seat and looked to Liam. "How off?"

Liam applied a felt-tip marker to the laminated map and drew the bearing from the camp's main gate. "Ten degrees from the center of our triangular fix."

"Oh, dear."

The realization hit the young hunter like a sledgehammer. "You know what this means, don't you? A moving target."

"Indeed I do, lad. Both opportunity and danger."

Diane sounded nervous. "You guys are scaring me. What's going on?"

Liam inhaled deeply to calm himself. "Every dagger any hunter's ever used against a wraith has always pointed towards the site of his latest kill. It's always been stale data, but the locations have been simple to find, since sites don't move. People move. Since it looks like your dagger's pointing at a moving target, the logical conclusion is that it's pointing to the wraith."

"I was afraid you'd say that."

Connor sighed. "We should all be feeling a healthy fear. Any wraith is dangerous, and this one's the least understood of their kind. But we're prepared for this, and we've worked well as a team against two savages already. Tom, as our newest member, you'll have to follow our lead. Whatever you do, don't take him on alone. Don't be a hero."

As the gravity weighed upon the moods of the Jeep's occupants, the liaison spoke in a respectful tone. "I hope to live up to your expectations." As the police vehicle, a Ford Kuga, passed through the opening chain link gate, Tom drove into the camp, two car lengths behind.

While the Jeep crept into the camp, Liam reached into a canvas bag behind his seat and grabbed pistols. "Since we don't know what to expect, it's time to arm ourselves."

Connor agreed. "Correct. Pistols for now."

"I'm already on it." Liam checked for empty chambers on three weapons and then passed two of them into the forward seats. He kept the third, its safety engaged, in his hand. He glanced at Diane.

The empath tapped her dagger. "I'm good."

Nothing had prepared Liam for the sight of Moria. As its gates closed behind him, the enclosure became a camp, a slum, and a prison. The first vision to capture his attention was a woman kneeling in a patch of dirt, wearing a dress of orange and red floral patterns, and watching her hands with dark eyes peering out from a yellow hijab. She washed clothes in an orange bucket, and the makeshift shelter behind her required a rope tied around a hanging stone to hold down its roof.

If his father suffered the same cultural shock, he hid it. "Take a bearing now. Remember that we're chasing a moving target."

Liam flattened the laminated map on the console between Connor and Tom. "Since he's moving, let's track him here where we can all see it." The young hunter then turned to Diane, who had readied her dagger on the floor. He connected with her, read the line of bearing from the GPS compass, and drew a felt-tip line on the map. "Maybe my father should drive so that you can review our fixes and communicate with the police?"

Tom agreed. "Sure." He lifted his handheld radio to his mouth and announced his intentions in Greek. Both vehicles stopped, and Connor crossed in front of the Jeep to take the wheel.

As the convoy moved forward again, Liam saw a little girl outside the window. She had long hair in a pony tail, and she wore a dark blouse and faded jeans. Her small hands seemed incapable of exerting any gripping force beyond that which she applied them to–making slight curls of her fingers while waving. Her smile melted the young hunter, and he decided at that moment to aim his weapons with excessive care and to avoid collateral damage to the refugees.

CHAPTER 24

The squalor surrounding Diane depressed her, and she felt the sadness of the refugees. They'd escaped rapid and violent deaths from tyrants in their homeland to meet slow and decaying deaths at the hands of bureaucrats.

She let her fear of the wraith focus her thoughts, and she clasped her dagger in her hand. Leaning into Liam, she confessed her feelings. "Why am I so scared?"

He shook his head. "It's beyond me. I'm afraid, too, and I never get this scared. Father's putting up a good front, but even he's scared. I can tell."

She kept her voice at a whisper. "I can sense it in both of you like I've never sensed it. We're all terrified, except for Tom."

"Yeah. Poor bloke doesn't know any better."

"But what do we really know?"

He glared at her. "You're the empath and the Lady of the Dagger. If you don't know, nobody does."

She looked ahead at the vehicle of police officers who remained ignorant of the dangers they approached. "Crap."

"We'll have to trust each other like never before."

His encouragement sounded trite, but she excused it. "We'll face him together, like always."

"Let's get another fix."

She put her dagger on the floor next to his GPS compass. His grip was warm on her wrist, and the blade rotated.

After the trance, Liam added a line to the laminated map. "He's moved again."

Connor looked at Tom. "Is it possible that he's been warned? How fast does the presence of the police spread across the camp?"

"It can be almost instantaneous. Some of them have cell phones, and I imagine the extra news about a second vehicle with armed civilians would get his attention. Even though we're holding our weapons low, I'm sure a gate guard shared the gossip."

The elder hunter's voice trailed as he fell into deep thought. "Indeed."

A minute later, Liam pointed to his compass on the floor. "Let's get another fix."

Diane leaned into the routine to let time stop, the dagger move, and time start again.

Liam drew the latest line. "He's south of our original fix."

Tom eyed the map. "We need to turn." He lifted the radio and called his police escort. The Ford turned down the next road, and Connor aimed the Jeep behind it.

Liam studied the map. "We're driving into a better geometry for a tighter fix."

Tom glanced at the map and back to the road. "We'll be turning right two streets from here."

"Diane, we'll get a fix exactly when we turn."

When Connor turned the wheel two streets later, she placed her dagger on the floor. The young hunter clasped her wrist, time stopped, and the dagger moved.

After time started again, Liam penned the update. "That's three tight lines! He's in a house right there." He tapped the map.

The liaison evaluated the young hunter's fix. "Yeah, that's a real good fix. I don't remember all the residents, but I know this street. It's a bunch of Syrian families. Never any trouble."

Connor's voice was strong with the anticipation of combat. "It's a great place for a wraith to hide. If we're storming a dwelling, we need to know the entrances, and we need to shift to rifles and shotguns. Jackets off."

"Got it." Liam holstered his pistol and passed the larger, powerful arms forward from the cargo area. "Lean forward, Father." The young hunter slid a shotgun into a sleeve high on the back of the driver's vest.

While the assault team upgraded its armaments, Tom offered a logistical summary. "All these houses have just one entrance in the front. They're quite basic. A man could slip out the back under the walls, but the police will catch him if he tries that. He'd be on his belly."

Connor took charge. "Tell them to stop in front of the house and set their perimeter. For our assault, I'll go in first and move left once inside. Liam, you'll be on my back and move right. Tom, you'll be three paces behind us with Diane behind you. We'll start at the hatchback where we'll get our shields and helmets. Any questions?"

Overwhelmed, Diane watched the Ford stop in the road, beside a Lighthouse Relief volunteers utility vehicle. "Is that truck going to be problem?"

Tom looked to the vehicle and back to the map. "Maybe. It's parked in front of the house with the wraith."

Liam's voice rose half an octave. "Bloody hell. If there are volunteers in there with him, that could mean hostages. That could be why he's stopped."

Connor remained calm. "It complicates matters, but we expected innocent civilians. This is a family dwelling, like Tom already mentioned. But if there is a hostage, aim carefully, and think twice before shooting."

"I'll exchange my shotgun for a sniper rifle."

"No, lad. Keep the firepower. Diane, how confident is your aim with that dagger as a throwing knife?"

"I... uh... it's perfect when it works. It's the dagger doing all the work, though. Not me. I suck without it."

Liam added his cynicism. "That's an understatement. She's practically spastic without magic."

She wanted to enjoy a moment of playfulness, but fear prevented it.

Connor parked the Jeep. "The volunteers don't change anything. Just expect most people in the house to be innocents, and pick your targets carefully. Meet in the back of the Jeep. Everyone out!"

Standing fourth in line, Diane watched the men strap on helmets and grab bulletproof riot shields. She lacked a shield, but Liam lowered a helmet over her head.

He tried to hide his nerves behind bravado, but she sensed his true apprehension. "Just another day on the job. Then after work I can take you to a great steakhouse I was reading about."

As he walked away, she wanted to say something witty, but she could only share her food preference. "I don't like steak!"

From the corner of her eye, she saw four uniformed Greek policemen surround the dwelling.

His shield in one hand and his rifle in the other, Connor crouched and marched towards the door. In a similar posture, Liam matched his father's stride.

Tom then moved behind the younger hunter. "Stay right behind me, Diane. I'm your shield."

Walking behind the crouched liaison, she couldn't see the hunters' entrance into the dwelling. But the front entrance was nothing more than a privacy curtain through which they passed without hesitation. The only indication of successful entry was the horrified shriek of a woman within the structure.

With the hunters inside the house, Tom continued towards the entrance. "Follow me in!"

As her eyes adjusted to the gentle lighting under the roof, Diane realized she stood in a single-room shanty. A quick tally of inhabitants revealed two young uniformed volunteers, two small children, and a husband and wife. Connor and Liam aimed rifles at the only unfamiliar man, who was lowering his belly to the earth upon repeated commands from the hunters.

Gaining courage, Diane lifted her dagger to her ear in preparation to throw it, in case the captive tried to resist. She stepped towards him as the hunters debated their next step. They were in obvious shock of having captured a wraith alive.

"I'll cuff him. You guard him."

"No, lad. Cuffing's dangerous work. I'll handle it. But drop your shield and use both hands on that rifle."

Connor strapped his rifle over his shoulder, dropped his

shield, and climbed aboard the refugee's back. He fumbled his hand across his vest to find handcuffs, and he needed several awkward seconds to locate the rarely used restraints. "There we go." He took the man's hands into the chains and stayed on his back.

Liam pointed his weapon to the ground. "So, now what?"

His father appeared uncertain. "Well, I've never heard of such a thing. A target of ours who gives up without a fight."

The restrained refugee's children were crying, and their mother attempted to comfort them. As she turned her attention towards the intruders, she spat her anger in Arabic. "What's the meaning of this? My husband's a physician! Why are you monsters treating him like animals?"

Diane sensed a horrible mistake.

The young hunter echoed her thoughts. "What if he's not our target? We don't know what Diane's dagger's pointing to. What if this is the site of his last kill, and we need to start filtering our clues?"

"I'm not sure, lad. Perhaps it's best if we get another fix."

One of the volunteers recognized the liaison. "Tom?"

"Yes. Hi. Um... Emma?"

Diane assessed the lady as an attractive blonde-haired woman in her mid-twenties who spoke English with a German accent. "Yes, I'm Emma. What's going on?"

"We're looking for a wanted criminal."

"I doubt it's Doctor Aziz, and even if it is, did you need to bring a small army?"

Tom raised his voice for the hunters' benefit. "What do you think, guys? Did we get our man, or do we need to move on?"

Liam stepped forward, took a knee beside the young doctor, and tapped the back of his hand against the man's neck. "I don't see it or feel it."

Connor moved himself from his captive and helped him to his feet. "Bah. Neither do I. Diane, can you discern the identity of our new colleague?"

Keeping her dagger in her hand, she walked to the man and addressed him in her Iraqi Arabic dialect, which she expected him to understand in a simple conversation. "What's your name?"

"My name is Nashuan Simeon."

"What's your occupation?"

"I am a medical doctor, or at least I was. God knows what I can be now that I've been condemned to this camp."

She moved the dagger to her left hand and extended her right. "Take my hand."

He shook it.

Feeling nothing, she released his grip. "Unless he's under some sort of magical protection, he's not our guy."

Liam knelt in the dirt in front of her. "Let's get a fix."

Diane joined him on the floor and placed her dagger on the ground facing the doctor. The young hunter's touch was warm and revealed his fast heartbeat.

Within their shared trance, he spoke in her mind. "What the hell's going on? This is a bloody mess."

"I don't know. I'm as clueless as you are."

"Damn it. Our empath can't be clueless."

"Well don't blame me, smartass. I told you I had no idea what my dagger was pointing at."

"Alright, alright. I didn't mean to be accusatory. Check out the knife, though. It's about to break your hand off."

She saw her entire arm twisting backwards. "It can only go a hundred and eighty degrees, right?"

"Logic would say so. Does that hurt?"

"How the heck should I know? It's never rotated so much, and I can't feel anything until it stops."

"Well, if something does break, or snap, or feel sprained, trust me to help you. I'll give you first aid."

"How romantic."

"Just don't panic."

"Do I sound panicked?"

"With your arm being twisted around, yeah, a little, and I don't blame you."

"I don't like this, Liam."

"No matter how much it hurts, remember to let go immediately. We want to protect your arm. You'll minimize the damage to your bones and ligaments if you let them naturally snap back where they want to go."

"Okay. I'll try."

The dagger stopped, time started, and a searing pain consumed Diane's joints. She opened her fingers and let her arm unfurl itself while she howled in pain.

In a flash, Liam was on her and stabilizing the fire in her flesh she wanted to revolt against. "Don't move! Don't move! I've got you now."

"It hurts!" A tear rolled down her cheek.

"Where's it hurt the most?"

"My wrist. Ow!"

He palpated her bones and then gave her hand gentle twists. "If none of this causes you horrible pain, I think you escaped without a break."

"It still hurts."

"I know. I know. But if it's no worse when I poke and prod, you've escaped with a sprain. I'll tape it up for you."

Glaring at the young hunter, the German volunteer interrupted the triage. "What the hell just happened?"

"Tom was telling the truth. We're looking for a wanted man."

"No, I mean the part where you just grabbed her hand and then that weird-colored knife just flipped around like lightning."

Liam appeared trapped. "I... uh... if I told you, I'm not sure you'd believe me."

The German put her hands on her hips. "I think you should tell me exactly why your strange knife nearly broke your friend's hand and why the hell it's pointing at me!"

CHAPTER 25

The next day, futility, anger, and sadness weighed upon Ethan as he entered the Mytilene police station. At the reception window, he stood in line behind an elderly couple complaining in Greek of a stolen purse. Since the wraith's command of the local language was weak, his thoughts drifted to what he would say at the window.

When his turn came, a female uniformed officer looked at him with ambivalence and greeted him in Greek. "What can I do for you, sir?"

"I wish to confess to a crime."

Her eyes opened wide. "What sort of crime?"

Ethan steeled himself and forced out the words. Fearing his Master would thwart him, he was shocked when they issued from his lips. "Murder. I killed three women on this island."

She cleared her throat. "Wait here. I'll have an officer escort you inside."

Ethan's wait was short, as the local police appeared to take seriously volunteered confessions of homicide. Within seconds, a uniformed middle-aged male officer passed through a doorway and commanded him in Greek. "Come with me."

The wraith entered the station's inner workspace and saw rows of desks. While most workstations were empty, some supported cops talking on phones, tapping computer keys, or interviewing persons of interest.

His escort stopped at a desk, sat, and gestured for the confessor to sit. The name on his uniform matched that of the plaque facing the wraith.

"Officer Kontos, do you speak English?" Ethan wanted to confess in his native language.

"Yes. So, you wish to confess a murder?"

Although he knew his revelation equated to a suicide attempt, the wraith wanted death after being cheated of it during his rescue effort with the refugees. "Three of them, or any one of the three, whichever is most efficient to take me into custody. I am a threat to society, and I must be incarcerated immediately."

The officer was unimpressed. "Let's start with your name."

"Ethan Smith." He pulled his passport from his pocket and placed it on the desk.

Kontos took the document, examined it, and typed the name into his computer. He then swiveled in his chair and placed the identification face-down on a scanner. After sliding the passport back to the wraith, the officer glanced at his computer screen. "You must be joking."

"I don't understand."

"You're the same Ethan Smith who saved dozens of lives in the latest refugee boat capsizing."

The wraith knew the answer, but he had to protest. "How can you know that?"

"Your name showed up in a paramedic report. It took seconds to cross reference and show up for me, and I know the details from word of mouth. You came very close to drowning. If it weren't for your American colleague, you may not be here."

Ethan blamed his young volunteer companion for saving his life, but he suspected his Master had helped the American pull him from the water. "Yes, that's me. He saved me from drowning, but that's irrelevant. I killed three women."

"Here, on Lesbos?"

"Yes."

Kontos tapped his keyboard and scanned his monitor. "I see only two unsolved murders with female victims on the island this year. When did you commit these supposed crimes?"

Ethan's anxiety rose as he realized he faced an uphill battle against the officer's resistance. "The most recent was a week ago. The other preceded that one by four weeks, and the first was four weeks earlier than the second."

"Can you give me the names of your supposed victims?"

"No, I picked them all randomly."

"Can you describe them? Let's start with your most recent supposed victim."

"Please stop calling them 'supposed'. I killed them."

"Mister Smith, I represent the law. Until I have evidence of a crime, we're talking about supposed homicides. Plenty of people walk into police stations and confess murders they didn't commit."

"But I did kill them. You have to believe me."

"Whom did you kill most recently, then?"

Ethan reflected upon his latest tribute. "She was young, probably mid-twenties. Beautiful. Brown hair, brown eyes."

The officer frowned as he tested the story. "Remind me again, when you killed her?"

"About a week ago."

"About, or exactly?"

"June twenty-eighth."

Kontos nodded. "There's a precise detail. That was Friday, wasn't it?"

Ethan recognized the test of his memory. "No, it was Thursday."

"Right. My mistake. Yes, it was Thursday. Now, about what time of day was it?"

"Very early in the morning."

The officer grunted. "Can you take me to the victim's body?"

"No, I threw her into the sea. I tied a heavy block around her ankle and threw her overboard from my boat."

Kontos wasn't even pretending to take notes. "I see. And how did you acquire your boat?"

Sensing his confession failing, Ethan tried to remain calm. "I leased a boat and dock when I arrived on the island."

"Why did you do that?"

"To dispose of the bodies I would kill. I disposed of all their bodies in the sea."

"If you were going to lie about a homicide, you'd be wiser to tell me that you buried the body. I can investigate burial sites with a methane sniffer and a dog, but it costs a lot of money to send divers into the water, and they're always busy elsewhere."

On his lap, the wraith balled his fists to contain his frustration. "I'm not lying."

"I see. So, this was pre-meditated for months, your claim of being a serial killer, and only now you're confessing?"

Ethan nodded.

"Very well, then. How did you kill her, the last one?"

"I stabbed her in the heart. May I show you the knife?"

"You brought a knife into a police station?"

"Yes. I imagine I should've mentioned that."

"Yes, you should have, but our metal detector also should've caught it. Slowly put your knife on my desk."

Ethan unsheathed his dagger and placed it in front of the officer. "It's made of bronze, which explains why your old metal detector missed it. It's a nonferrous metal."

The officer opened a drawer, pulled out a rubber glove, and slipped it over his fingers. He reached for the weapon, lifted it to his face, and admired it. "This is a handsome artifact. You keep it amazingly sharp and polished, I'll give you that."

"It's not an artifact. It's a brutal weapon, and I wielded it without mercy. You must believe me."

Kontos examined the blade at the tip of his nose and grunted. "I see no blood with my naked eye. Not even a trace. If I take this to a lab, will I find any?"

Ethan lowered his gaze. "No. I cleaned it with oxygen bleach."

"Mister Smith, I'll be blunt and tell you that there's no unsolved murder or missing person's report for a woman in her mid-twenties on this island all year, much less last week."

Defying physics, the blade assumed its own power and slid across the desk. As the wraith felt the metal in his palm, he looked up and saw red irises flash and then return to their normal brown color within the officer's eyes.

The eerie sanguine glow from his interviewer told Ethan that his Master worked against him, but he kept arguing for his guilt by revealing his final, riskiest clue. "She was a refugee from Moria. I paid a guard to help me sneak her out."

Kontos exhaled and rolled his eyes. "You're losing my interest, Mister Smith. Missing persons reports for Moria residents are questionable at best, and unless witnesses press the issue, they're always considered to have reached the mainland. I don't suppose you could produce a witness to your crime?"

"No."

"Can you at least tell me why you did it?"

"You wouldn't believe me."

The officer scoffed. "I've heard every motive imaginable."

"No, not mine. I... I believed that killing them would make me immortal."

Kontos raised his eyebrows. "I've heard of such delusions, but that's a new one for me personally."

"I'm not deluded."

"You've confessed to a crime that has what we'll call a 'mystical' motive. There's no missing person, you have no name for any of your victims, and you can't produce a corpse. You have no witnesses, and your murder weapon is a sterilized, bloodless museum artifact. Did I miss anything?"

"You have my confession."

Kontos stripped the glove from his hand and tossed it in a wastebasket. "No, Mister Smith, I'm afraid I don't. I believe I have the ramblings of a man suffering from some sort of delayed shock from your effort rescuing the refugees. I'm neither qualified nor obligated to give you psychological support, but I recommend that you seek help."

"I don't need psychological help. I need to be separated from society."

"Not for murder, based upon the evidence, or lack thereof, I should say. We need more people being heroes like you were this week, not snapping under stress like you are now. Please, Mister Smith, you appear completely harmless, and I can't arrest you. But I urge you to seek help."

Ethan wanted to threaten Kontos with harsh words and violent gestures to prove the officer wrong. But the lording spirit of his dagger restrained him. He sheathed his knife and remained silent while the officer escorted him from the building.

CHAPTER 26

Sitting in the Renegade's back seat, Liam turned to Diane and spoke softly. "She's got to be his next sacrifice."

She leaned towards him. "I would agree, but I don't feel it."

"You haven't touched her yet. You should learn something when you do."

"I was going to, but your dad stopped me."

Liam glanced at the driver's seat where the elder hunter held the steering wheel. He considered asking his father about his intentions but opted instead to let him focus on trailing the volunteers' truck out of Moria. The young hunter decided Diane's perspective of Connor's intent would suffice. "Did he say why?"

"He just said to wait and try it somewhere safe."

Unsure what his father considered safe, he trusted the elder hunter. "Fair enough. God knows what's going to happen." He glanced at her wrist, reached into the back of the Jeep for a medical kit, and then balanced the plastic case on his lap. From it, he withdrew a roll of athletic tape.

"I'm fine now. It only hurts a little."

"Oh, really?" He closed the medical kit and held it out. "Grab your dagger and press its edge into this kit like you're trying to slice it open."

She frowned but obeyed. As the knife hit the plastic, her wrist bent, and she grabbed it with her other hand. "Ow! You knew that would hurt. Why'd you make me do that?"

"Because I knew it would hurt. You're slow to accept your disadvantages."

"So, I'm too stupid to know when I'm injured?"

"No, too stubborn."

She returned her dagger to her purse and then flopped her

wrist over the armrest. "I won't argue that. Here. You can play nurse, but stop playing psychologist."

"I don't mean to be rude, but I need to be honest." He mentally appended 'if we're going to spend our lives together', but he kept the qualifying sentiment to himself.

"Just fix me."

"Lean towards me and press your palm gently into my armrest."

She extended her hand and bent it backwards against his seat.

"Can you wiggle your fingers?"

She fluttered her elegant digits below his face.

"Okay, here goes." The tape screeched as he extended a length and wrapped it around her wrist. He worked towards her elbow and then back to her hand, creating layers. As he reached her thumb, he pulled it back and immobilized its lower joint. When finished, he bent into the tape and ripped it from the roll with his teeth. He lifted her forearm and tested her hand in various directions. Confident he'd limited her range of motion, he gave her back her arm. "You're good now."

She retracted her hand and tested its mobility. "It feels weird."

"Haven't you had your wrist taped before?"

"Not that I remember. I'm not much of an athlete. So, I don't get injuries often."

"But you're a spastic klutz. Haven't you sprained your wrist by just tripping over yourself?"

She scowled and backhanded his upper arm, which remained in a cast from healing bullet wounds. "There. You did a great job. I hardly felt that."

As the chain links of Moria drifted into the distance behind the Jeep and the police vehicle turned towards the center of Mytilene, an inconsistency landed in Liam's mind. "Your dagger cauterized my wound in Istanbul better than a surgical team. Why isn't it healing you now?"

"It's got to be a matter of emotional state. I was going crazy with panic when I thought you were dying." She pointed to her taped wrist. "But this is just an annoyance."

"You haven't had any strong emotions about our wraith yet, have you?"

"Well, no. Just fear, like everyone else, and that usually just clouds things."

"Could our fear be blocking us, or be blocking you, more specifically?"

"Maybe. Now that we know where my dagger's been pointing, maybe we can all be less afraid. That could clear things up."

Liam nodded and thought of the German volunteer who'd attracted the dagger's interest. "You want to try a fix again, just to see if it's still pointing towards her?"

"Sure."

Having learned from seeing the dagger twist the empath's arm, Liam recommended a new technique. "This time, don't hold it, but let it rest in your hand."

She took the dagger from her purse and balanced it her palm, just forward of the tape.

Liam moved his hand underneath hers and lifted his callouses into the soft skin behind her knuckles. Time stopped, the dagger made a slight adjustment towards the volunteer's truck, and time recommenced. "It's still pointing at her."

Diane returned the dagger to her purse. "I think she's the next sacrifice, but I don't feel it."

The volunteers' truck pulled into a grocery store parking lot, and Connor guided the Jeep next to it. From the truck's passenger seat, the German woman exited the vehicle and walked to the liaison's door on the Renegade's passenger side.

Tom rolled down the window. "What's wrong?"

"My partner needs to get back to the Lighthouse Relief camp with the truck. It's a long trip during traffic. If you want me to help you and your friends, you need to do it quick."

Tom glanced at Connor. "I can walk home from here. Why don't you let Emma take my seat and take her wherever you need to go?"

The elder hunter looked at the German. "Is that alright with you, young lady? Our introduction was rather unorthodox, and I would understand your hesitation."

She shrugged. "You had a police escort with Sergeant Rouphos, and I trust him. Tom's been volunteering around the camp for a couple years, too. So, you don't scare me, despite the SWAT team behavior. But you're going to have to tell me what you want from me before I go any further."

"I would like to discuss our affairs in the safety of a Catholic church. I was thinking of Saint Therapon."

The German frowned. "How did you get from a commando raid on the camp's best doctor resident to a Catholic church?"

Connor continued his explanation. "We should be on holy ground to explore this further."

Emma's face flushed. "Explore what further?"

"Perhaps a demonstration. Emma, if you'll be so kind as to watch my son and his friend in the back seat. This time, watch the dagger closely. I suspect you had too many distractions when they did this in the doctor's home. Liam and Diane, can you point the dagger away from Emma and take a fix?"

Diane pointed the dagger away from the German while holding it in her palm.

Liam lifted his hand into the empath's knuckles, entered the trance, and spoke into her mind. "I can't wait to see her face when this is done."

"You seem to like watching her."

"What? Come on. You're not jealous, are you?"

"You practically undressed her with your eyes when she walked to our car."

He was guilty, but his intent had been harmless. Guarded from lust by the divine essence protecting his bloodline, he'd been noticing how each sacrifice had been young and beautiful. Emma was his third data point supporting his observation, after Diane in Michigan and an attractive Iraqi woman in Istanbul. "I was just observing."

"Uh huh."

"No, really. I'm prevented by divine privilege from lusting

after women. I see how other men leer, but I simply can't do it."

"Oh, so you've tried?"

"A man doesn't try to lust. It's a reptilian function. How can you possibly be trying to turn this against me?"

"I'll be the judge of your divine privilege."

The complexities of courtship were confounding the young hunter, and he was thankful the conversation ended upon the dagger's settling upon the German woman.

Time started again, and Emma blinked. "It's pointing at me, just like in Doctor Aziz' house. That was like magic."

Relieved he didn't have to talk to the German and invite Diane's jealousy, Liam let his father explain.

Connor twisted to talk to the startled woman. "We can repeat this demonstration all day. It's a divine power we can only partially explain. But, as you can see, with this dagger constantly choosing to point at you, we can only conclude that you're someone special for our cause."

Her voice was gravelly as she wrestled for understanding. As she swore in German, Liam caught half the nasty words, like 'devil' and 'liars'. Then she switched to English. "Your cause? What is it?"

"We're hunting a serial killer. We had thought the dagger was pointing towards him, which is why we assaulted the doctor's home, but now we know it was pointing to you."

She shook her head. "This can't be true. It's trickery. It's a magic show." Backing away from the vehicle, she shook her head faster.

Liam called to her through his open window. "Emma. If you run, the killer will find you. You need our protection. You're the next victim."

"No, this is crazy." Emma marched towards her truck.

Liam placed his hand on Diane's shoulder. "You have to stop her."

"Me? Why me?"

"You're the least threatening and the most trustworthy. Get out there, stop her, and calm her down."

"Then what?"

Liam had an idea. "Then call for me."

CHAPTER 27

As Diane trotted towards the volunteers' truck, she tripped and staggered. Her clumsiness nearly cost her a sprained ankle, but she recovered her stride without damage. Instead of an injury, she garnered the German woman's compassion.

With her hand on the truck's passenger door, Emma called to her. "Are you okay?"

"I think so. I trip over myself once in a while."

"What do you want?"

"I want to explain what's going on."

"I've seen enough."

"But you haven't heard everything."

"I'll listen from inside the truck. You stay three steps away." Emma sat in the pickup truck's passenger seat, closed the door, and yelled out the window. "You've got sixty seconds."

While walking to a spot three meters from the truck's door, Diane reached into her purse and clutched her dagger. "I need to hold my knife while I talk to you."

"Why?"

The empath offered a partial truth. "It's been blessed. It works like a good luck charm."

"Keep it behind your back, then."

Her sore wrist protesting but holding firm with its taped support, Diane swung her dagger to the small of her back. "I know this is weird, but it all makes sense."

"You have fifty seconds left."

Diane sensed the German woman's strong defiance, which aligned with her expectation of a wraith's chosen sacrifice. "I believe you and I are both from a special bloodline dating back to Upper Mesopotamia and the city of Nineveh. Because of this, we're linked to a serial killer who targets selected members of our line."

"That's crazy."

"But you saw the dagger."

"I saw something."

"You saw it twice. You saw it nearly break my arm in the doctor's house, and then we showed you in the Jeep."

The woman's curiosity was overcoming her resistance. "Can you show me again?"

"I need my partner."

"Yeah, okay. Have him leave his weapons in the car, though."

Diane turned to call for Liam, but the ghost in front of her stopped her.

With an unseen wind flapping a milky gown over her, the Maiden of Yorkshire floated inches above the pavement and spoke in medieval Middle English. "Embrace our sister."

Diane sensed herself in a trance, the world beyond her and the apparition on hold while they talked. "You mean Emma?"

"She is of the line of Nineveh."

"Is she the next sacrifice?"

"Yes."

"How is she any different from the last sacrifice? I spent a lot of time with Nadine in Istanbul, and nothing special ever happened when I touched her."

"You will need our German sister to defeat the savage."

Diane felt the kinship bond with the ghost every time she alluded to the sisterhood. "How can I need her? It's been just me and my friends and family against the last two wraiths."

"You used Nadine as a distraction in Istanbul."

"So, Emma's a distraction now?"

The mist forming the apparition's frame began to drift upward into the sky. "All will be revealed when you embrace our sister."

When the trance ended, Diane looked to Emma. "This might work without him, if you'll agree to take his place."

"What do you want me to do?"

"Just hold my hand."

"I'm not leaving the truck."

"I'll come to you, if it's okay with you." Diane extended her hand and walked to the vehicle.

Emma reached out the truck's window. "Is this going to hurt?"

"It's never hurt me before, except for that mistake you saw in the doctor's house. Take my hand."

The German wrapped her fingers around the empath's digits.

Reality stopped, and Diane entered a dream within a dream, observing the trance of the German woman. Watching from above, she saw Emma burning on a crude woodland crucifix, blood pouring from her heart's puncture wound.

Then Diane was the sacrifice, hanging from the cross and aware of Emma observing her. Finally, the Maiden of Yorkshire became the restrained, bleeding and burning victim. As the empath tried to call out in protest, the killing scene vanished, and she stood, marking an equilateral triangle with the German woman and the ghost.

Wide-eyed, Emma stared at the apparition and called out in German words that Diane understood. "Who are you?"

Diane tried to answer, but a supernatural force silenced her while the ghost responded. "We descend from the same line, the line of Nineveh."

"What's going on?"

The black pools of the ghost's eyes narrowed as her misty brow furrowed. "Believe everything Diane says. She speaks the truth. A savage hunts you."

"Why me? I haven't done anything!"

"You are an empath. You know."

The old answer Diane had hated took on a new meaning when addressed to someone else, and whatever force had been silencing her released her into the conversation. "She's an empath, too?"

"Yes."

The German was stymied. "I'm a what? This is crazy. I'm going crazy."

Diane addressed her new sister. "No, you're not. I've been through this before. It's going to be okay."

The Maiden of Yorkshire dismissed the empath's platitude, her voice carrying a hint of cold venom. "Be not complacent, but beware! This is the most dangerous wraith known. You must work together, and you each must risk yourself for others. That is love. Love is the power of the empath."

Emma's urgency grew. "You're telling me a bunch of stuff that doesn't make sense."

As she revealed her ancient anger, the apparition furrowed her brow, and her eyes became black. "I've been denied passage since he killed me seven centuries ago. I need your help."

"How can I help? I'm totally confused."

"The other empath will explain everything." The maiden's eyes softened as she looked to Diane. "You understand."

The path forward was murky, but Diane understood the rules. "Yes, I do."

The apparition looked upwards while drifting into transparency. "Avenge me."

Time started again, and the parking lot became Diane's reality.

Emma burst out the truck's door and into the Chaldean empath's arms. "I don't understand!" She started sobbing.

Diane held her new spiritual sister. "It's going to be okay."

"You say that, but she... that entity... said we were in danger. I... I'm going crazy."

"You're not. You have to trust me."

"Was that a ghost? Did we just see a ghost? You saw her, didn't you? That wasn't all in my head, was it? Please tell me it wasn't!"

"I saw her. She is a ghost, killed by the man that's coming for you. She's real."

Mortal horror focused the German empath, and she pushed back from the empath's shoulder. "What should I do, if there's really a killer coming for me? I need to hide!"

"No, nothing yet. He only kills under a full moon. We've got a few weeks to get ready."

"How can you be so sure? What if it were you instead of me? Would you be so calm?"

Diane leveled her stare into the German empath's eyes. "It was me already, and I survived. I can't make any promises, but I know your best chance of survival is to join me and my team." The Chaldean empath looked at the hunters. "They've been through this before with me, and we've risked our lives for each other. You won't find better protection anywhere."

Emma nodded, turned to her truck, and called out to her volunteer companion. As the vehicle rolled away from the German empath, she walked past Diane towards the Jeep.

"I guess this means you're coming with us?"

"After what I just saw, I'd be a fool not to. I'm going wherever the hell you are."

CHAPTER 28

At lunch, Liam watched Emma tip back her third cup of coffee. The German empath was shaken and trying to nurse her shock with caffeine. The young hunter made eye contact with Diane across the table and nodded at the caffeine addict seated beside her.

Diane shrugged and half-whispered, half-pantomimed her response. "What?"

Giving up on subtlety, Liam blurted out his concern. "Emma, do you normally drink so much coffee?"

The German empath was anxious and cynical. "No, but I don't normally get told I'm being hunted by a serial killer at the same time that I'm introduced to a friendly ghost."

"I'm sorry. I didn't mean to–"

"And have that ghost tell me I'm an empath half an hour after armed commandos storm a friend's home with automatic weapons." She grabbed a passing waiter and ordered a refill.

"Again, I'm sorry if I'm trivializing this, but suicide by caffeine won't help, either."

Diane intervened. "Let's see how she feels after a few sips of her next cup. Four cups can't be fatal."

Liam shrugged. "No, I guess not."

"So, we'll let her enjoy her next cup, and we'll see how it goes. Is everyone okay if I order a platter for all of us?"

As the two hunters folded their menus, Emma kept staring at the one she'd never opened.

The Chaldean empath continued. "It's settled, then. I'll order lunch for everyone."

A short but lean waiter refilled Emma's coffee and took Diane's order for the foursome.

As the server marched away, Liam looked to Diane and started his inquiry on a light note. "So, when you chased after Emma, did you trip on purpose?"

"No. Why?"

"Because if you'd staged that, I was going to call you a genius."

She flicked her uninjured wrist at him.

Liam scanned the restaurant for nearby diners, but since the lunch rush had passed, the adjacent tables were empty. He considered it sufficient privacy since anyone eavesdropping on their conversation would consider it delusional talk. "But let's get on with understanding where we are and what we're up against." He looked beside him at the elder hunter. "You don't mind if I take the lead, do you, Father?"

Tipping back a cup of tea, Connor grunted and waved his fingers.

The young hunter started with a leading comment. "From the Jeep, we saw Emma grab Diane, and then she let go. A second later, Emma was in Diane's arms, like you were best friends."

Ignoring his invitation to expound upon the trance, the German empath gulped coffee.

Liam probed directly. "Emma? What happened?"

As she lowered her cup, she looked into the distance, reminding Liam of the post-traumatic thousand-yard stare.

Placing her hand over that of her colleague, Diane took over the investigation. "Emma?"

The German empath's long, blonde ponytail shifted behind her shoulder as she looked at Diane. "Yes?"

Diane treated the new teammate with the same patient skill she'd developed with her autistic brother. "Can you tell us what happened in the trance, Emma?"

"I already told you. I met a ghost. She said I would die."

"Did she really say that, Emma? I didn't hear her say anyone would die."

Emma gave a hasty, nervous laugh. "She didn't have to say it. When a ghost shows up to warn you that you're being hunted by a serial killer that nobody can stop, it's a logical conclusion."

"No, Emma, the ghost said we can work together to stop him."

"Really? How? You're supposed to explain it all to me. That's what she said."

Liam raised his eyebrows. "That's going to be a challenge. We're still making sense of everything and formulating a plan."

Diane glared at the young hunter. "We're working on the details, but we know the basic approach, don't we, Liam?"

The young hunter cleared his throat. He'd shared an idea with his father in private and then with Diane in a quick dagger-induced trance, and they'd all agreed on a plan. But he needed to be sure of Emma's identity and of her willingness to cooperate. So, he moved slowly. "Well, there's a lot of techniques we normally use to track the killer, who we call 'the wraith'."

"Why do you call him that? I don't like it. Not at all."

"He steals life from some of the women he kills."

"You mean, he wants to steal my life?"

"Yes. For him, it would mean that he wouldn't age until the next blood moon, when he'd kill someone else, and so on and so forth with every blood moon."

She reached for her cup, tipped it back, and plopped it onto the table. "Just when I thought this couldn't get worse, or crazier."

"It still gets a little bit worse before it gets better. We know that he's capable of finding you with supernatural guidance. He's always found his victims, but we have an idea of how to hide you from him."

"I'm listening."

"Diane wears a pendant that protected her from her wraith being able to identify her. We want to try it on you."

"You mean there's more than one?"

"We killed the last two, but there are a few more. Don't worry about the others, though. Their killing cycles are much longer. We have years before they kill again, and the chances of them targeting you are astronomically slim."

"That's not very comforting."

"Forget the others. We have only your wraith, our wraith, to deal with. We think we can hide you from him until the blood moon and then set up a trap for him."

"What happens if it doesn't work and you can't hide me?"

"We protect you. We lock you in a fortress and employ every tactic we know against him. Truth be told, that's our plan for you anyway."

"Lock me up for weeks?"

"Yes. I'm sorry."

Emma chuckled. "Have you seen the living space at the volunteer camp? It's not exactly a four-star hotel."

"We won't be putting you in a four-star hotel, but we have the means to provide to a nice, safe place."

"So, I'll be detained like the people I've been trying to help."

"Yes, but with access to everything you could need or want, including visitors, if you so choose."

Appearing calmer as the picture settled within her mind, the German empath sipped her coffee and pondered her fate. "So, why bother with the amulet at all? If I'm going to be in a fortress, what's it matter?"

"Timing. We can prepare quite a welcome for him if we know exactly when he's coming. If the amulet can hide you until just before the blood moon, he'll be unprepared, desperate, and scrambling to get to you. We'll have every tactical advantage, and you've seen us in action. You know we're professionals."

She looked to Connor. "No offense, but he's really old for a commando. And why's it just the two of you?"

"He's my father, by adoption, which explains the fifty-year age difference. But we're of the same line from a holy tribe, and we're among a select few ordained by divine fate to protect those of your line who are targeted."

She gave Liam a blank stare but then sounded perkier. "There's the first piece of good news I've heard today." Then she became pensive. "If the amulet works, what would happen if I just wear it forever? Would this killer just starve, for lack of a better word?"

The young hunter inhaled deeply and measured his answer.

174

He knew his father would bail him out if needed, but he wanted to provide Emma the choice. "Not exactly. If you wear it and it works, it would protect you, but the evil spirit that drives the wraith would pick another target for him."

She nodded slowly as she absorbed the gravity. "So, you have something that could save my life, but if I keep it, someone else will die in my place?"

"Yes, unless Father, Diane, and I can stop him. But we've run out of options for finding him, other than you."

"No wonder you want me in a fortress. If I run with the amulet, I sentence an innocent woman to death."

"You wouldn't just sentence her to death, you'd throw away the first chance we've had in a thousand years to trap him."

"A thousand years?"

"We're not the first to hunt him, but we hope to be the last." Liam looked across the table to employ a subtle recruiting technique. If he could get Emma to accept the amulet, it would be an incremental step in lowering her resistance and building her commitment to their team's goal. "Diane, can you give her your pendant."

"It's an amulet of protection." The Chaldean empath reached behind her nape to unlatch it. She lifted a strong chain of white gold over her long brown hair, and then she placed the amulet on the table. The pendant was a disk of silver holding a milky iridescent ovular moonstone, which lacey, gothic metal twists surrounded with a sharp point at the bottom. The silvery structure and the stone's setting within it suggested a dagger underneath a full moon.

Emma cocked her head and frowned. "Keep it."

The Chaldean empath raised her voice. "Don't say no. It could be a lifesaver for you."

"I mean I don't need it. I already have one." Emma reached behind her neck.

Liam yelled. "No!"

She froze. "Why not?"

"If you have one like it, it could be protecting you right now as we speak. Don't take it off. In fact, Diane, put yours back on."

"I'm not his target!"

"But you're his natural enemy. Don't risk giving anything away."

"Fine." Diane put her chain around her neck.

Liam stood, walked to the opposite side of the table, and crouched between the empaths. "Can I see yours please?"

Emma lifted the pendant to her collarbone.

"Yours, too, Diane."

The Chaldean empath obliged.

Eyeing both pieces of jewelry, Liam thought they were exact replicas, and it solved the question of Emma's identity as an empath for him. "Bloody hell. What were the chances of this happening?" He took pictures of both pendants, went back to his seat, and handed his phone to his father.

"Good gracious, lad. They do look identical."

Emma volunteered her first unsolicited insight. "My mother gave me mine. She said to never take it off since it would protect me from evil spirits. I obeyed her..."

Liam probed. "Why'd you obey her?"

"Because I knew she was right. I just knew it. I wanted to rebel like any teenager, but I couldn't. I've worn it every day of my life since then."

"Have you had episodes where you thought you knew the future, or you had feelings about people you couldn't explain?"

"I assumed I was just sensitive. I was always afraid to explore it."

Diane shared her experience. "I used tarot cards for years, and I was afraid to go deeper until I had no choice. But you have a choice. If your amulet protects you, you might be able to hide forever. But I hope you can trust us and join us."

Emma scanned her new colleagues' faces. "Join you where? What's your next move? You never said why you're even here on the island."

Liam fielded the question. "I'm glad you asked. We need to take you to the safest place we know that also includes the wisest counsel available to us. Now, in case anyone in service of the enemy happens to be listening, I'll write down where we're going." He yanked a felt-tip marker from his shirt pocket, wrote a place on a napkin, and slid it to her.

The German empath read the napkin and slid it back to him. "I'd love to go there, but something tells me I won't see any of it."

The young hunter agreed with her concern. "You might be able to see some of it when we get there, before any would-be pursuer could catch up." He looked to his father. "Maybe half a day of tourism before sweeping her away to safe confines?"

"Perhaps. Under our constant watchful eyes, of course."

"Of course, Father."

Emma frowned. "But I'm not convinced you all know what you're doing."

Liam protested. "Why not?"

"Because you're all afraid."

The young hunter admitted his trepidation to himself, but he'd considered his mask of bravado impregnable. "Why would you say that?"

Her condemning look suggested acceptance of real and unavoidable danger. "Because I'm an empath. I know."

CHAPTER 29

That evening, Diane sat in the back of the Jeep with Emma while watching Connor, his rifle aimed in an innocuous downward angle, inspect the perimeter of the private hangar of Mytilene International Airport.

Carrying his firearm in the same posture as his father, Liam stood outside the Renegade on Emma's side and yelled to his father. "How's it looking?"

"Clear so far. I'm checking behind the jet now." The elder hunter disappeared on the far side of the Embraer Phenom jet, which glimmered under the hangar's powerful lights. He reappeared from behind the aircraft's nosecone. "All clear."

"Copy, all clear." Liam opened Emma's door. "Please follow me, Emma."

Diane cleared her throat–loudly. "Don't worry about me. I'll let myself out." She stepped from the vehicle and slammed the door, but when Liam called to her from the hatchback, she realized her theatrics had lacked venom.

"Hey, Diane. Aren't you forgetting your luggage?"

"I thought a big strong caveman like you could carry it for me."

"Nope, sorry. You and Emma are taking two pieces of luggage each, since Father and I are giving our full attention to protecting you." He winked and smiled.

"Seriously?"

He cast a suspicious look around the hangar, pausing to examine its few entrances and robbing Diane of the satisfaction of eye contact during his brief rebuttal. "Don't whine. It's hardly twenty meters to the plane."

"Jackass."

"I love you, too."

"Yeah, I know. The secret council knows. Everyone knows, except me, until I was the last to know."

"Don't blame me. You're the one who blurted it out."

Emma handed Diane a bag from the back of the Jeep. "What was all that fuss about love?"

"I'll explain when we're alone."

"Are you two... a thing?"

Diane groaned. "Ugh. I don't know. It's complicated."

"I can't wait to hear about it."

The Chaldean empath escaped the conversation and rolled two suitcases towards the chartered airplane. As she admired the aircraft, she stumbled.

Three paces behind her, the young hunter heard her clopping and turned. "Are you alright?"

She recovered. "I'm fine."

Beside her, Emma slowed, absorbing the extravagance of the chartered flight. "Do you guys always travel like this?"

Diane eased her pace to parallel that of her empathic sister. "Never, but that's a good question for Liam. I thought you took a vow of poverty, buddy."

His head swiveling alertly, he moved beside the German empath to shield her with his body from unseen surprises. "I did, but you don't expect Father and me to chain ourselves to Emma, do you?"

"Don't be weird. Of course not! What are you talking about?"

"That's the only way I'd feel safe taking her through public transportation without knowing if her amulet's hiding her. Father agreed that we needed to splurge on the privacy and the speed to get to Rome tonight."

"I think your poverty contract needs a legal review."

He waved a dismissive hand and mocked her klutziness with his dexterity, his head in constant movement while his feet moved in a perfect kinesthetic cadence towards the Embraer.

Diane was afraid to reveal her ineptitude in geography with Liam, but she felt comfortable whispering to her empathic sister. "How far's Rome from here?"

Emma shrugged. "I have no idea. I flew from Frankfurt to Athens to get here. The rest was on a ferry."

Diane closed the short distance to the jet and handed the luggage to a steward at the bottom of the deployed airstairs. "Yeah, me too. But I've got a feeling we're going to get to the city real late tonight."

"So?"

"So, Liam and Connor are so paranoid about protecting you that they're going to lock you up the second we get into town."

The German empath handed her bags to the flight attendant. "I hadn't thought of that. I'll be an immediate prisoner. No sightseeing for me at all."

Diane tried to perk up her partner. "You mean no sightseeing for us. I'm not going to have any fun without you. I'll save it all for the day after the full moon, when this will all be over and we can tear up Rome together—with Connor's credit card!"

Emma smiled for the first time Diane could remember. "I would like that very much."

"By the way, where did you learn English? You speak it better than me."

"It was my concentration of studies in university."

The second rented SUV pulled into the hangar and parked beside the Jeep. Tom stepped from the Ford Kuga's driver's seat while Josh and Nana emerged from the back row. The liaison hoisted the bags of the Chaldean empath's family over his shoulders, letting her brother read his tablet while walking and letting her grandmother struggle unencumbered against her aging joints.

With the hunters patrolling a paranoid perimeter around the group, Tom managed the introductions and then shook hands with all whom he'd met. As quickly as he'd entered Diane's life to help her find a wraith, he turned his back and departed.

As the Chaldean empath boarded the jet, the peculiar thought struck her that the order's liaison on Lesbos faced the difficult task of returning two vehicles to the rental agency by himself.

But as she took her seat in the plush, living-room-styled cabin designed for wealthy passengers, she turned her thoughts towards her family. "How was the architecture tour?"

Nana flicked her fingers. "Wonderful. We saw old castles, old churches, old... what's it called?"

Josh concealed his face behind his tablet. "Aqueducts. The Romans built them some unknown time after they took control of Lesbos in seventy-nine BC."

"Right. Old aqueducts. Older than me. That's what we do all day. What'd you do all day?"

Diane fielded the question. "We... um... met Emma."

The grandmother lacked a diplomatic filter. "Who is she, and why are we all of a sudden flying away with her?"

"She's an empath, like me."

Staring down her nose, Nana eyed the German. "No kidding?"

"That's what they tell me?"

"Who tells you?"

"The same ghost your granddaughter talks to."

Nana continued her evaluation. "What's your family name?"

"Um... Zeigler."

The grandmother frowned. "No, I mean your mother."

"Her maiden name was Graf."

"No, keep going. Your mother's mother."

Emma paused to reflect. "It was... Stein, I think."

The grandmother frowned. "No, you need to keep going."

"That's all I know."

"You call your mother and find out as far back as you can."

"I guess so." Emma shrugged and asked Diane for guidance with her eyes."

"You'd better call your mother and get an answer. I know my grandmother, and she won't stop until she's satisfied."

While Emma lifted her phone to her ear and kicked off a conversation in German, the steward asked the cabin's occupants to fasten their seatbelts for taxiing and take off.

As the plane rolled from the hangar, the German empath extended her phone from her cheek to give Nana an update. "My mother's looking through a family album for names now."

"Good."

Diane glared at her grandmother.

Nana took the hint and added her politesse. "Thank you and thank your mother."

Emma nodded as the view from the windows turned from illuminated sheet metal to a dark canvas painted by stars and runway lights. When the jet reached the runway, the German empath slipped her phone into her pocket. "My mother says her grandmother's maiden name was Kraus. Does that help?"

Nana shook her head. "No. What else you got?"

"My mother's great grandmother's maiden name was Malak. It means 'painter', and it's from Bavaria. That's it. That's all I can give you."

Nana frowned. "What's that? Milk?"

"No, Malak."

The old Chaldean woman pursed her lips, flicked back her wrist, and raised her nose in victory. "That's Diane's great grandmother's maiden name, too. It means 'angel' in Arabic. I knew it. I knew you were related. I could tell."

Diane was thrilled. "Yay! A distant blood cousin and an empathic sister, all wrapped into one person." From the corner of her eye, she saw Liam, seated next to her, frowning. She reached into her purse, grabbed her dagger, and commanded a telepathic link with the young hunter. For a moment, time stopped, and she was in his mind. "Don't ruin this with whatever you're about to say."

In their controlled trance, he was defensive. "Come on! This isn't proving anything."

"I said don't ruin it. Every lady on this plane's in a great mood. If you open your mouth to screw it up, so help me you'll pay for it."

"Is this what marriage to you would be like? Every time you don't like what you think I'm about to say, you run for your dagger to give me a telepathic tongue lashing?"

"And you'd be lucky if that's all I did. It beats being passive aggressive or screaming at you."

"Well, yeah. I guess you've got a point there."

"Okay. So you'll calm down?"

"Yeah, I'm calm. And I'll keep my doubts to myself, but I do want to compare your DNA ancestry when we get to Rome. I'm sure the council will want to anyway."

"No problem. Just be quiet for now."

"Yes, Oh Great Lady of the Dagger."

As Diane released her weapon, Nana was scowling at her. "If we have two women with special powers and two hunters, then why are we running away from the killer?"

"We're not running away, Nana." The Chaldean empath looked to the young hunter. "How long's the flight?"

"About three hours."

"That should be enough time to satiate Nana's curiosity. I'd better start explaining, but be ready to jump in and help me if she gets too rough with her questions."

CHAPTER 30

The next day, Ethan felt lethargic as he stepped into the shack, anticipating the conclusion of his watch shift.

His young American colleague eyed him. "Hey, Ethan. You don't look so good. You feeling okay?"

Long protected by his domineering spirit, he'd never been ill. "I feel... quite strange."

"Maybe you should sit down."

"Yes. Perhaps."

Billy slid a plastic chair towards his colleague's backside. "Here you go. I'll do the watching for the rest of our shift. You just take it easy."

As the American stepped into the sultry mid-afternoon air, Ethan felt the walls of the shack closing in. The sensation was miserable, his muscles aching, his appetite nil, and a tickle developing in his throat. He coughed to get temporary relief, but then the annoyance returned, and he coughed again.

The young American patrolled several back-and-forth laps across the shack's causeway, and then he returned to check on his comrade. "You're not looking any better. Mind if I feel your forehead?"

Ethan grunted and nodded.

Billy's knuckles touched his skin. "Awe, man. You're burning up. You need a doctor."

Although one thousand years old, the wraith was a novice at being sick, and the young American's suggestions seemed like wisdom. "If you think it's best."

"Damned right I do. You're a mess."

"I should kill you for saving my life."

"Oh, don't act like you're dying now. You're not that sick. I've seen worse. My brother had pneumonia when he was twelve, and I swore he was going to cough out a lung."

Ethan hacked phlegm from his throat and spat it on the floor.

"Awe, come on, man. Don't do that. Swallow it."

The concept of ingesting the slimy wad disgusted Ethan. "I'm sorry. You mentioned a doctor. Is that the protocol for an episode as this?"

"Episode? Shit, Ethan, you've got a bug or something, that's all. Some antibiotics or whatever ought to clear you right up."

Recognizing the illness as an attack from his Master, Ethan realized he was at war—with himself, with his lording spirit, with the hunters, with the world. "If you say so."

At the end of his shift, he defied his encroaching sickness and summoned the energy to run an errand he'd planned.

Billy seemed surprised to see his colleague walking away from their bunkbeds. "Where are you going?"

"I have something I need to take care of."

"You need to take care of yourself, first."

Ethan gave his colleague a dismissive wave and then powered through a three-mile walk to the nearest dive locker. When he arrived, he found the small waterfront property abandoned except for one man clinking empty oxygen tanks behind a small shack. He called out to the worker in his best Greek. "Hello!"

Wearing tight shorts and a tee shirt, a young man with an athletic build walked to him. "Yes, can I help you?"

"I want to rent scuba gear."

"We rent by half-day, day, or longer, but you need to have a certification."

Ethan did not. "Do you offer training?"

The man's eyes lit up. "Of course. We have a three-day course that leads to an Open Water Scuba Diver Course certification through Scuba Diving International. If you take the course, you'll be able to dive with a partner anywhere to a depth of sixty-six meters."

The chart Ethan had purchased online showed the depths near the Lamnas Shoal north of Lesbos where he'd dumped his victims' bodies as shallower than sixty-six meters. "I want to dive alone."

"We offer a solo diver's course, which you can take after the introduction course."

A tickle in the wraith's throat made him cough. "I would like to take both courses."

"Come with me to the front desk, and I'll sign you up."

Ethan followed the diver to the shop's door, but a coughing fit struck him.

"Are you sure you're not too sick for this? You won't be able to dive with a cough like that."

The wraith attempted to answer, but his coughing became more violent. "No, you're right. I will come back later." He turned and walked towards the volunteer camp with the intent to crawl into his bed.

Lumbering through a mental daze, he expelled phlegm onto the beach's dirt path while gasping for air. Several steps later, a heavy queasiness billowed deep within his stomach, and he moaned.

"Is this just a taste of true human suffering?"

His Master's silent answer was a mocking confirmation with a hint that more suffering would come. The defiance he'd shown to his domineering spirit required punishment.

Falling to his knees, Ethan felt his innards gurgling and revolting against his being. He dropped forward to his palms and began convulsing. After several heaves, he retched, and his heart raced with panic when the vomit choked his windpipe. His first experience regurgitating was terrifying as each lurch strangled him while he spewed noxious bile onto the dirt.

Astonished at the pile of puke below him, he stared at it. He'd seen such wretchedness from others, but emptying his own stomach was traumatizing.

He spat the remnants of partially digested food and gastronomical acids, but the acrid taste lingered. He stood and walked to the water, cupped a handful, and jammed the liquid into his mouth. Swishing the water around his cheeks left a salty taste but alleviated the sourness.

Gathering his waning strength, he stood and headed towards the dormitory. The habitually easy walk became an uphill climb through molasses as his muscles protested. Beads of sweat tickled his brow, and a cool sensation enveloped him, causing him to suspect dehydration.

He lumbered into the dormitory and found his bed. Although exhausted, he took his toiletry kit and plastic drinking cup to the bathroom and filled the container with tap water. He tried to guzzle the liquid, but his stomach protested. Backing off, he took a couple light sips, set the cup down, and brushed his teeth.

Such misery was new to him, but having seen much worse as a caretaker, he knew his Master had great leeway in inflicting more agony.

Movement at the door to the communal restroom caught his attention as his young American colleague joined him. "You seen the doctor yet?"

Ethan lowered his head and shook it.

After saving his watch partner's life, Billy had taken on a new confidence. "Well, shit, Ethan. You must be either really stubborn or really dumb."

Lacking the energy or desire to argue, the wraith waved a dismissive hand.

"You want me to help get you to a doctor?"

Again, Ethan shook his head.

"If you're going to be that stubborn, at least let me tell our supervisor to get you a watch relief for tomorrow.

With a slow nod, the wraith accepted the offer to take the next day off from looking for refugee boats.

"Well, at least you got that right. You need some help getting back to your bed?"

"No. I'll manage."

"Suit yourself, but don't expect me to carry you if you pass out."

A debilitating weakness overcame Ethan, and he grabbed the sink for support. "Maybe I should take your help."

Billy stepped to him, took his arm around his neck, and bore the wraith's weight. "Leave your stuff, buddy. I'll come back for it."

"I'm thirsty."

"I'll get you some water. Let's get you to bed first."

As the young American helped him lay in his bunk, the relief Ethan expected eluded him, and he groaned.

"Just be still. I'll get your water."

Closing his eyes, the wraith felt the world spinning and realized the misery of his illness would keep him awake. Sleep would remain distant and offer no reprieve.

Billy returned and tipped the cup against Ethan's lips. "Small sips, buddy."

Through his tender throat, Ethan forced water into his queasy stomach.

"Keep taking sips and drink as much as you can."

The American's words provided minimal comfort since he knew nothing would spare him from feeling horrible. "Thanks, Billy."

"No problem."

As he wallowed in his suffering, he made a silent resolution. No matter what his Master did to him, he would defy him.

CHAPTER 31

Careful to avoid bumping the German empath, Diane whispered into the young hunter's ear. "Do you really need to be so paranoid… and so close to her?"

Holding a pistol under his windbreaker, Liam kept his back to Emma like a moving human shield while surveying the street for the wraith, but there were only quiet storefronts under the electric streetlights. "We're most vulnerable on the move. I'll relax when we're inside."

Diane groaned and shifted her gaze to the elder hunter, who tapped a code into a keypad and opened a door. Walking into the building, she followed Connor into the order's headquarters and saw Friar Don behind the reception counter.

Since it was midnight, the sterile lobby was empty except for the friar. He stepped around the counter, revealing his black robe with a white eight-pointed cross, and then he greeted the arrivals in his British accent. "Welcome back familiar acquaintances, and greetings to our new guest." He shook hands with each arrival, brought them into the elevator, and then tapped a code into a keypad.

Diane's stomach moved upward as the elevator descended. When it stopped and the door slid open, the friar led the entourage into a familiar subterranean chamber with leather sofas in the room's center. A door on each wall offered exits, and Friar Don led the group around the seating area to the far portal.

The friar tapped a code and then pushed open the portal to the long hallway leading underneath adjacent buildings. Moving through locked doors and several turns that Diane found familiar but still dizzying brought the group to a final waiting room attached to the sanctum, where the friar aimed his palm at couches. "Please sit. I will return shortly." He tapped a code into a keypad, pushed open a door, and disappeared into the courtroom.

Her eyelids droopy, Emma appeared worn as she sank into a leather chair. "Someone please explain this to me again."

With her adrenaline subsiding inside the safety of the order's fortress, Diane empathized with her new sister's fatigue. "This is the guts of some secret society that likes to boss us around."

Emma frowned.

Liam countered. "Don't be so crass. This is the inner sanctum of the order which governs our hunt for the guy who's trying to kill you. I suggest you pay it a bit more reverence than Diane."

The Chaldean empath was too tired to argue.

Emma crossed her legs. "I understand that, but wow. I feel like I just entered a military bunker run by clerics."

Diane shrugged. "You may have."

The wooden door swung open, revealing Friar Don. "The council is ready. Everyone please enter the sanctum."

Diane followed the friar and the hunters into the refuge-courtroom-temple and was surprised to see the overhead lights radiating and five of the seven council members seated behind their arcing table. As she walked down the central aisle between the empty wooden benches, she noticed the bronze casting of the order's eight-point cross already planted in the center of the council's semicircle.

Friar Lucio, the council's chairman, spread his arms but displayed a stern expression while addressing the room with an Italian accent. "Welcome, members and guests of the order."

Friar Don stopped between the witness benches and ushered the hunters and empaths to the right. He asked Nana and Josh to stand behind them, and then he stepped to the center of the semicircle. "Esteemed members of the Council of Paranormal Activities, we are gathered for an ad hoc session to investigate the episode of enlightenment shared yesterday between Miss Diane Yousif, Honorary Dame of Honor, and Miss Emma Zeigler, Guest of the Order. Before you stand Miss Yousif, Miss

Zeigler, Connor Brady, Knight of Honor, and Liam Brady, Knight of Honor. I begin the session with the verification of identity of Connor Brady."

Still standing, Friar Lucio hastened the process. "The abridged version will suffice."

"As you wish, Master Chairman." Friar Don stepped to the stubby column and unlatched the dagger's hatch. Hinges groaned, and then he stepped away.

Friar Lucio called Connor to the bench, and under the hunter's gaze, the chairman summoned the dagger's glow. "Upon invocation, the cursed dagger glows in his sight. This man is a hunter of wraiths, descended from the Tribe of Naphtali, and ordained to represent this council in battle against the enemy." As the glow receded, it yielded blackness over the column.

Connor returned behind the witness desk, and the chairman called for Liam, who strode from his stance beside the Chaldean empath's left shoulder to the bench.

While the young hunter passed the same test as his father, Diane tuned out until the old friar finished approving Liam's identity.

"...Tribe of Naphtali, and ordained to represent this council in battle against the enemy. Be seated, everyone."

While Liam returned to the witness desk, Emma turned to Diane with astonishment in her face and whispered into her right ear. "The daggers glow?"

Diane whispered back. "Some of them. We probably should've mentioned that already. There's still a lot to explain."

The chairman sat. "Given the late hour and the minimal preparation for this council, we'll be convening without our full membership. However, five elders are sufficient to render a decision."

The German empath whispered. "About what?"

Diane shrugged. "I have no idea."

Friar Lucio continued. "Although we lack the enchanted twin to the fifth wraith's cursed dagger, we hunt him, expecting the empath's dagger to guide us. However, less than twelve hours ago, we learned that our empath's dagger does not point to the wraith but instead points to Miss Zeigler. We are here to determine Miss Zeigler's identity with regard to the fifth wraith."

Diane's kinship with her distant cousin and empathic sister was growing stronger by the minute, and when she learned the purpose of their presence, she drew a breath to protest.

Like a vice, Liam clamped his hand around her upper arm, immobilizing her. He glared, and his voice was ice. "Don't."

"But this isn't–"

"Just... don't."

Shocked that he'd predicted and policed her defiance, she yielded to his judgment. "Fine."

He released her.

Adding insult to injury, Friar Lucio targeted her. "Miss Yousif, please place your dagger on the table so that we may observe it."

Before she could protest, Liam echoed the friar's command with a low, cold voice. "Do it."

Silently, she moved the blade from her purse to the table, but before letting it go, she made a quick telepathic link with the young hunter and demanded an explanation. "What's going on?"

With the room around them frozen, the young hunter answered in her head. "I don't know, but the council doesn't convene this fast unless there's something big going on."

"Who set this up?"

"Who do you think?"

"Your dad."

"Yup."

"Did he request it, or were we summoned?"

"He didn't say."

"Did you ask?"

"No."

"Why not? You're always so quick to fall in line with whatever rules are thrown at you."

"Because I trust my father, and I trust the council. If you invaded my head to nag me, can you do it later?"

"I'm not nagging. Ugh!"

"Can we just get on with the council? It's obvious they don't want you playing around with your dagger down here."

"I'm not playing..." Although the subterranean chamber remained suspended in motionlessness, Diane saw the council chairman look to his left and then to his right, his jaw moving at half speed. Terrified to see an interruption to her employment of the dagger's power, she watched him in awe.

Like a lethargic dream, he looked up and extended his hands to the council members beside him. They accepted his grip and clasped the hands of the outer two. As five pairs of eyes turned upward, they held hands and chanted in Latin, and a faceless humanlike form of milky white appeared over the bronze eight-point cross, spread its gossamer wings from wall to wall, and then disappeared in a blinding flash.

Against her will, the council and their angel broke the link with Liam, and Diane's world returned to reality. She dropped the dagger like a burning coal.

After his summoning of supernatural power, Friar Lucio amazed her with his calm demeanor. "Thank you, Miss Yousif. And please, invoke no more trances within the sanctum unless requested."

CHAPTER 32

Diane noticed Liam's calm demeanor and whispered into his ear. "Didn't you see it?"

"See what?"

"At the end of our link?"

He shook his head. "It ended normally like always."

The angel was intended for her vision alone. "Never mind."

Unable to make immediate sense of the angel who'd broken her link, she shut down her analytical mind while watching the German empath walk towards the council.

Emma stopped at the center of the semicircle, where the black-robed friar awaited.

Friar Don poked a swab along the insides of her cheek, tucked her saliva sample into a bag, and thanked her for her cooperation. He then marched up the aisle and out of the room.

The council chairman addressed Emma but cast his voice for all witnesses to hear. "Thank you for giving us your DNA sample. We'll have results from our lab by sunrise to verify your lineage. However, this is our only piece of scientific evidence. Henceforth, we rely upon your testimony and the testimony of our members. Please tell us, Miss Zeigler, why you believe you are here."

Despite her fatigue and recent traumatic discoveries, the German empath stood with erect posture and spoke with an assurance reminding Diane of her own strength. "It started when the three people seated behind my right shoulder barged into the home of a doctor I was visiting at the Moria refugee camp. Connor and Liam arrested the doctor, but they seemed confused." She paused to draw a breath and gather her next thought.

Friar Lucio encouraged her onward. "Why do you think they

were confused?"

"I can only speculate."

"We're trying to determine if you're a targeted sacrifice of a wraith, but it's also important for us to better understand your empathic abilities. They may be germane to our determination. Please feel free to speculate."

"I was terrified when they stormed the room, but I still noticed their zeal. They weren't there to capture anyone. They were there to kill. When the doctor offered no resistance, they were caught off guard."

"That's understandable since every wraith has either run for his life or fought every hunter to the death for a millennium."

"After they handcuffed the doctor, Diane and Liam used her dagger as a beacon to look for something, and I was shocked when it pointed at me."

"Everyone was shocked. Can you give a reason why you believe it pointed at you?"

"I had no idea until half an hour later when Diane took my hand, holding her dagger, and we saw a ghost who called herself the Maiden of Yorkshire. The ghost said I was an empath and also the next target of the wraith for sacrifice."

"What were her exact words?"

Emma replied without hesitation, bolstering Diane's growing belief in her empathic abilities. "No, she called him a savage. She said 'a savage hunts you'."

"And she called you an empath as well?"

"She said we descend from the same line, the line of Nineveh, and when I asked her why I was being hunted, she said I was an empath and that I know."

The council chairman looked to his colleagues, but none voiced a concern. "That concludes our questioning. Do you have anything you wish to add?"

"What going to happen to me?"

"Our purpose is to protect you. Depending upon our findings, we'll deliberate how to best accomplish that."

"Thank you. I've been going through a lot since I last woke up, but I can see that I'm in danger. I don't know what I'd do without your team."

"It's our honor to serve you, Miss Zeigler. Please be seated."

The German empath went back to her seat.

Friar Lucio looked to Diane. "Miss Yousif, do you confirm Miss Zeigler's testimony?"

"Yes. All of it. I saw and heard the ghost, too."

"Do you wish to add anything?"

She cleared the buffers in her brain that were still choking on the order's angelic display, and a relevant memory surfaced. "Yes. The Maiden of Yorkshire was the wraith's victim on the first day of July in the year of our Lord, one thousand three hundred and forty-nine. She told me that in a prior visit with me, and I remember it vividly, which is why I'm stating it verbatim. That sort of clarity of memory from a trance or visitation is part of being an empath, and Miss Zeigler has it, too. I'm sure she's an empath and the wraith's next target."

"Thank you, Miss Yousif. Liam Brady, do you wish to comment upon Miss Zeigler's testimony?"

The young hunter appeared eager to race to a conclusion. "No, Master Chairman. I can't comment on the visitation by the ghost, but everything else Miss Zeigler and Miss Yousif said is true, and any detail I would add is included in the report my father filed."

"Thank you, Liam Brady. Connor Brady, do you wish to comment upon Miss Zeigler's testimony?"

"I do not, Master Chairman. All that has been shared is truthful and complete to the best of my knowledge. Although I met Miss Zeigler only yesterday, I trust Miss Yousif implicitly."

"Thank you, Connor Brady. Does anyone else wish to add anything? No? Very well. The evidence seems straightforward based upon the divine intervention of a ghost."

Diane relaxed her guard, assuming the council would hurry to the conclusion that Emma was targeted and in need of protection. Then Friar Lucio challenged her hopes.

"However, there are inconsistencies we must address. For example, we–"

Diane sprang to her feet, making her chair screech against the floor. "Don't say it!"

"Excuse me?"

"Don't say it. Give her a chance first."

"You presume much, Miss Yousif."

"Um… may I talk to you in private?"

Friar Lucio thought for a moment. "Do you wish to speak with me personally in private or do you wish to approach the council?"

"The council. Please. It's urgent."

"Very well. Approach the council."

She marched to him and spoke in a soft voice, forcing the other council members to crowd him to hear. "I know what you're about to say, but you can't say it. You need to give Emma a chance to volunteer what happened to her."

"How can you know?"

"I'm an empath. I don't know everything, but when it's urgent like this, I have no doubt. When I was targeted as a sacrifice, I felt chest pains of the tributes. You know this from Connor's report of the sixth wraith. You were going to say that Emma should've felt the pains, too, if she's both an empath and the fifth wraith's sacrifice."

Friar Lucio nodded. "Very impressive. Yes, I was going to say that. Do you believe that Miss Zeigler felt the pains?"

"Yes."

"Have you discussed this with her yet?"

"Not yet. We've been moving so fast since we met her. There's still a lot we need to tell her and that she needs to tell us."

"Very well. I will explore this, based upon your insights."

"Thank you." Energized by the old man she found endearing despite his administrative and supernatural power, Diane trotted back to her seat.

"Miss Zeigler, Miss Yousif has redirected my line of questioning. Please tell the council if you've had any recent telepathic experiences prior to your shared vision of the ghost with Miss

Yousif?"

"Recent? Not really. I've had them my entire life where I felt someone's pain or joy, or I could tell if someone should or shouldn't do something, but it's been a couple years since I last experienced that."

Diane wanted to lead Emma to the answer but bit her lip.

Friar Lucio showed his flexibility in guiding the German empath. "More specifically, during the last week have you felt any abnormal sensations that you couldn't explain?"

"Do you mean like chest pains?"

Diane gave a silent cheer.

"Yes, Miss Zeigler. Chest pains. Did you have them?"

"Pretty badly about a week ago. So bad, they woke me up. I've actually had them for a couple months now, but they're so rare that I didn't think much of them."

"How many episodes did you have?"

"Three."

"Do you remember when they were?"

"The latest was June twenty-eighth, in the morning, around five in the morning."

The timing aligned with Diane's vision of the last tribute.

"What about the episode of chest pains before that?"

"I can't believe how clearly I'm remembering this, but it was May twenty-ninth in the early evening."

"And before that?"

"April thirtieth, in the middle of the night, after midnight."

"Were there any other episodes, or just the three?"

"Just the three."

"Were these pains near your heart?"

"Yes, all of them. What's it mean?"

"I'll trust Miss Yousif to explain the significance to you. It's better to hear it from someone who's lived through it herself. The pattern is clearly pointing to the full-moon cycle that Miss Yousif outlined from her original vision with the Maiden of Yorkshire. The evidence with your chest pains corroborates that of her vision."

The other members of the council offered slow nods.

Friar Lucio continued. "The evidence suggests that Miss Zeigler is both an empath and the target of the wraith's next sacrifice under the blood moon that begins in the late evening of July twenty-seventh and continues to the early morning of July twenty-eighth."

Diane sighed but realized the proceedings had accomplished nothing more than agreeing with what she already knew. But her hopes rose when the council chair announced the next steps.

"Connor Brady, can you think of a safer place to protect Miss Zeigler than within the walls of these headquarters?"

"I cannot, Master Chairman."

"Very well. Draft a plan to protect Miss Zeigler within the walls of these headquarters and to draw in the wraith to his destiny. The order must protect her, the order must stop this wraith, and we must risk a siege against our own walls to accomplish our divine duty."

CHAPTER 33

Two weeks later, Liam awoke in the middle of the night.

After a spell of disorientation, he remembered he was sleeping on a cot in the waiting room outside the courtroom-sanctum. The other members of the team who'd confined themselves to the order's headquarters had declared him an unwelcomed occupant within the sanctum during sleeping hours.

Apparently, he snored like a jackhammer, and his would-be roommates wanted none of it.

Checking his phone, he noted the time as one o'clock in the morning. As he rolled from his cot, the room's quietness mocked him as the night's banished loner, but he consoled himself with his short trip to the restroom. Those sleeping in the courtroom were closer to the order's holy epicenter, but they faced an uphill walk and a locked portal between themselves and the facilities.

Several paces brought him to the men's room, which he and his father had commandeered as their personal space, and he relieved his bladder. When done, he crept to the courtroom's keypad and tapped the code Friar Don had shared. He pushed open the heavy oaken door and looked at his sleeping colleagues.

Matted brown hair identified the Chaldean empath as the lump under a gray blanket on one cot. Flickering candlelight painted blonde hair amber and marked Diane's distant cousin, the relation verified by a DNA test, as the mound atop the mattress closest to the semicircular bench. Nana and Josh slept in cots abutting the far wall. Between the empaths and the entrance, Connor slept and emitted a gentle snore.

Liam whispered to himself while closing the door. "Bloody double standards."

Alone again in the waiting room, he sought sleep in his crude bed, but the makeshift command center drew him to its closest keyboard. Eight laptops, four stacked on a metal shelf above the other four resting on a workbench, gave views through security cameras. With the pending sunrise looming over him like the dawn of a war, Liam flipped images across the screens showing the building's street entrances, air vent penetrations, roof exits, and interior doors.

He then toggled icons showing the status of motion sensors attached to the newly installed window bars and to the other penetrations through the headquarters' roof and through its three-foot-thick stone walls. Paranoia was rising within him since he was hours away from inviting a one-man siege.

At sunrise, he'd reveal Emma to the Wraith.

With the cameras and motion sensors affirming the expected safety, the young hunter crawled into his bed and fell asleep.

An hour before sunrise, his phone alarmed, and he sprang with zeal to conduct his morning toilette. As he stepped from the men's room, he saw Diane carrying her clothes on hangers and wearing pink pajamas he found adorable. "Good morning."

Though beautiful to him upon awakening, she was coy and raced by him into the ladies' room. "Morning."

Across the room, a lock clunked open, and his father entered through the door leading to the entrance hallway. He balanced a bag of bagels and a box of coffee from Dunkin Donuts.

"Need some help?"

Connor stepped to the foldout table serving as the team's dining area and then plopped the food onto it. "Spread out the plastic cups and utensils. Friar Don should be back soon with breakfast sandwiches and fruit, and I'll head back upstairs to meet him." The elder hunter departed through the route he'd come in.

The order's headquarters had become a prison to Emma, and in a show of solidarity, Diane and the hunters remained incarcerated with her. Wearing jeans and a blue tee shirt, Emma emerged from the ladies' room. "Good morning."

"Hello. Are you ready for breakfast?"

"Sure." She strode to the table and sat. "Just bagels? Where's the fruit?"

"Father's getting it."

"Why not? I can handle a few carbs." She stuck her nose into the bag, plunged her hand into it, and pulled out a whole wheat bagel.

Liam lifted the heavy box of coffee and poured the steaming liquid into a polystyrene cup. "Would you like some?"

"Sure."

He poured a second cup, slid back a chair, and joined the German empath. Hungry, he reached for half a sliced bagel, smeared cream cheese over it, and shoved a third of it into his mouth.

"You do understand that eating like a caveman isn't romantic."

His cheeks puffy with unleavened bread, he grunted. The definition of 'romantic' still eluded him, and the only thing he considered worse than having two women coaching him was having two empaths trying to train him.

"Don't you want to be more of a gentleman around the ladies in your life?"

He swallowed. "Yeah, I guess."

"If you take smaller bites, you'll impress Diane, and you might even taste your food."

"I taste it. Sort of. Enough with the manners lessons. Are you ready for your big moment?"

"As ready as I can be."

"Are you sure today is the day?"

She sipped coffee. "Diane's still far better at this than me, and she may always be. But for my part, I believe we're doing the right thing. If I get an uneasy feeling while we're doing it, I'll speak up."

"Right. Good." He chomped another mouthful of the bagel. While he wrestled with the bread to position a big lump between his molars, Diane approached the table.

202

"What are you guys talking about?" The Chaldean empath pulled back a chair.

Emma slid a coffee cup in front of Diane. "The big reveal."

"We're still doing it after breakfast?"

"Unless Liam or Connor say otherwise."

The young hunter gulped his mouthful. "Nothing's changed. We're doing it right after breakfast. I assume you still have good vibes about it, so to speak."

Diane frowned. "That's about all I have. Nothing definite other than a feeling. But if we wait any longer, I feel like his Master will pick a new target, like he did with me."

Since Liam saw no point in arguing the past, he silenced his concerns about the possibility of them already being too late. "Then right after breakfast, it is."

Behind him, a latch clicked, and his father carried a tray of breakfast sandwiches and fruits. "Who's still hungry?"

Three hands went up.

"Then I've arrived in time." The elder hunter lowered the food to the table and then sat with his team. "Where are Nana and Josh?"

Diane sipped her coffee. "Let's let them sleep in. They don't have any part in this."

"So be it, young lady. So, is everyone ready for the big moment?"

Three heads nodded.

"It's really not that big a moment, Father. It's what happens next that's the challenge."

"Agreed, but we'll take the necessary precautions. Speaking of which, let me fetch our gear." The elder hunter disappeared into the sanctum and returned with a minimal equipment loading. He handed his son a vest and a holster carrying a solitary pistol.

Liam stood, donned the gear, and continued eating. As the foursome consumed breakfast with minimal chatter, he suspected from their pensive silence that each member was wondering how the wraith would respond to their pending call to battle. As plates emptied, he prodded the team. "Are we ready?"

The gang stood and gathered at the exit to the hallway.

Liam pushed open the door, let his father lead the march, and filed in line behind him. The empaths followed, reinforcing the habit of keeping the hunters between danger and the ladies.

After traversing the underground maze and riding the elevator to the ground floor, Liam wondered if any friars would oversee his team's actions.

His father answered the unspoken question. "Let's wait here in the lobby until Friar Don shows up." The elder hunter approached the lone steward who manned the reception desk. Upon Connor's prodding, the clerk lifted a landline intra-building phone to his cheek, held a quick conversation, and hung up. The elder hunter returned to his lingering team. "He'll be here in five minutes."

The steward excused himself and walked out the front door.

When the elevator opened five minutes later, the lean friar appeared, wearing his black robe with its white cross. "Sorry to keep you waiting."

Liam kept quiet, letting his father talk.

"It was no bother at all. We weren't waiting long. Are we clear to go? Once we do this, there's no going back."

"Yes. I verified that the building's abandoned."

Connor voiced the plan. "So be it then. I'll go first, then Liam, and the door gets locked behind us. Three rapid taps followed by two slow taps on the door means it's safe to open. At that point, Diane comes outside. Finally, if she doesn't sense danger, we'll reverse the knocking sequence. It will be two rapid taps followed by three slow taps that brings Emma out. Friar Don will hold the door open when Emma is outside."

The moment's gravity required leaving nothing to chance, and Liam reinforced the plan. "Quiz time. What's the sequence, Emma?"

"Three rapid, two slow knocks is Diane. Then two rapid, three slow knocks is me."

Wearing jeans and a golf shirt under his vest, Connor stepped to the exit. "Let's go lad." As the elder hunter pulled open the door, Liam saw sunlight for the first time in two weeks.

The young hunter followed his father into the sidewalk lining the Via dei Conditti. As he departed holy ground, his mind registered the change in venue from the building which elders of the order had blessed to the unprotected street of Rome.

A ten-foot-high wall of dirt rose on either side of him, serving as buttresses to narrow the point of entry. Horizontal lines of rebar shaped his exit, the upper bar running over his head and the lower one beneath his boots. The vertical metal rods to which they attached were invisible, buried within the dirt mounds. To his right, sections of concertina wire he'd cut to coiled lengths of six feet lay on the ground.

While his father Connor marched around the left berm, Liam checked out the view to the right. With the order having used its political clout, the sidewalk was cordoned off for a fake construction job. A chain link fence diverted pedestrians to the road's far side, and the tarps stretching over the links prevented the wraith from spying on the ground-level windows.

"Check the clothing store."

Obeying his father, Liam scanned the windows across the street but saw no movement or suspicious visions. Downward-sloping shingles covering the high-fashion women's clothing building prevented a rooftop sniper. A final look upward showed a clear view of the morning's cloudless sky. "Clear!"

"Agreed, lad. Clear. Summon Diane."

Liam trotted to the door and knocked the sequence.

Diane's head emerged from the doorway, and then she stepped between the earthen berms. She held her dagger in her hands. "I don't feel any danger."

"Give it a second. There's no hurry."

"It feels weird out here. I forgot what it was like."

"Just chill for half a minute."

"I am chilling. There's no danger."

"Okay. Clear, Father!"

"Copy, clear. Bring out Emma."

Liam rapped on the door, Friar Don propped it open, and the

German empath stepped out. Silent, she looked to the young hunter for guidance.

"Do you sense any danger?"

Emma shook her head.

"Okay. Diane, get a stopwatch ready."

Shifting her dagger into one hand, the Chaldean empath manipulated her phone with the other. "I'm ready."

"Start it when Emma takes off her amulet. Yell when the time reaches one minute. Go ahead, Emma."

The German empath unclipped the necklace from under her hair and handed it to Liam.

He studied Emma's unmoving features and body. "Do you feel anything?"

"No."

"Diane?"

"Not me."

Ten seconds later, the German empath's eyes became glassy, and her eyelids drooped.

Liam stepped towards her. "Emma?"

She lost consciousness and collapsed.

The attentive young hunter extended his hands under her armpits before the sidewalk could claim her. "Father!" Liam lifted Emma's light frame and carried her through the door. He then hoisted her to his chest and cradled her while Connor and Friar Don locked the door behind them.

She opened her eyes and was half-awake. "What happened?"

Liam lowered her into a leather armchair. "Tell us what you remember, before you forget."

"Where am I?"

"The lobby of the order's headquarters."

Tears welled in her eyes. "I... I'm remembering. It was like a union of souls, but it was with a monster, a demon. It was a nightmare, right? A vision? It can't be real."

Liam knew it had been real. She'd broadcasted her existence to the wraith, and he'd accepted the transmission. The call to battle had been successful. "You're safe now, Emma. And you accomplished the day's mission."

CHAPTER 34

The coughing fits had forced Ethan to quit the volunteer group. With nausea, a fever, and the constant clearing of the tickle in his throat, he'd become useless to help himself, much less others. To allow his dorm mates the rest they needed to care for the refugees, the sick, loud, and distracting wraith had quit the team.

For two weeks, he'd endured his suffering alone in a hotel. Barely eating, he'd lost fifteen pounds while surviving on juices and breads. Dizzy with malnutrition and the chronic ailment of supernatural origins, he rolled to the side of his bed to sleep. But a coughing fit denied him his rest.

His throat cooled, giving a necessary reprieve from its tickling and scratching. For a moment, he drifted into sleep, but it was fleeting–enough to keep him alive. He awoke to a recurring migraine headache, the brain-splitting pain his tormenter had added a week earlier to the repertoire of agony.

Grasping his head, Ethan realized his dire lot. No medicine could help him. His capricious Master would continue the sickness to his satisfaction, and he saw relief coming only from his lording spirit's hand, either through mercy or through appeasement.

Instead of appeasement, Ethan would resist the supernatural entity. A life lasting beyond one thousand years, killing innocents to fuel an emotional exile of loneliness, was a curse, and he'd tolerated enough. If his Master would continue forcing him to remain alive and to suffer, then he would endure it. Immortality had been tempting, but he refused to continue serving the evil behind it.

The wraith's willful role in killing had ended.

And since mercy was unknown to his domineering spirit, Ethan entered a standoff. Will versus will. Torture versus endurance. He steeled himself to survive the worst misery he could imagine for nine more days, until the blood moon passed.

Then, in a flash, the headache disappeared, the nausea subsided, and the tenderness lifted from his throat. He whispered to the spiritual companion of a millennium he now considered his enemy. "Are you giving me relief to free me, or are you teasing me before further torment?"

The unspoken answer bloomed in his understanding. His Master was relenting temporarily to prepare him to receive a message. Ethan was to eat, sleep, and regain his strength for one day, and then he was to listen.

Unable to resist, the wraith ordered a feast from room service, devoured it, and then slept for twelve hours.

When he awoke, darkness enshrouded the hotel room's windows, but the nutrition and rest invigorated him with the optimism of a new day. For a moment, he dared to believe he'd outlasted the demon spirit's wrath.

At the apex of his hope, the silent revelation struck. The identity of the blood-moon sacrifice was known.

"You see her, Master."

Temptation ransacked his every fiber. One more kill. Freedom from sickness. Life until the following blood moon. Renewed possibilities for life eternal.

No.

Ethan reminded himself of his decision. The renewed hunting line had scared him into seeing the truth about himself, and nothing he could do would change his mind.

"I still refuse to serve you. Do what you must, but I will endure your worst torment until I die. You are no longer my Master."

A pounding pain invaded his skull, the migraine intolerable. He collapsed onto the bed and pressed his palms into his head.

Then, his arms took on a life of their own, and he dug his fingernails into his scalp. He extended his hands and saw blood at his fingertips.

"What is this madness?"

The answer came as a single convulsion, his body stiffening from head to toe with his back arched. Helpless and terrified, he suspected his predicament.

The Master was possessing him.

He opened his mouth to verbalize a protest, but he instead blurted out a cackling laugh that rose to a self-mocking falsetto.

Barely capable of discerning his own thoughts from that of the invading spirit, he observed his body writhing in unnatural movements. Haunting, discordant sounds came from his throat and mouth as he rolled and shuddered on the bed.

He blacked out.

His consciousness became aware of an alternate reality, neither worldly nor divine. Trapped in a fabrication his Master had constructed for his punishment, Ethan writhed in pain, the noncorporeal nerves of his ethereal body burning under the domineering spirit's spell.

Compounding his physical punishment, the lording spirit fed the wraith's shame.

A milky white female form appeared, her black eyes glaring at him. Despite her lack of defined human features, he recognized her as the first victim he'd killed more than one thousand years ago. Her voice carried deep, chilling tones. "Why did you kill me?"

Unable to move, he conveyed a response through the mist enshrouding their shared experience. "I was wrong to do so. I had no right. I am sorry."

Her voice boomed with glacial frigidity and then rocketed to a torrid shriek. "I reject your apology. You betrayed me. I will be avenged!"

"Leave me! I can no longer endure your torment."

"Leave you? Very well. I open the way for the next victim."

She became a cloud and then evaporated, but the ghost of his second kill appeared, threatening him. "Why did you kill me?"

Again, he answered through the mist. "I was wrong to do so. I had no right. I am sorry. I beg you to accept my apology."

The voice of the second apparition reached its scorching crescendo. "I reject your apology. You betrayed me. I will be avenged!"

One by one, all the victims of his dagger attacked, pelting him with their wailed warning. "I reject your apology. You betrayed me. I will be avenged!"

Hyperventilating as the phantom of the last refugee he'd murdered disappeared, he sensed himself back in the earthly realm. As he saw the morning sun at the window, he realized his ordeal had lasted the night. His first impulse was to feel anger towards his victims, but he caught himself and redirected his thinking towards his Master. "Damn him."

In a moment of self-control, he reached for the hotel phone and dialed the reception desk.

A man answered. "Front desk."

"Please. I need a priest."

The receptionist paused in apparent thought. "Would you like directions or transportation to a nearby church?"

"No. Please. A Catholic priest. To my room."

"This is an unusual request. May I connect you with a local Catholic church?"

"Yes!"

"Hold please."

"Hurry."

After a minute, the receptionist announced his success in establishing the conference call. "Mister Smith, I have Deacon Demitrius from the Assumption of Virgin Mary Catholic church. He speaks English."

The deacon's voice was soft. "I understand you seek a priest. How may I help you, Mister Smith?"

Ethan groped for a plausible argument. "I can't leave my room. I suffer from a terrible cough… migraine headaches…. I'll donate a sizeable sum to the church in exchange for a house call."

"There's no need to pay. Father Kristos is doing house calls for the homebound today and can stop by the hotel after lunch. Is that acceptable?"

"Yes. Yes. Thank you."

After hanging up the phone, the wraith questioned why his lording spirit had allowed the call. Perhaps, he hoped, seeking divine intervention invoked a loophole through the demon spirit's oppression.

A surge of energy inspired Ethan from the bed, and he made his way to the bathroom. After days without bathing, he cleaned himself in preparation for the holy man's visit. He then lost control of his faculties, becoming again a prisoner in his body.

He packed his backpack with wads of cash, his passport, and the case containing the enchanted dagger he'd stolen long ago. The cursed dagger, the source of his long life, was sheathed against his leg. As his final preparations for the priest, he unlocked the door and lay a spare blanket in front of it. He then sat in the room's only armchair and waited.

An hour later, he heard a knock at the door and the priest's greeting. "Hello. This is Father Kristos!"

"The door's unlocked. Please enter, Father Kristos."

Wearing a suit with a white clerical collar, a man of average build entered the room. "I'm here to help for Ethan Smith."

"I am he. Please, close the door."

The priest looked downward. "Why is there a blanket here?"

His possessor compelling him, Ethan stood, withdrew the dagger, and flung it towards his guest's heart. With unnatural guidance, the blade found its mark, and the priest collapsed into the blanket.

The wraith rolled the body in the blanket, hoisted it to his hips, and lugged it into the bathtub. In the wash basin, he scrubbed blood from the blade and then returned it to its scabbard. Deep within himself, he heard his waning vestiges of humanity shrieking in protest, but the dagger's dominating spirit moved his hands like those of a puppet.

After gathering his backpack, Ethan marched from the crime

scene, down the hallway, and to the hotel's back staircase.

Taking a side door on the ground floor, he left the building. A brisk walk brought him to a street corner convenience store where he purchased all the energy bars he could fit into his backpack. He then hailed a cab, which brought him to the island's north end and to his former volunteer organization's watch tower.

He jogged to the shack and found his prior American colleague with his new partner, a middle-aged man with a haughty expression and an expensive haircut. The new volunteer invoked Ethan's judgment as a wealthy businessman performing self-inflicted penance for a life of success that had come on the backs of others' labors.

Billy's eyes opened wide. "Ethan! You're back."

The wraith brushed by the young American and his new watch partner. He grabbed the boat's keys from a table and darted out the shack's door.

Behind him, he heard the American yelling. "Ethan! Did someone tell you to take the boat? Is there a dinghy out there I can't see? Is there a rescue? Take me with you!"

Passing the site where he'd attempted suicide, Ethan wanted to fall on his dagger, but anything remaining of himself was trapped inside a body his lording spirit controlled.

In the beach's dirt, his stride slowed, and he sensed the demon spirit's indecision about killing Billy and the businessman. In a flash, the debate raged and ended.

A stolen boat warranted a much milder law enforcement response than a double murder. He knew the priest's body would be found soon, but he expected to reach open water before any pursuers could determine his whereabouts and summon a coastal force to apprehend him. Plus, he had supernatural intervention.

The wraith commandeered the twenty-seven-foot cuddy cabin utility boat his volunteer organization kept lashed to a small pier. Before starting the engine, he leaned over it, ripped off its magnetic anti-theft GPS tracker, and threw it into the water.

Behind him, the powerful outboard motor revved with urgency. Standing at the wheel, he aimed the bow north, and spray hit his face as the small ship bobbed over successive waves.

As he navigated over the Lamnas Shoal, the demon spirit pasted a sardonic grin over his face and forced him to remember the three tributes he'd dumped in the water.

The strong engine propelled the cuddy cabin into Turkish water within minutes of leaving Lesbos, and the wraith turned west to parallel the nation's southern coast. When he reached the western tip of the landmass, he verified over his shoulder that he was out of the watch shack's sight, and then he turned southwest towards Athens. The illusion he'd given Billy of having fled to nearby Turkey would buy him time for his escape.

Checking his gasoline gauge, he slowed to improve his fuel economy. Although he would need to refuel, he knew the demon spirit would help him find places with his required resources and restrict his travel to the seas.

All the way to Italy, where he would travel by land to Rome.

CHAPTER 35

The next morning, Diane heard three rapid raps followed by two slow knocks. She opened the door and stepped into the fresh air. In front of her, the two hunters wore full body armor and carried bulletproof riot shields while blocking the entrance to the headquarters. By her side, the dirt berms gave an eerie sensation of being underground, while at her feet rested three bags of groceries, delivered by a trusted source and inspected by the hunters.

Scanning the windows of the women's clothing store across the street, Liam cried out. "Do you sense anything?"

Holding her dagger in both hands, she needed to inhale and concentrate to tap the new signal. But for the first time in three days of trying, she picked up the wraith's telepathic scent. As the Maiden of Yorkshire had advised her, she sensed his sadness, self-loathing, and even his underlying compassion. And it frightened her. "Yeah. It's weak, but I got him."

The young hunter sounded excited with the news but irked with its incompleteness. "What do you mean 'weak'. What's going on in your head? Give me some detail."

She wished she understood. Nobody working against this wraith had even dreamt of him in hundreds of years, and now the hunter wanted instant details. "I can only tell you that I know he's out there."

"Where?"

"How should I know? Do you see my dagger pointing anywhere?" It aimed at the sky.

"You're an empath. That's what you do."

Connor turned his jaw towards his son and then back to the street. "That's enough, you two. Bring Emma out for one minute."

Diane gave the two-fast, three-slow knocking signal, and then Friar Don propped open the door with his foot while dragging the bags of supplies into the lobby.

The German empath walked from the holy protected site and stopped behind her empathic sister.

Diane spun around to face her. "I feel him."

Emma's eyes opened wide. "I don't. I feel nothing."

"You never have felt anything except when you take off your amulet."

"Why can you feel him with your amulet on?"

Diane pondered the question. "I've had practice at this. It comes easier for me the more I do it. It'll probably do the same for you."

The German empath was nervous. "Is he close?"

"I can't tell. I'd assume not since I barely feel him, but I'm just guessing."

"Am I to really take off my amulet?"

"Connor said to."

Emma leaned into Diane. "He's no empath. He's a noble man, but he's blind to what we see, especially to what you see."

Liam glanced over his shoulder. "We don't have all day, ladies. The less time out here, the better."

Though uncertain, Diane voiced her conclusion with conviction. "Trust me. You're safe right now. Take it off."

The German empath removed the necklace and clasped it around Diane's wrist. Having forgotten to start a countdown with her phone, the Chaldean empath started whispering the countdown. "One Mississippi. Two Mississippi."

"What's that about Mississippi?"

"Four Mississippi. It's how we count seconds in America." Having skipped the fifth count to answer the German's question, she skipped to the sixth. "Six Mississippi."

Emma's eyes glazed over.

Her dagger loose in one hand, Diane grabbed her sister's shoulders. "Stay with me. Eight Mississippi."

"I'm… I'm fine. But he's out there. I feel him now."

"Eleven Mississippi. Good."

"He's coming for me."

"Thirteen Mississippi. Be brave. We're here for you. Fifteen Mississippi."

Emma raised her voice. "He knows I'm here. He knows exactly where I am. We don't have to do this anymore. Can we please stop this now?"

"Nineteen Mississippi. Can you make it forty more seconds?"

"I don't want to." Tears welled in her eyes."

"Twenty-two Mississippi." Diane raised her voice. "Can we wrap this up, guys?"

While the Chaldean empath twisted to see the hunters' reactions, Liam shot a glance over his shoulder. "I think that's enough for today, Father."

Connor looked at the empaths. "Very well. That's enough, Emma. Head back in. We'll follow you."

Diane's count hit thirty seconds as she reached the lobby. The hunters followed her, sealing the door behind them.

Strong enough to have endured the shock of exposure without her protective pendant, Emma stayed conscious throughout her revealing. But within the lobby's safety, she broke down into tears, crumpled into a leather armchair, and sobbed.

Diane gave her back her amulet. "You're doing a brave thing."

"Brave? I feel like a baby for crying about it."

"You're crying because a supernatural serial killer's stalking you. You're allowed to cry. But we have the best defenses in the world protecting you, including me and my dagger. If he comes for you, he'll have to deal with me!"

The German empath forced a smile. "I appreciate what you're doing, but it's still frightening. Are you sure it's best that I stay here in this building?"

"Of course. Why would you doubt that?"

She wiped her tears with her fingers. "I can tell from the friars that they don't like the idea of bringing a wraith to their secret headquarters. From what I can tell, it's inviting trouble."

"Don't overthink it. It's their job to protect us."

"But consider if the wraith..." she inhaled and exhaled slowly through her nose. "... if he succeeds and then shares our location with others like him. Three retired daggers could be stolen and create three new wraiths."

Diane agreed with the risk. "The order has failed to protect retired daggers before."

Interrupting the conversation, Liam extended tissues to Emma. "Those loses were in a distant past."

The gravity of the wraith's approach toyed with the Chaldean empath's fears. "He's smart. They all are. Would he come here if he doubted he'd win?"

Although lifting a veil of bravado over his face, his anxiety was obvious. "Wraith's always think they can win, and it's not like he has any choice. We're making the decision for him. Challenge us here where we have the advantage, or miss the blood-moon sacrifice and die." He forced a grin. "We owe that advantage to both of you. It was tricky timing, but apparently you've lured him here without him switching to another target."

Emma looked to Liam while running the tissue up her cheek. "I know I'm new at using my powers, but from what I know about them, I'm sure he's coming."

"I believe you, and I believe Diane. Your experiences corroborate, and today was a success. I don't mean to be a downer, though, but I think it's only going to get tougher."

The German empath's voice revealed her discouragement. "How?"

Flanked by Friar Don, Connor joined the small group forming around Emma and spoke with firm reassurance. "Now that you've ascertained that he's coming, you need to keep him coming. That means you need to appear attainable so that he doesn't give up and switch to a new targeted sacrifice."

"I know that. What did Liam mean, though, about it being worse?"

Diane recognized the problem from her own experiences. It was the boring drudgery of waiting for death's grip to arrive, not knowing if victory or defeat awaited. It was the danger of taking dangerous action by exposing Emma every day until the battle. "I think he meant the wait and the uncertainty."

"That's exactly what I meant. I didn't want to give him much leeway in his arrival timing, but I conceded to the feelings of the empaths and agreed that we needed to reveal Emma when we did. What's done is done, but we have anywhere from now to seven days from now until he chooses to attack. Like Father said, we need to reveal Emma periodically to entice him. So, we can't fully seal ourselves in with a complete defense."

Diane had an idea, and she grabbed Emma.

The German empath wore a quizzical expression but got up and followed her sister's lead. "Where are we going?"

"Outside again."

Liam darted ahead of her. "Not without a proper escort."

"Then give me the proper escort."

"Wait. I didn't mean to scare you. Let's calm down and talk about it, first."

Diane stopped and faced the young hunter. "But you did scare me." She looked at the concern in her sister's face. "You scared both of us, because you were right. We don't want to expose ourselves to him at all this week to reveal Emma again. So, we should do it one last time, right now."

As his father reached his side, Liam rested his riot shield against his hip and crossed his arms. "How can you expose Emma just one more time and guarantee he's coming?"

"Because I'm putting myself alongside Emma as bait, and I'm also offering him two hunters. Everyone the wraith and his Master could hate will be challenging him, waiting in one spot. It's an offer he can't refuse."

CHAPTER 36

Liam blocked the Chaldean empath's passage. "I forbid it."

She glared at him. "Seriously? You'll never forbid me from doing anything. Got it, buddy? That's a bad habit you need to break right now."

He realized he'd gone overboard trying to protect her, and if he wanted to spend his life with her, he needed to heed her warning. "You know what I meant."

"That's the problem. I know exactly what you meant. It's what you always mean. You always think you're in charge of everything. But you're not."

Although Liam didn't think he was in charge of everything, he saw himself as responsible for everyone's safety, and the subtle distinction was important for a future wife to understand. But he agreed with the empath that his father was the leader, and there were better places and times to argue the distinction. "You're right. My father's in charge of this mission."

Connor took the hint. "Liam has a valid concern. We revealed Emma two days ago, and that's two days our wraith may have been planning, moving, and plotting against us. Every second that we spend outside this building is a chance for him to send a bullet or a cursed knife into one of us. We'll discuss this rationally before anyone goes outside again."

"I'm smarter now, and my dagger and amulet protect me."

"Perhaps, young lady, but let's regroup and act based upon what we just learned from you and Emma."

As Connor stepped towards the chairs, the empaths followed.

The group sat in attentive postures, but Liam remained standing. Hoping his father would let him lead the questioning, he began by reconstructing their status. "Let's start with Diane.

You felt nothing until today, right?"

She nodded.

"And today you felt his presence, but nothing else? Nothing about his intent, his location, or his emotional state?"

"You make it sound like a failure. Nobody except Emma's even contacted him for like seven hundred years, and I just detected him. I think that's pretty impressive."

He considered her information useless given Emma's awareness of the threat, but he withheld his criticism to avoid negating the Chaldean empath's value. "Of course, it goes without saying that what you did was impressive. Now, let's see what sense we can make of it combined with Emma's experience. Emma, remind us what you noticed each of the three days."

"The first time was so intense that I just passed out. I remember sensing his presence, but it was too much, too fast. Yesterday, it was like he was gone, and I wondered if I'd been mistaken the prior time. But then just now, it was horrible. I did feel him. He's coming for me."

Diane corrected her. "He's coming for us. You may be his target, but we're all his enemies. We're with you."

Liam's pulse quickened. "Diane's right. We're all with you. But how can you be sure he's coming?"

"His emotions. He's prepared for battle."

Diane interjected. "You sensed arrogance? Conceit? Right?"

Emma shook her head. "No. You might expect that, but I sensed the opposite. Hopelessness. Sadness. Bitterness. Finality."

The young hunter rejected her report. "That can't be possible. That's not a wraith, is it, Diane?"

The Chaldean empath expounded. "No, I'm afraid it's not. The first two we beat were arrogant and haughty big time. I don't know how you can live hundreds of years by killing people without developing a huge ego. These monsters are narcissists."

"I hear what you're saying, but I felt what I felt."

"I don't doubt your experience or your truthfulness." Liam looked at Diane. "But this doesn't make sense."

"Which is exactly why I need to contact him, with Emma, to be sure."

Succumbing to his desire to protect the woman he loved, Liam refused to let her endanger herself. "We can't risk both of you trying to contact him, especially since we've lost you to trances for days at a time."

"But you just said it's not making sense. We need to go after him. Let's take the offensive. You should like that, Mister Warrior."

The young hunter indeed liked the way she thought, but he wanted to mitigate her danger. "You said you'd expose yourself and two hunters to him. So, if you go after him, you're trying to accomplish three things. You want to verify it's really him, you want to learn what you can about him, and you want to expose all of us as bait."

Diane shrugged. "Yeah. Pretty much."

"Then you should take Father and me with you."

"Four people in the same trance?"

"Do you know of any rules against it?"

"No. But it sounds exhausting."

It was the first downside of her sessions Liam remembered her claiming. "Trances wear you out?"

"A little. I have less energy after them, but ours have been quick and with only two people. I don't know what happens with four people going after a wraith. I'm learning as I go. This is happening so fast."

"I know. But I'd feel better if we were with you."

"I guess it's okay." She looked to the German empath. "Do you see a problem with it?"

"You're the master. I'm just the apprentice."

"But you're the target. Your feelings count, too."

Emma shook her head. "I don't see a problem with it, and I don't want to sense him again by myself. I would welcome the team."

Connor stood. "Well then, no need to belabor this. We've reached an agreement. We'll repeat our procedure for exposing

Emma, except we'll all position ourselves in a square and hold hands. Diane will be behind Liam, Emma behind me. I suggest that the empaths both join us outside upon the first knocking signal and then hold the dagger together."

Diane and Emma nodded.

"Good, then. Liam, check your gear and get behind me."

The young hunter followed his father into the fresh air, which smelled earthy between the ten-foot-high mounds of dirt. While Connor marched around the left berm, Liam checked out the view to the right. The chain link fence diverted pedestrians to the road's far side, and the tarps stretching over it kept the sidewalk abutting the order's headquarters in shadows.

"Check the clothing store."

Obeying his father, Liam verified the windows and roof across the street free of gunmen. A final look upward showed a clear view of the morning's cloudless sky. "Clear!"

"Agreed, lad. Clear. Let's back up now."

With his assault rifle aimed outside his riot shield, the young hunter moved next to his father and then backed up with him.

"Crouch behind your shield and summon them."

Liam leaned his shield against his shoulder, reached backwards to the door, and gave the knocking signal. The empaths emerged from the building and squatted behind him and his father. One bronze dagger and eight hands went up, sought each other's fingers, and became enjoined.

Like his prior trances with Diane, time stopped, and Liam slipped into an alternative reality. Unable to move, he sensed his three companions with him.

Within his head, the Chaldean empath's compassionate but strong voice soothed him. "Um… let's do a roll call. I'll call your name, and you say 'hello' if you can hear me. Liam?"

"Hello."

"Connor?"

"Hello."

"Emma?'

"Hello."

Diane continued the trance's logistical management. "Liam, did you hear Connor and Emma?"

"Yes. I heard them both."

"Connor, did you hear Liam and Emma?"

"Yes, indeed, young lady."

"Emma, did you hear Connor and Liam?"

"Yes, I did."

"Great. We're all connected. Does anyone have any last thoughts before I reach out for him?"

Emma spoke out. "What should I do? I don't feel him?"

"My dagger and our amulets are insulating you from him. I don't think there's anything you need to do until we're connected."

"But once we're connected with him, then what?"

"After we contact him, if we can at all, I have no idea. We'll be making it up at that point."

CHAPTER 37

Ethan vomited over the cuddy cabin's side, leaving a trail of undigested energy bars along the hull. The swells in the Mediterranean Sea northwest of Crete tossed the vessel like a cork, and the seasickness served as an easy method for his Master's infliction of misery. He reached into a rising swell, cupped seawater, and cleaned his mouth.

He rolled back onto a cushion. "I am truly damned."

Weak from nausea and caloric deprivation, he walked in a daze towards the driver's seat. While kicking the idling engine into higher revolutions per minute, he desperately considered what little freedom remained available to him, but he uncovered only one thing.

His thoughts.

He assumed the wicked spirit of his dagger who'd gifted him long life was a powerful demon, far beyond his ability to defy in the material or spiritual realms. But he knew human thoughts were invisible to even the most powerful of his kind.

As the ship powered over a swell, Ethan realized the folly of his single solace. His thoughts were powerless until they became actions, but his Master could see his movements faster than the wraith could command his hands and feet into motion.

A demon's puppet, he was helpless to stop himself from carrying out the spirit's will. He would chase down his sacrifice, steal her life, and kill all who resisted him. Then he'd continue his condemned life until his Master tired of using him, which could be the end of time itself. "I am worse than damned."

A female voice echoing in his head reminded him of the Sirens of Greek mythology, and the coast of Kea off his port beam spurred his recollection of Odysseus as the hero of Homer's

Odyssey.

But the soothing, compassionate voice became stronger, and he discerned its words. "Speak to us. I command you. Speak to us. I command you."

Considering the experience a new form of his Master's trickery, he grabbed his head and yelled. "Get out of my head."

The voice continued. "Speak to us. I command you."

"I told you to leave."

"Speak to us. I command you."

"Damn it." They hadn't heard him yelling, and he conceded he'd have to respond within his mind, or the voice would taunt him incessantly. He thought his words. "I'm here. Who are you? Who wishes to torment me?"

The voice carried surprise. "We know who you are. We know what you are. We are your enemies."

With his only unseen enemy being a voiceless demon, the threat coming from a female voice confused him. "I have no invisible enemies. The ghosts of whom I killed appear before me when tormenting me. Since I don't see you, you cannot be such a ghost. Now, speak the truth. Who are you?"

An old man's voice pushed itself into Ethan's mind. "Should I address him now?"

"You already are."

"I am your enemy. My son and I. Do you recognize who we are?"

An exhilarating mix of fear and awe overcame Ethan.

The old man's voice rose with authority. "I said I am your enemy. Speak!"

The wraith suspected his Master's trickery. "How can I be sure it's you? What can you tell me that my Master does not know?"

"I... I cannot tell you what your Master knows. Therefore, I cannot tell you what he doesn't know."

"You sound rather unsure of yourself for a mortal enemy."

The old man countered. "I'm appalled that you're incapable of recognizing your enemy."

"How would you expect me to recognize you?"

"Young lady, perhaps you should reconsider if we've found our target. This cretin sounds like a jokester, not a serial killer."

"I'm sure it's him. Who else could it be?"

The old man redirected the questioning. "What does our other empath perceive?"

Ethan found the confusion of his assailants a refreshing change from the certainty of his Master's attacks, and he took note of the allusion to two empaths.

A second female voice flowed in his mind. "I feel horrible. It's him."

A young man's voice then rolled around his head. "That's consistent with your experience, but it doesn't identify him."

Ethan's frustration with the authenticity of everyone's identities boiled over. "Enough! My name is Ethan Smith, born on the fourteenth day of May in the year of our Lord, one thousand and sixteen. I was thirty-three years old when I killed my first sacrifice to my Master in the year of our Lord one thousand and forty-nine. Two of your kind managed to wound me before I killed them in the year of our Lord, one thousand two hundred and ninety-nine. Now, if you bantering idiots still have doubts about me, get out of my head. Otherwise, state your business."

All four voices remained silent.

"Well? Say something. One of you must have the intelligence to state your points."

The first female empath spoke into his mind. "We hear you. This isn't what we expected."

"What did you expect? Defiance? A bold call to bloody battle?"

"Well, yeah."

"Don't be so presumptuous or naïve. I've been a monster in my past, but I recently gained a new perspective. I cannot continue."

"You cannot continue... what?"

"Killing!"

"But, you'll die. This doesn't make sense."

Ethan glanced around his earthly surroundings and noticed

the waves rising and falling at a small fraction of their natural speed. "You've trapped me in some sort of dream state."

"Yes. That's one skill I have. I have many more, like sensing lies. Tell me, why do you all of a sudden want to give up on immortality?"

Her allusion to multiple skills suggested she was the huntress who'd joined the rekindled line. "A ghost, the one whom I killed in Yorkshire in the year of our Lord, one thousand three hundred and forty-nine, told me the line of hunters had been recreated. Faced with the fear of my own mortality, I realized the folly of seeking immortality for a life of infinite loneliness and killing of innocents."

The owner of the young voice, the hunting son, spoke. "Don't believe him. It's classic misinformation. He's probably across the street getting ready to ambush us."

The second empath countered. "No, he's telling the truth. I can feel it."

The old hunter hushed them. "Silence, all of you. We'll deliberate our perspectives in private. Mister Smith, would you have us believe that you wish to stop being what you are?"

"Yes."

"Then throw down your daggers and surrender yourself."

"I've tried, but I can't. My Master won't let me."

"Come on, Father. That's such an obvious lie that it's insulting."

"Don't be so harsh to judge me, young hunter. If you'd ever been under the influence of a demon, you'd know my challenge."

The elder spoke. "Under the influence is one thing. To be possessed is another."

"I am possessed."

"Then how is it that I'm talking to you? Why am I not talking to the demon spirit who controls you?"

Ethan was exasperated. "Are you trying to learn from me or test me?"

"Answer the question."

"A demon can neither read nor control thoughts."

"Precisely."

"You're not buying into any of this, are you, Father?"

"Not at face value, lad, but I will ponder it."

"While you're pondering whether I'm lying or not, remember to ponder what damage I can inflict with a powerful demon controlling me and two daggers, one of which I stole from your brethren."

The elder hunter thought out loud. "Supernatural damage. The possibilities are limitless."

"Yes. I fear I'm unstoppable and the doom of you all. I would urge you all to run, but there's nowhere you could go to evade his wrath."

The elder became the only member of the four capable of conversing after the wraith had stymied their plans to taunt him into battle. "We're aware you have great power, but we'd always considered you and your Master as one. This bifurcation is unexpected and significant."

In his mind, Ethan scoffed. "You have no idea."

"If you speak the truth, what would you have us do?"

"You must kill me, of course. Let's at least agree upon that before we discuss anything else."

"For the sake of argument, we'll assume we believe you. How do we kill you?"

"As a gesture of good faith, I won't ask you to reveal your weapons or your tactics. I simply ask that you use everything at your disposal to destroy me."

"That's noble of you to recommend, but it achieves nothing towards the supposed common goal of liberating you from your Master. If you give us nothing else, we've gained nothing. Can you at least tell us when you'll attack?"

Ethan was disgusted in his weak ignorance. "I cannot. He hasn't revealed that to me."

The elder hunter grunted.

"However, I can tell you that I am in a boat northwest of a Greek island named Kea, and I believe he intends for me to make for the eastern Italian shore by sea. I killed a priest in a hotel in

Mytilene yesterday, and I'm sure Greek authorities are looking for me on land and in airports."

"The Italians may be, too."

"I doubt it. A British drifter killing a priest within walking distance of Moria's daily human tragedy is hardly worthy of Interpol."

"Then you're at least two days away."

"Yes."

"Bullshit. Don't believe him, Father."

The first empath pushed her voice and will above the others. "Let me test him. Mister Smith, let me see the world through your eyes."

Having lived to control others during his entire thousand-year life, Ethan doubted he could yield his senses. "I'm not sure how."

"Just let me."

"I'll try."

"It's not working."

"I told you he's lying."

Ethan tried to draw a breath, but his physical body moved in the same slow motion of the waves, the spray, and the rest of the real world. "This is a foreign concept to me."

"Keep trying. Work with me."

"I'm trying to let you hear, see, feel, smell anything you want. This is harder than I imagined."

"Got it!"

"What? I didn't feel anything."

"You wouldn't, but I saw your boat. Your right hand is on the steering wheel, and you've got something nasty on the back of your index finger. It looks like... barf."

"I just vomited over the side. Seasickness."

"He complied. He let me see."

"That's wonderful and all, but it doesn't prove that he's telling the truth. We can't let him bullshit us."

"Easy, lad. We're almost done. Mister Smith, is there anything else you can think of to help us... overcome your Master's hold on you?"

Ethan ransacked his mind. "There's nothing he won't see other than my thoughts... our shared thoughts, like this conversation. But it's pointless because no matter what we might agree to, we can't do anything without him seeing it and countering it."

"We're on sacred ground, which is hidden from his sight. We'll set up a trap. It should be quite simple."

"No! Don't you understand? Your ground may be sacred, but he sees."

"Do you mean he can see inside our encampment now?"

"No, he's not that powerful. I know your site's protected, but once I'm there, he'll see and hear through my body, and his supernatural powers will sniff out anything you've set against me."

"Then we'll have to set a trap you can't detect."

"Yes. I beg it of you. Otherwise, this will end as a tragedy for all of us."

CHAPTER 38

Liam backed into the building, helped his father lock the door, and dropped his riot shield. "I'm not believing any of it."

Beside him, his father placed his shield on the floor. "I'm not sure what to believe about his intent, but we learned something quite valuable about his identity."

Liam shrugged. "Okay, I'll grant that. We confirmed who he is."

"We also confirmed he's coming. There's no need to risk further exposure. We can finally button down our defenses and wait."

The young hunter remained skeptical. "What if the whole thing's a ruse? What if he just convinced us to button down the building while he turns tail and goes after a substitute sacrifice far away?"

"What of it? If he shifts to a substitute sacrifice, what would you do about it?"

"I'd send Emma and Diane right back outside tomorrow to invade his mind."

"And then what? Ask him to tell the truth? Beg him to come for Emma? No, lad. He's either coming here, or we're not seeing him until after the blood moon."

Liam sighed and slumped his shoulders. "I suppose you're right."

"Don't worry about the veracity of his claims. We'll spend the rest of the day perfecting our defenses, and then we'll talk about extra options that may exist if we believe his suicidal claims."

"I wish we could do more to be sure about his claims."

"We can't."

He accepted his father's wisdom and glanced at the two-byfours and packaged concertina wire piled in the lobby's corner. "Fine, then. Let's do a final equipment and provisions check, and then we'll work through our defense checklist."

An hour later, the young hunter and his father finished inventorying the weapons, ammunition, food, bottled water, armor, clothes, computers, and communications equipment. Routers in each subterranean room offered wired and wireless Internet Protocol links throughout the floors, and they were ready to seal themselves within the sanctum and its waiting room, which served as their command center, with hardwired lines as their only connection to the outside world.

He grabbed a backpack filled with tools, lifted his shield, and followed his father through the labyrinth of hallways. Outside each security door, he helped the elder hunter check the supplies they'd need to barricade each access point on the path leading back to the inner sanctum.

After riding the elevator, he reached the lobby and marched towards the entrance door. "Are you ready?"

A riot shield in one hand and a Heckler and Koch 416 rifle in the other, Connor nodded.

Liam opened the door, followed his father into the open air, and shut the way behind him. After doing their rehearsed clearance checks, the young hunter took his tools to the concertina wire while his father watched for intruders.

Since the sun was risen, employees of the women's clothing store were straggling into the entrance across the street. While Liam uncoiled a helix of concertina wire around a straight line of razor wire he'd clamped taut between the top and bottom bars, his father called to him. "Movement."

The young hunter lowered his pliers, tore off a glove, and grabbed his rifle. As he looked up, he saw a lean man's silhouette. His arms in front of his body, the walking figure crossed the street. "Good morning!"

Connor lowered his rifle. "It's just Friar Don." He raised his voice. "Careful how you approach armed men. You could've gotten yourself killed."

"Sorry. I wanted to get you gifts before you sealed yourselves in there." He lifted a set of beads with a crucifix. "I know a street vendor near the Vatican. His rosaries are the best. I used one when my nephew was fighting cancer, and Friar Francesco used one when his sister was caught in a bad marriage. Let's call them good luck charms, for lack of a better word. I got one for each of you."

Connor kept his focus on the street. "That's very thoughtful of you. Liam will take them."

The friar stepped to the young hunter, who pocketed the gifts. "Thanks."

Friar Don eyed the handiwork. "Can't he just cut through that?"

Liam recalled the specifications of his fence. "The strongest tool on the market exerts seventy-five thousand PSI of cutting pressure. This wire can take up to three times that. It's reinforced with carbon steel running along its spine. And if he did cut it, it would snap out like a whip and give him a rapid education on what it feels like to be cut by a dozen angry razors. That's what the tension in the line's for."

The friar frowned. "But he can take his time and work slowly and carefully."

Liam pointed to the sky. "Not after I set up my rifle on the roof."

"What rifle? Who's going to operate it?"

"I am. Remotely. I've got a workbench and vices up there. I've got a computer on the network that runs a solenoid, and that pulls the trigger. I'll have the same thing waiting for him in the lobby."

"Fascinating."

"You have to embrace technology or get beaten by it."

The friar studied the sky and then looked back to the young hunter's work site. "How do you aim it?"

"I'll secure the rifle and shoot a spotting round or two to make sure I know where it's aiming."

"But you can't change where it aims?"

"Well, no. I have to time it to hit him when he's standing under the barrel."

"But if he works on one side or the other of this wire fence you're putting up, you won't be able to hit him."

Liam shrugged. "I know, but it's just a free chance to shoot him."

The friar stood straight. "Can I be your rifleman up there instead of using remote control?"

"I can't ask you for help."

"I just volunteered. I spent two years in the British Army."

"This guy has powers we don't understand. If you miss, and he gets in, you'd be stranded on the roof. We'll be putting a fence on the stairs heading up there."

"I can escape to the building next door, if you give me some rope. Its roof's about three meters lower than ours and less than a meter away."

"I'm okay with it. Father, he wants to pick up a rifle and help us."

"I heard, lad. There's nothing in our governing laws preventing it. Work out a plan with him, and thank him for his help. Who knows? Maybe he'll kill a wraith for us."

The young hunter stood. "You got your own rifle?"

"No. I was hoping to borrow one of yours."

Liam had allotted a spare rifle to the empath's grandmother, who'd be hiding in the sanctum. He'd considered letting Nana and Josh hide outside the headquarters, but if removed from his protection, they'd become liabilities the wraith could find and hold hostage. So, they needed to stay, and Nana had earned her right through past battles to carry a weapon. "I could lend you the old rifle I was going to use remotely on the roof, but its sights are off, and it jams about every couple hundred rounds. That's why it's going up there."

"I imagine from that distance, the sights won't be a problem."

"No, I guess not. You know what? Better yet, I'll let you take a couple grenades."

The friar's eyes opened wide. "I haven't thrown a grenade since my basic training."

"You'll be fine. Just pull the pin and drop them. Now that I think of it, that's our best chance to kill him."

"Then why do I feel silly for volunteering?"

"I call it the willies. We all get it."

"I guess that's what I have now."

"Logically, there's nothing to worry about. We'll have every air vent, the stairs, and the elevator blocked with wire. I'll have a remote-controlled rifle waiting for him if he gets through the front door, and now we have you waiting for him with a surprise from above. No mortal man can to get to Emma without a significant military arsenal on his back. But instead of an arsenal, he's bringing a demon. That's a huge illogical question mark."

The friar looked upward again. "That's a perfect position, and I'll have an escape route."

Liam gave him one last chance to back out. "There's no body armor. It's all accounted for."

"Bah. Only my head and arms will be exposed, and what good am I if I can't face the evil I've dedicated my life to stopping? I'd consider myself a coward if I ran now. I'm getting on in years, anyway. I'd rather die as an aging hero instead of decaying into old age as a man who shied away from danger."

The hunter extended his hand. "Welcome to the team. Diane knows where we keep the weapons. Go take a few dry fires with the rifle to get used to it, but don't touch the grenades until I get there."

"I can feel the excitement already. It's electrifying."

As the friar stepped towards the door and tapped in his code, Liam mulled over their exchange. The new volunteer had given him an idea. "Friar Don?"

"Yes?"

"Before you seal yourself in there, I'd like to run an idea by you and Father. I may need you to get some special supplies."

The friar turned. "Of course."

"I'll keep my eye on the street, but I'm listening, lad. Go

ahead."

Liam summarized. "After we seal ourselves in the command center, four security doors of two-inch-thick steel barricaded by razor wire traps will be between us and the wraith."

The friar corrected him. "Not if he comes from the roof."

"Right. It's only three doors in that case. I don't expect him to climb to our roof, but that highlights my point. What's the difference between three, four, or even more impasses?"

Connor spoke over his shoulder. "If it takes him a few hours to break through each one, it could mean the difference between life and death. When the moon sets, it's over. He's working against a clock."

"If he's coming on the blood moon. If he comes earlier to take Emma away and kill her later, the redundancy in our barricades won't matter."

"Fair point. Go on, lad."

"What if I set up something different for him at the entrance to the sanctum? If he can get to the command center before moonset, I want to hit him with something he won't expect."

"That's in line with what he recommended for overcoming his Master, if you care to believe him."

Liam smirked. "It doesn't matter what I believe, other than believing in my team and in my ingenuity. Wait 'til you hear what I'm planning."

CHAPTER 39

The next day, Ethan saw a private fishing dock on the outskirts of Otranto, Italy. He draped his backpack over his shoulders, lifted the two daggers from their scabbards, and knelt. He stabbed the bronze blades through his boat's keel, and with his Master strengthening him, he cut fatal slits into the hull. As the boat sank, he sheathed his weapons and leapt into the water.

Exhausted from scant sleep and malnutrition, he swam to a creaking wooden pier. Water dripped from his clothes as he climbed up a ladder. Woozy while standing on the dock, he examined the yard and its nearby house but saw nobody. He ambled to a ten-year-old Fiat sedan parked next to a boat trailer, and he found the keys under the driver's visor.

Fearing his Master would force him to murder while stealing the car, he plopped his sopping pants into the seat. He turned on the engine, cranked up the heat, and drove away. As the fisherman's house disappeared into his rearview mirror, he understood the demon's wisdom. Leaving a trail of corpses belonging to the nation in which he'd hide for six days would be an intolerable risk. So, his lording spirit had guided him to an empty home with a waiting vehicle.

The seven-hour drive to Rome began uncomfortably while Ethan wiggled in his wetness. As he reached the outskirts of Lecce, the world froze, and he slipped out of time. Hope and fear rose within him. "Hello? Yes?"

The primary empath's voice was weak and distant. "Mister Smith? ...hear me?"

Although conversing through a telepathic link with a mortal enemy, the wraith welcomed the intrusion. Any human spirit trumped the bondage of his Master. "Barely. It's much less clear than last time."

"I'm within the headquarters... holy ground. I'm lucky... you... at all."

"Don't leave."

As quickly as she'd touched him, she diminished.

Left alone, he drove onward.

Two hours later, he pulled into a rest stop and parked at a gas pump. His clothes still sloshing, he walked into the convenience store and saw touristy tee shirts and shorts for sale. He grabbed his new wardrobe and marched to the counter.

A young clerk stared at his wet shirt. "What happened to you?"

Ethan had last spoken Italian three hundred years ago, but he remembered the basics. "Long story. Fishing. Late for important meeting. Need fuel." He handed a wad of wet bills to the attendant, took his change, and then went back to his stolen car.

While refueling, he changed into dry clothes, although his underwear remained wet. After filling the gas tank, he drove away from the rest area and towards Rome.

Four hours later, he saw a pond off the road. He angled the Fiat towards it and parked by its edge. Slinging his backpack over his shoulders, he scanned the surrounding countryside for witnesses but saw nobody.

He shifted the car into neutral and pushed it into the water. Gravity took hold of the vehicle, and then water overcame the seals of its cabin. While Ethan took off on foot towards Rome, he looked over his shoulder at the sinking car.

He took backroads throughout the remainder of his trek until reaching a small inn at the outskirts of the nation's capital. After checking in and paying for six nights with cash, he locked himself in his room.

Exhausted, he fell asleep.

He awoke the next day, amazed his Master had allowed the slumber.

While he remained in bed, suffering the aches of travel and

sickness, the empath stopped time and attempted contact again. "Mister Smith?"

"Miss... Empath?"

"You may call me that. I sense... closer. Easier..."

"Yes, I am near. Ten kilometers from you, staying at an inn."

"When... attacking?"

"I don't know. My Master won't say. Please, defend yourselves."

She faded.

He spent the day resting and eating his energy bars, which he managed to digest. By allowing him to recuperate, his lording spirit was playing a game he failed to grasp, but he accepted the restoration of his strength. To pass time, he rummaged through worn paperbacks in the inn's hand-me-down library, selecting several palatable titles to protect his sanity while cooped up for days.

That evening, he slept again.

He awoke refreshed, held another meaningless telepathic conversation with the empath, and finished his energy bars. Risking being seen, he walked to the nearest convenience store for more food, and then he returned to his room.

Two more nights, he slept, finally awaking on the morning of the blood moon.

Time stopped, and the empath harkened. "It's now or never. When are you coming?"

"I don't know. I can only hope he's released me from this torment, letting me die with a mortal destiny."

"I'll sense if you move towards me. When I contact you, make yourself receptive."

She faded.

He cried out in his loneliness. "I am not your enemy by choice!" Knowing his demon adversary would decide his fate this night, he tried to distract himself by reading, but his eyes flitted back and forth over the same sentences.

The sun set, and then darkness covered the countryside while he stared out a window. At nine o'clock, he dared to hope he'd sleep through the night and awake as a mortal man. But when his head hit the pillow, his Master imprisoned his spirit deep within his human body.

Against his will, his limbs moved, renewed with the strength of several days of rest. Leaving the backpack, he tapped the daggers at their scabbards while walking towards the door.

In a waking nightmare, he strode into the summer evening air towards Rome. He covered the distance to the inner city in a daze of fear and helplessness.

At the midpoint of his journey, time stopped, and the empath invaded. "You're coming."

"I cannot help myself. He forces me."

"Let me see through your eyes."

He allowed it, letting the empath view the city's nighttime skyline from his perspective. "Do you see?"

"Yes. I will return."

Time moved again, and he marched into Rome. The architectural beauty and timeless artistry of the city hinted at a history of the shared human experience that eluded him.

As he turned onto the street of the order's headquarters, the empath again invaded. "Give me your eyes."

He allowed her access.

"I see where you are. You're very close."

"Can you not save yourselves?"

She became haughty. "Stop threatening us. We've got some surprises for you."

"I hope they're brilliant, Miss Empath, for your lives and for my death."

Abandoning him to his fate, she left him.

Seeing the construction zone, he marched down the opposite side of the street and stopped in front of the closed women's clothing store. He waited for a taxi to zoom by, and then he crossed the road.

Standing between the berms at the razor wire, he looked up at a security camera.

The empath invaded again. "You found us. Now what?"

"I cannot stop. He'll force me in."
"You have no weapons. No armor."
"I have the daggers. Please, kill me."
"Trust me. We intend to."

As she released him to reality, he snapped his jaw upward. Two dark objects fell from the sky. Crossing his arms, he grasped both daggers and then flung them up. With impossible power and accuracy, the bronze blades defied metallurgy and sliced the cast iron shells of the grenades. As the inert halves clunked into the sidewalk, the daggers landed in his palms.

Someone swore from the roof. "Damn!"

He looked up again, and a rifle barrel pointed at him. In slow motion, he saw the muzzle flash, and he spied the first bullet's silhouette. As the round came towards his head, he lifted one dagger and swatted away the deadly projectile. He lifted his other dagger and smacked the next bullet off its mark. Feeling the deep throb of bones fracturing in his hands under the strain of supernatural speed, he wielded the knives as impenetrable deflectors, knocking away round after round.

The volley ended, and smoke wafted over the rifleman.

With one underhanded toss, Ethan hurled his cursed dagger upward into his attacker's eye socket and through his frontal cortex. As the man's head slumped over the roof's edge, the bloody dagger fell back into to Ethan's hand.

The wraith cringed inside himself. While he anticipated his inevitable doom under his Master's dominion, he aimed the bloodied blade at a coil of concertina wire.

The knife grew hot, searing his skin, but he maintained the grasp. He smelled his burning flesh while sliding the dagger through the wire and cutting it like butter. As the coil's tension lashed the razors outward, the second dagger rose and deflected the deadly whip.

Stepping through the gash in the fence, Ethan eyed the key-pad. The lock was part of holy ground, but the fingers that had tapped them hundreds of times had been standing on a public street, open to his Master's view. Like a puppet, the wraith pressed the proper code into the pad, and the latch clicked.

Disgusted and terrified, he pushed open the door into the lair of his mortal enemy.

CHAPTER 40

Standing in front of the computers of his control center, Liam adjusted his body armor. After watching the wraith survive the hand grenades and rifle attack, he found the weight of his gear uncomfortable. "Is Friar Don answering?"

Beside him, his father lowered his cell phone, which he'd been using through an Internet Protocol to speak with the friar. "I'm afraid he's dead. We must assume the worst."

"And I'm dishing out my worst." He glared at the computer screen, and through a security camera, he watched the wraith enter the lobby. "Firing!" He stabbed his finger into a computer key, and tracer bullets sped towards the intruder. As had happened outside, the daggers moved like lightning, protecting their owner from fatal wounds.

"Stop. It's pointless."

"Bloody hell." Liam shut off the lobby's remote-controlled rifle. "Conventional firearms aren't working."

"Let's see how he does against the next barrier."

The young hunter gazed at a new computer screen as the wraith walked into a different camera's field of view. The intruder threw a dagger into the grenade Liam had staged in the concertina wire in front of the stairs. Like a melon, the weapon split open, but the bronze blade remained out of the assailant's reach.

"At least his dagger sort of obeys the laws of physics. It didn't boomerang back to his hand."

His father crowded him at the computer monitor. "What happens next will be interesting."

The second dagger glowed, and smoke rose from the wraith's palm.

Liam cringed. Fear prevented him from speaking, other than short spurts. "I believe him. He's being controlled."

"Why so sure now?"

"His burning flesh. Nobody can take that much pain on purpose."

The wraith swung the hot blade through the coiled wire, and an arc of razors lashed out at him. Crimson spots dotted the intruder's shirt, and rivulets of red flowed down his cheek.

"Bloody hell. It cut right across his chest and face, and he didn't even flinch."

"No question, lad. He's absolutely under a demon's control."

The realization encouraged Liam and reduced his fear. "It took our fourth obstacle, but we finally made him bleed."

"Right. That means there's hope."

"Shit, Father. Remember when I said the number of barricades didn't matter? Well, I was wrong. Let's back up into the sanctum and set up a razor fence right outside it."

"I see your point. It's a valid one, but what about our command center? Information is power. It helps to watch him."

"I'll take care of that. You grab spare razor wires and start setting up the fence. Hurry, Father!" Liam tucked two laptops under his arm and draped an extension cord into the courtroom, which lacked outlets. In the semicircle enclosed by the council member's arced bench, he found the ladies and Josh huddled in their armor behind riot shields. "I'm moving the command center back here."

With fear and defiance, the Chaldean empath looked at him. "Why? What's wrong?"

While setting his equipment on the council's abandoned bench, Liam drew in a breath and spoke with the most courage he could muster. "He killed Friar Don, and he's broken through the stairs."

Surprised, terrified expressions landed on the listeners' faces.

"Don't worry. We made him bleed at the stairs. He paid for passing through. It may not be much, but it could weaken him, and it shows he's vulnerable. Father and I are setting up another fence for him at the entrance." He pointed up the aisle towards the sanctum's doorway.

Diane sounded strong. "Can we help?"

"No. Father and I will go as fast as possible. A third set of hands would slow us down. Speaking of which, I need to get going. Diane, hand me two grenades."

The Chaldean empath reached into a canvas bag resting on the floor behind her and pulled out the requested weapons, which she carried to him. When within whispering range, she addressed him. "Are we going to die?"

"I don't know."

"How scared are you?"

"I was practically pissing my knickers when I saw him do what he did, but when he bled, I felt a lot better." Groping for something assuring to say, he thought of nothing but felt a pressing need to make progress. "I need to go." Carrying the grenades, he trotted up the aisle and joined his father at the worksite.

Connor tapped a nail into the doorframe. "We'll have to string the wires horizontally, and we'll have to jury rig it with nails."

"Agreed. Let's hurry." Liam lowered the grenades, reached into an equipment bag, and put on a pair of Kevlar work gloves. He pulled a line of wire tightly across the doorway.

His father struck a nail completely into the frame, pressing its head against an exposed barb, and then he walked to the other doorjamb.

Liam held the line as his father hammered a nail over a razor's edge to hold the horizontal wire in place. "Not bad."

"It'll have to do." Connor returned to the other doorjamb. As he hammered down his end, Liam pulled the wire, and his father moved to his side to pound it tight. "That's two, lad. Three to go."

Diane called to him. "You've got to see this. Come here."

Liam took off down the aisle. When he reached the empath, she stood with a small crowd in front of the computer. He moved to the screen and ogled it. Sanguine gashes along the wraith's arm revealed the injury he'd received reaching through the fence to retrieve the dagger he'd thrown at another grenade. Continuing his assault, he stabbed both burning daggers through two inches of steel. "He doesn't have the codes to the interior doors."

Watching the supernatural display, Diane was in awe. "He doesn't have to. He's cutting through it. *Yulla*, get back to work."

Liam trotted up the aisle and helped his father string the wires. Then he helped him roll the concertina coils under tension across the taut horizontal razor lines.

Time passed faster than he'd hoped, and Diane announced the enemy's progress. "He's through the next door. Only one more before he's in the waiting room."

"How bad's he bleeding?"

"He shredded his other arm."

"Good! Keep working, Father."

"Almost done... and. Yes. Clipped the last piece in."

Liam gestured for his father to leave. "I need to do this last step myself." The unstated reason was so that a mistake would blow up only himself.

"Good luck lad." Connor retreated to the room's far end.

The young hunter reached into the equipment bag and withdrew a roll of duct tape. He pressed a grenade against the doorframe and secured it with long strips of the adhesive. Satisfied with the weapon's placement, he grabbed a spool of fishing wire. He tied several lengths to different layers of coiled wire, and then he tied the lines to the grenade's pin. Though the lines slacked to prevent blowing Liam up, he trusted the whipping of any cut wires would set off the trap. "The first one's done, Father!"

"Damn! No time for a second. He's coming." Connor trotted to the entrance and handed his son a riot shield. "Ready?"

Liam drew a deep breath. "Yeah." He lowered the shield sideways to the floor and then lay prone behind it. Aiming his rifle outside the edge of his bulletproof barrier, he verified his field of fire across the waiting room.

His father joined him.

Diane called out. "He's torn his left arm up really bad, but he's still coming. He's going for the door now."

Like flowing ore, the inner steel of the waiting room's door turned orange and melted. The enemy cut an arc over his head and then sliced two vertical lines downward. He kicked down the cutaway piece and then stepped over the bent metal into the waiting room.

Connor struck first, his rifle cracking in the young hunter's ear.

Liam shot next, pumping a dozen rounds at the assailant until he lost count. Every round ricocheted off a bronze blade, and he stopped and yelled. "It's pointless! Retreat!"

It wasn't until he'd given up that he noticed the intruder's appearance. A disgusting demon, the man's face was a twisted aberration of sagging and torn skins. Fangs protruded from the slimy mouth under a long, crooked nose. He had a body of scarred and blighted leather, and at its extreme ends, horns, a pointed tail, and cloven hooves. To Liam, all wraiths looked the same.

He rolled to one side of the doorway and then pushed his half of the door closed.

His father mimicked his actions and then locked the entrance. "Find your positions, everyone. Liam, take off your amulet. Let him see us for who we are. You all know what's coming next."

CHAPTER 41

Ethan's hands were numb, the searing blades having burned his nerves. But the sliced flesh of his arms and the broken bones of his wrists sent debilitating signals to his brain. As the hunters shut the entrance behind the razor wire barricade to the inner room, he braced himself for more suffering.

With his Master manipulating him, he lifted the enchanted dagger he'd stolen long ago and then hurled it at the duct-taped grenade. As with the prior impasses, the blade defied physics and severed the weapon into halves. Momentum carried the knife to the locked portal, and then gravity pulled it to the floor behind the razor wire.

Stopping in front of the coiled lines, he extended his least-shredded arm through the nest of metallic barbs, which carved new red traces into his flesh. Within his imprisoned mind, he cursed his Master, who could have returned the dagger to him but preferred to subject him to the razors. He grasped the handle and suffered the heat of new, burrowing cuts as he withdrew it.

Clutching both knives within the goo of his palms, he brought the enchanted dagger, glowing with heat, down through the wires. As concertina coils whipped towards him, he blocked them with his cursed knife.

He raised the hot tips and stabbed them through the door. This barrier lacked a core of steel, and smoke wafted from the burning wood. As he carved an arc and then traced vertical lines on either side of him, time stopped, and he sensed the empath. "I told you to run, Miss Empath."

"We're not running."

"What else can you do? I've defeated every obstacle. My body's breaking, but his control is absolute."

"We'll take our chances."

Ethan shared a desperate thought that had been tormenting him. "You can still defeat me if you kill the other empath."

The primary empath digested the concept in silence and then countered. "You'd find a substitute nearby. There's too much time before moonset."

"A virgin of the proper lineage? Finding one on short notice may be harder than you think."

"We're not killing her. We're killing you." She faded.

He hoped she was right, but he doubted it. Wood fibers cracked when he kicked in the door, and then he used the fallen planks as a ramp leading into the room.

A gentle mist enveloped him, and he wondered if he'd stumbled into a telepathic trap. But real-world moisture landed on his skin, and he tasted water on his lips.

The unexpected gentle spray caused him to slow and inspect his surroundings. To either side, shelves of small green plants rose in a terraced shape, explaining the misting system. But the oddity which struck him was the sloppiness of the spray's coverage, since it draped both the greenery and the room's entrance. Anyone entering the space, which resembled a courtroom with the slight downward slope of a theatre floor, would be moistened.

The oddities continued as his Master sensed cursed daggers that had once belonged to others of Ethan's kind. To either side, rising from the terraced plants, a bronze blade pointed straight upward. The knives would have escaped the wraith's detection if not for the demon's recognition of their divine empowerment.

A final view compounded his confusion, and he sensed it also caused his Master to hesitate. He stood motionless while staring at four people.

Their rifles over their shoulders, the hunters flanked his sacrifice, who stood facing him. The men had skin of glowing azure and oversized eyes of pure white, and their backlit sky-blue auras seemed angelic. Between them, the young lady issued a red aura. Her sanguine light blossomed in his vision, and she became an intoxicating view. The temptation to kill her overwhelmed him.

But the fourth person's posture stymied him. Giving her own shifting, multi-colored aura, the primary empath knelt in his path. With one hunter holding the back of her bulletproof vest, she rested her right hand over the hunter's wrist. Her other hand extended before her, and she exposed a dagger, one his Master recognized as enchanted, in her lowered palm. "We surrender. I yield my dagger."

The hunting son yelled. "Now!" He crouched and began to spring sideways and backwards, his tensed arm attached to the kneeling woman. His other hand held that of the sacrifice. In a team effort that appeared choreographed, the standing woman also held the other hunter's hand as she and the hunting father turned and jumped away.

The kneeling empath invaded his mind, stopping time. "Mister Smith."

"What's all this?"

"Our final stance."

"I begged you to run. Now you can't stop me."

"Did you hear me surrender?"

Her bronze blade appeared stationary, friction holding it to her skin against gravity. "I don't understand. What mercy do you expect from me? From him?"

"No mercy. My surrender was for your Master to hear. But now, can you see all around you?"

With his physical body frozen, he used his peripheral vision and his memory from having scanned the room. "I see what I need to see."

"I don't think so. Can you see the ten car batteries stacked behind the plants?"

He could not, and he was shocked that his Master had failed to. "I don't. Batteries? Do you hope to electrocute me?"

"Not hope. Do. Watch my dagger."

"I am. It's not moving."

"Be patient. Keep watching."

As motivated legs drew the three jumping people away from Ethan in slow motion, the dagger slid down the empath's palm. He remained confused. "What's happening?"

"Do you see where my dagger will land?"

He noticed coppery squares below her hand, and thick insulated cables that had escaped his detection ran from either piece of exposed metal. "I see it. You're closing a circuit with your knife?"

"Yes. And when it's closed, one hundred and twenty volts will run from the cursed dagger to your right, through the mist you're standing in, and into the other cursed dagger."

Exhilarated and terrified, Ethan needed to understand more. "How could my Master have not seen this?"

"Greed. When he saw two possible empath victims, two possible hunter victims, and two cursed daggers, it overwhelmed his cravings. He desires vengeance and power, and we gave him a sensory overload."

"It's working."

"Yes. We've tested this circuit. It will work."

"Will I die?"

"I don't know."

"I'm overcome with temptation now. I crave my sacrifice. Please make sure I die."

Her voice sounded strained. "We'll do... what we have to."

"What's wrong?"

"This telepathic link. Five people. Draining."

"Do you need it? When we reenter real time, will your trap not spring?"

"Yes. But you must fight your Master. Resist any power he has to make you to jump away from the mist."

"I can't do that. I've been trying. I'm helpless."

The falling dagger reached her fingertips. "I will hold this... as long as I can. Exhausting."

He felt her energy waning. "Please. Hold this. Don't let him spare me. If you fail, I fear none will ever succeed."

"I'm holding it. Not much longer."

"Please. I beg you. Don't let me escape."

A gap formed between the bronze blade and the empath's hand, and her life force flickered and faded. As time recommenced its cruel march, he steeled his will for a final stance against the demon. Within himself, he mustered every shred of his essence against the lording spirit, and he demanded his body to remain rigid within the mist.

Arcs shot from the dagger to the exposed copper.

His Master overpowered Ethan's defiance and sent him diving backwards. He feared the demon's will would overcome the laws of physics, but he saw arcs expanding like sideways lightning in the mist. Branches of lightning reached out and tickled him in his paths of least resistance–his open wounds.

His body became rigid, and every muscle tensed. Feeling the cramping pain, he became helpless. A final vestige of weakness within him lamented his defeat, but as he slipped into an abyss of nothingness, his higher consciousness registered a resounding victory over his former Master.

CHAPTER 42

As the young hunter had instructed, Diane clamped her eyes shut and let her legs go limp. He'd warned her to avoid kicking for fear of her toes extending into the electrified mist.

Electricity cracked, and she rose upward and sideways with the young hunter's bullish arm strength. As she descended behind a bench, she extended her hand to brace her fall against the hard floor.

But the hunter turned himself into a human pillow and drew her over him. "Are you okay?"

She was fine. "Yeah."

"Get off me." He pushed her up.

She stood, and as he brushed by her, she turned to watch him. But the horrible image of the wraith writhing in a helpless electric dance drew her vicarious attention.

Liam picked up a staged piece of wood, lowered it next to Diane's dagger, and then kicked it with his boot. The blade slid across the floor, and the arcing stopped.

The Chaldean empath looked at Connor and Emma, who were rising from the floor. "Are you okay?"

They both nodded.

Liam stepped towards the motionless wraith and kicked his two dropped weapons down the aisle. "Father! Get the cases!"

"Right." Connor trotted away.

Diane's gaze drifted back to the intruder. "Is he dead?"

Liam knelt and examined him. "Let me see."

She hated the wraith for what he was, but she pitied the man who'd wanted redemption. Walking to him, she felt the mist on her face and stood over the young hunter.

"His heart's stopped, but he's still breathing."

She surprised herself with her request. "Save him."

"I thought you might say that." He leaned over the wraith and began chest compressions. "Can you turn off the mist, so that we don't end up like him?"

She ran to the mister's power cord and turned it off. The background hiss subsided.

Carrying two cases, Connor knelt in the aisle and locked the disarmed assailant's knives within them. "The daggers are sealed."

"Bring your handcuffs, in case I bring him back."

The elder hunter darted to the wraith's feet and bound his ankles within the metallic restraints. "You'll have to bind his hands if you revive him."

After a third round of chest compressions, Liam pressed his fingers into the victim's neck. "He's alive." He grabbed handcuffs from his vest and locked them around the wraith's wrists.

Remaining on the ground, the wraith writhed, and Diane pitied him for his suffering. But the writhing grew in its violence, and she realized his motions were unnatural.

Connor diagnosed the danger. "He's still possessed. Get the rope, lad. Quickly! Before he breaks the cuffs."

Liam darted down the aisle towards the equipment bag and came back with inch-thick nylon. "Lift up his torso."

The elder hunter pulled the wraith's shoulders while his son wrapped rope around their captive.

Seizing, the wraith rolled his eyes back in his head, and then his body stilled while he glared at the elder hunter. His voice was a haunting mix of deep bass coupled with hisses and squealing. "Old man, do you think you've won?"

Connor raised his voice. "Nobody speak to this monstrosity! It's not a man but a demon. Empaths, attempt no telepathy! Liam, hold him down but say nothing, no matter what vulgarities issue from him. I'm calling the council." He lifted his phone. "Yes. We've won. We lost Friar Don, I fear, but the rest are okay. No, he's alive, but possessed. Yes. That's exactly what I believe is best. Thank you." Connor lowered his phone. "Friar

Lucio will be here for the exorcism in ten minutes."

The wraith glared at Diane with scorn. "You'd be safer if you lost your virginity. Come here and I'll relieve you of it." He wiggled his tongue.

"Let Liam and me handle this beast. Everyone else step outside."

Diane stepped over the broken door, through the shredded razor wire, and into the waiting room. She sat on the soft cushion of an armchair and let relief wash over her.

While Nana and Josh landed in a sofa, Emma sat next to her. "I guess it's over. We survived."

"Apparently. This whole exorcism thing sounds like they're just mopping up a mess."

"Do you think we should check on Friar Don?"

Diane sensed the loss of their colleague. "No. I'm sure he's gone."

"I can't get used to the fact that the man who's killed thousands of innocent women and wanted to kill me is tied up in the next room and possessed by a demon."

Diane let the comment linger unanswered as she sank deeper into the cushion. Holding her team and the wraith in the long trance had proved exhausting. As her adrenaline waned, she drifted in and out of sleep until she heard footsteps through the busted door to the hallway.

A huge tome under his arm, Friar Lucio stepped into the waiting room. "Oh my. What a battle this must have been. You ladies must be traumatized."

Diane flicked a dismissive wrist. "I've been through worse, sort of. This was the scariest, but at least this time nobody got close enough to stab me."

"He would have attacked you mercilessly, had you not succeeded. This is a great victory, and I understand that you've apprehended him alive."

"And possessed by a demon."

"I trust Connor's judgment, but I must determine that for myself."

Curious, Diane rose from the chair and followed the friar to the courtroom's broken door. "Connor! Can we come back in with Friar Lucio?"

"Yes. That's fine. Just remember not to speak to the demon, no matter how he taunts you."

Diane led her family and the German empath to the semicircle, where the wraith sat in a chair facing the bench while the hunters wrapped bandages around their captive's wounds.

Friar Lucio stopped in front of the possessed man. "Oh my, are all his injuries from the wires?"

Connor bragged. "My son proved his expertise in setting up the razor wire properly."

Friar Lucio grunted. "Determining if someone's truly possessed is normally a complex process, but given what we know and what I see, I'll skip ahead to the exorcism. Nobody can speak to him. Nobody should talk unless I ask you to pray with me. Connor and Liam, please step behind him and make sure he stays in the chair."

The hunters moved behind the wraith.

Friar Lucio began his work. "I am an exorcist within the order, and I will begin with the instructional phase of the Rite of Exorcism. Please, empaths, refrain from sending your consciousness into the divine realm, and Miss Yousif, please hold my manual."

The empaths nodded their agreement, and Diane held open the heavy book in front of the friar.

Friar Lucio continued. "All, please join me in the Lord's Prayer."

Remembering the words, Diane contributed to the team's incantation. She then assisted with the Hail Mary but stood in silent ignorance while the friar invoked the words of a prayer he introduced as the Athanasian Creed.

The exorcist then touched the captive's neck with the hem of his stole while pressing his palm on the wraith's head. He then uttered a long litany for prayers while his subject–the energumen–glared at him with defiance.

"I will now command the demon by repeating demands in

three repeated groupings." Friar Lucio redoubled his attention on the energumen. "In the name of Jesus Christ, tell me your name."

The wraith's voice was a mix of deep bass and discordant screeching. "Tell me yours, cheater."

"In the name of Jesus Christ, tell me your number."

"Cheating in golf again this week?"

"In the name of Jesus Christ, tell me why you entered God's servant."

"Why, fool? You haven't figured out my pleasure in killing the women you can't protect?"

"In the name of Jesus Christ, tell me when you entered God's servant?"

"This wretch told you already, old fool. It's been a long time in your pathetic human reckoning."

"In the name of Jesus Christ, tell me how you gained access to God's servant."

"You've forgotten the dagger already?" The wraith curled and squirmed in his seat, a sadistic smile plastered on his smug face.

"In the name of Jesus Christ, tell me if you are held in him by necromancy, by evil signs or amulets."

"If you need me to spell it out for you, you're dumber than you look."

"In the name of Jesus Christ, tell me the sign of your departure, so that I'll know when you have left God's servant."

The wraith's eyes rolled back in his head, revealing the full whiteness that separated energumens from those suffering natural seizures. The veins in his face and neck bulged, and then the eyes rolled forward with dilated pupils glaring at the friar.

Standing beside Lucio, Diane gasped, but she held her silence.

Friar Lucio rested his gaze away from the subject. "The demon answers with partial truths. That's progress, and I will send him straight to the foot of the cross." While reaching into his robe, he lowered his nose towards the demon. He pulled out a vial of holy water and sprinkled it on the energumen's face.

As unnatural sounds gurgled from the wraith's throat, his

cheeks extended and narrowed towards a wolfish snout and then returned to normal.

Shocked looks on her comrades confirmed to Diane that the restructuring of the bones had been a shared experience– whether an illusion or a paranormal event.

Friar Lucio seemed unfazed. "I begin the second series of commands." He stared at the wraith. "In the name of Jesus Christ, tell me your name."

The wraith ignored him.

As the exorcist repeated the commands, the energumen gave a mix of answers ranging from truths to threats. After another ten minutes of grilling his subject, the friar led the small team in prayer, completed the rite, and then asked Diane to close the book. "This concludes this session of exorcism. The demon remains in the subject."

Diane's curiosity got the better of her. "What's next?"

"We'll build a jail cell to hold him here on this sacred ground. This could take weeks or months of repeated sessions to banish the demon, or demons, depending if they're grouped."

"They come in groups?"

"Usually, with weaker demons hiding behind the stronger ones."

"What happens after you succeed?"

"We'll study him, as long as he lives. God only knows what will happen once the demon or demons leave."

"What about us?"

"We'll retire this wraith's dagger, after you have some time to go home and rest, of course. I'm sure this was exhausting."

CHAPTER 43

The next morning, Diane tipped back a cup of espresso while enjoying a slow, leisurely lunch of pasta and sauce with her family and hunting team. Everyone seemed fatigued but content.

Connor slurped spaghetti and then wiped his mouth. "Would anyone like to hear what's going on at the headquarters?"

Diane answered for the team. "Sure."

The elder hunter lifted his phone to his ear. Appearing jovial in his victory, he tried conversing in Italian. "*Ciao*, Friar Lucio."

The Chaldean empath nibbled on oil-dipped garlic bread while the hunter spoke in the foreign language. As Diane's mind drifted, she saw white haze and a human form floating within it. In a realm occurring outside the bounds of sidereal time, a female form materialized from the mist.

With an unseen wind flapping a milky gown over her, the Maiden of Yorkshire called out in medieval Middle English. "You have avenged me."

"I did?"

"I will soon pass."

"I didn't kill him."

The maiden smiled and looked upward as she rose and dissipated into the mist. "You showed mercy. You showed compassion. You showed love. Love is the tool of the empath."

"Wait!"

The ghost was gone, and Diane reentered time.

Connor lowered his phone to the table. "They have construction crews putting the building back together. From what they can tell so far, nobody outside the order witnessed any of the battle. We either got lucky or enjoyed divine intervention."

Diane swallowed her bread, the oil tasting fresh like the

olives had been picked that morning. "Cool."

"There's also a funeral for Friar Don tomorrow. Of course, we're all invited."

The Chaldean empath wanted to pay her respects. "Yeah, we need to go. He was nice. It's sad."

"He died the way he wanted to. I'm sure he's in a better place."

Diane continued the inquiry. "Anything else?

"Ah yes. The wraith. Mister Ethan Smith. He's alive, he's healing, and he's having moments of lucidity free of the demon."

The Chaldean empath's compassion poured out. "Wow. So, what's that mean for him? I know he's a beast, but I don't think it was all his fault."

Connor's voice became stern. "Don't be so quick to pity him. He chose his fate."

"I thought a demon attacked him. Maybe more than one."

The elder hunter revealed his deep knowledge of the dark arts. "Many demonic possessions begin with acts of the human victim's will. Outside of curses, most possessions involve an invitation, whether overtly or by ignorance, such as amateurish use of séances, Ouija boards, or, dare I say, tarot cards."

Wondering if she'd danced on the razor's edge of becoming a demon's toy with her tarot readings, Diane gulped. "But what about him? How'd he become possessed?"

"We'll learn that over time, but there's one thing of which Friar Lucio is certain. The Mister Smith who attacked us was indeed possessed, but he wanted to be freed, even at the cost of his own life. However, long before he desired to resist his Master demon, he was integrated with the beast. That means he was in a willing, symbiotic relationship with the demon."

"For centuries?"

"For a millennium. That's why I caution you to be stingy with your pity. However, he sends a message. Though I'm in no mood to accept his sentiments, he apologizes for Friar Don, and he thanks us all for our help, especially the one he called 'Miss Empath'."

Next to Diane, the young hunter gulped a mouthful of meatballs. "Dang. I never thought a wraith would thank us."

"We've accomplished a lot of things that I'd considered impossible when you showed up at my doorstep long ago."

"You didn't find me on your doorstep. Cut it out with the silly stories."

"No, lad. I didn't. Friar Don delivered you to my house. It was he who handed you to me the first time I held you in my arms." Tears welled in Connor's eyes. "Sorry. Ignore an old man's nostalgia."

"Bullshit, Father. The man deserves a toast." He raised his latte. "To Friar Don!"

Beverage containers clanked as the group cheered in unison. "To Friar Don!"

Diane reflected upon their lost comrade. "That may explain why he was insistent on joining us."

"I'm sure it was." Connor wiped his eye with his napkin. "Perhaps we should talk about something happier."

She knew the proper subject. "I know! Give me your credit card. Emma and I have some shopping to do. Nana, you're coming, too, right?"

The grandmother's eyes opened wide. "Shopping in Rome. Yes!"

Connor protested. "My credit card?"

Diane insisted. "Consider it a bonus from the order for a job well done."

"I wasn't aware of any payment structure."

"Well, you are now." The Chaldean empath extended her hand and smiled.

"I can't resist. I'm helpless." The elder hunter reached into his pocket, pulled out his wallet, and found the credit card. As he handed it to Diane, he put on a serious face. "Careful, young lady. The limit's only ten thousand Euro."

"How many dollars is that?"

"Enough for any mortal, but for two empaths and Nana in Rome, I can't be sure."

"Thanks!" She yanked the card from him and slid it beside her dagger in her purse.

Seated beside Nana, Josh scribbled notes onto a pad of paper.

"Josh, what are you doing?"

"I'm writing."

Diane rolled her eyes but reminded herself to be patient with him. "Oh, that's interesting. What are you writing about?"

"Our adventures."

"Do you mean our adventures hunting wraiths?"

"Yes."

She continued her coaxing. "Are you writing about all three of our adventures?"

Keeping his nose pointed at his scribbling pencil, he frowned. "I'm not lazy. I already wrote about the first two."

"Oh, I know you're not lazy. You're my productive brother. Do you need help writing about our latest adventure, Josh?"

"No."

She looked to Connor. "Did you know he was taking notes?"

"Why, yes. I did. I commissioned him as our team scrivener weeks ago. I suppose I forgot to mention that to you. When he's done, I'll submit his notes to the order for a calligrapher to update our original book."

"Huh. That's cool."

Josh lowered his pencil. "I've written as much as I can about this last adventure until Friar Lucio exorcises the demon from Mister Smith."

Curious about her brother's narrative, Diane wanted to study his work. "Can I read what you wrote, Josh?"

"Not until it's done."

"Oh, can't you let me see it? All you're missing is the exorcism, and I have faith in Friar Lucio to do that, Josh."

Her brother raised his gaze to the ceiling. "No. There's something else missing."

"What's that, Josh?"

He looked to Liam. "When are you going to marry my sister?"

The young hunter blushed. "First, let's agree that we want to be married."

"Oh, why is everyone so stupid? You want to marry her, she wants to marry you, and I want my brother-in-law. Why aren't you getting married yet?"

The ruddiness remained on the young hunter's cheeks. "Bloody hell, you're right, Josh. I do want to marry your sister, and I do want you as my brother-in-law. But the rules are unbreakable, and we need to bring down another wraith before it can happen."

Embarrassed and enamored, Diane looked to her potential husband. "So, buddy, what are you going to do about it?"

The color fell from his face as he weighed his words. "While you ladies ruin Father's credit today, I'll visit the order. Now that I know who's in charge, I'll be having a candid heart-to-heart with Friar Lucio about killing another wraith, bending over backwards, or doing whatever's necessary to marry the woman I love. Then I'll take her on our second date so I can get to know her better."

Diane smiled. "That was sweet!"

"Was that romantic enough?"

She shrugged. "Yeah. Not bad for a caveman."

THE END

ABOUT THE AUTHOR

After graduating from the Naval Academy in 1991, John Monteith served on a nuclear ballistic missile submarine and as a top-rated instructor of combat tactics at the U.S. Naval Submarine School. He now works as an engineer when not writing.

Join the Wraith Hunters to get news, freebies, discounts, and your FREE Prophecy of Eden (Book #5) early bonus chapter!

WRAITH HUNTER CHRONICLES:

ROGUE SUBMARINE SERIES:

ROGUE AVENGER (2005)
ROGUE BETRAYER (2007)
ROGUE CRUSADER (2010)
ROGUE DEFENDER (2013)
ROGUE ENFORCER (2014)
ROGUE FORTRESS (2015)
ROGUE GOLIATH (2015)
ROGUE HUNTER (2016)
ROGUE INVADER (2017)
ROGUE JUSTICE (2017)
ROGUE KINGDOM (2018)

John R Monteith

PROPHECY OF CHAOS

www.ingramcontent.com/pod-product-compliance
Lightning Source LLC
Chambersburg PA
CBHW030243200626
46816CB00002BA/487